Maria Bluni grew up in Huntington, New York and has an MA degree in English Literature. She holds a deep appreciation for the natural world and has been exploring the White Mountains of New Hampshire, the inspiration for *The Lady in the Woods*, for most of her life. She has two adult children and currently resides in Massachusetts with her husband, their spoiled golden retriever and the two cats that tolerate him.

For Scott

Maria Bluni

THE LADY IN THE WOODS

AUSTIN MACAULEY PUBLISHERS™

LONDON • CAMBRIDGE • NEW YORK • SHARJAH

Ordering Information
Quantity sales: Special discounts are available on quantity purchases by corporations, associations, and others. For details, contact the publisher at the address below.

Publisher's Cataloging-in-Publication data
Bluni, Maria
The Lady in the Woods

ISBN 9781649790705 (Paperback)
ISBN 9781649790699 (Hardback)
ISBN 9781649790712 (ePub e-book)

Library of Congress Control Number: 2021902350

www.austinmacauley.com/us

First Published 2022
Austin Macauley Publishers LLC
40 Wall Street, Floor 33, Suite 3302
New York, NY 10005
USA

mail-usa@austinmacauley.com
+1 (646) 5125767

First and foremost, I would like to thank my husband, Scott Bluni, for encouraging me to write a full-length novel. I could not have completed *The Lady in the Woods* without his steadfast love and support. Our two sons, Scott Bluni Jr. and Mark Bluni, cheered me on the whole time as well.

I also wish to thank Jessica Moreland for her professional guidance. Writing is clearly a solitary undertaking but throughout the process, I never felt alone. I am blessed with many supportive friends that encouraged me along the way. Please know that I appreciate you all.

And lastly, a huge thank you to Austin Macauley Publishers for believing in my manuscript and working with me. As a debut novelist, I am incredibly grateful for their guidance throughout the publication process. Their team has been supportive, encouraging, and above all else, professional. Thank you!

Part One

Chapter One

Mariah Talbot was in no mood to deal with the black Audi tailgating her this morning. She owed the dull ache behind her eyes to a restless night's sleep, despite the Ambien she'd taken just before climbing into her old bed. She glanced at her side mirror, trying to get a better look at the driver behind her. There was no mistaking the outline of a man.

"Great," she mumbled, reaching for her coffee. It was weak, and she frowned after taking a sip, making a mental note to bring her own, stronger blend the next time she dog sat.

She rarely slept well at her parents' house. But whenever they needed her to pet sit, she never hesitated. After all, Jake had been her dog, too. The yellow Labrador was nearing twelve years old now, and although he was still in relatively good health, he had begun to slow down. As a result, he'd started to put on extra weight. Before leaving, she'd given him a handful of dog treats, knowing once her parents returned home, he'd be placed back on a strict diet.

"What they don't know won't hurt them," she'd said, burying her face on the top of his head before kissing him good-bye. He'd devoured the contraband biscuits, something she *had* remembered to bring this weekend, in an instant. It was always hard to leave Jake but this morning it had felt unusually tough. He still had a few good years left in him, she knew, so why couldn't she shake the feeling that she would never see him again? When she'd walked out the front door to her car, she'd sensed he was standing in the living room window, watching her leave. It was something he'd done since he was a puppy. A lump had formed in her throat, and she had resisted the urge to look back, knowing his soulful eyes were watching her.

"They'll be home in a few hours," she reminded herself, thinking of her parents as she tightened her grip on the wheel. She checked her mirror again and groaned. The guy behind her was still driving too closely. Usually, idiot drivers didn't bother her, but this one was starting to get on her already frayed nerves. Visiting her childhood home was never easy. No matter how hard she tried not to think of the past, each visit chipped away at her resolve.

She'd loved that home, once. Her fondest childhood memories had been exploring every nook and cranny of the antique colonial house. Despite having had no siblings, she'd never felt lonely as a child. Somehow, there was always some 'mystery' to solve in the old house, some 'treasure' to unearth. Whether it be a shard of old pottery or dirt stained bottle she'd found in the original root cellar of their basement, or the hours she'd spend rummaging through old trunks in the attic, she was never bored. The massive Victorian trunks had been in her family for generations and were crammed with ancient looking books and dusty old family albums. A few of them were in color, but most were sepia toned. The stoic facial expressions and stiff poses of her long-dead relatives had provided countless hours of fuel for her imagination. Sometimes, she'd even invent elaborate stories about them to entertain her parents. Since most of the nameless faces were unknown even to them, Mariah would simply make them up. Her favorite photograph was a tintype of a young girl dressed all in black, standing beside a large yellow dog who Mariah had dubbed Jake. When her father brought home a chunky yellow Labrador puppy years later, Mariah knew *exactly* what to name him.

She pictured Jake standing in the window again and sighed as she downed the last of her coffee.

"It's a gorgeous day," she mumbled, shifting her attention to the beautiful morning around her. She lowered her window and savored the crisp breeze on her face. Although they were in the final days of August, there was no mistaking the hint of fall in the air. Some of the trees along the Massachusetts Turnpike were already dotted with colors and she knew it would only be a matter of weeks until they were bursting with bright shades of red and orange. She wondered if the trees in Vermont had begun to change. During her four years at University of Vermont as an art major, she'd painted countless landscapes. Some had been given from her to friends and family, but many of them had actually been sold in shops in downtown Burlington. It had been five years since she'd picked up a paintbrush but lately, she'd been toying with the idea of starting up again. She spied her hands on the steering wheel and imagined them splattered with colors. Mark used to tease her all the time about it, saying that manicures were a waste of money on her. It was hard not to think of him on days like these.

"Mark," she whispered quietly, as the smell of balsam tumbled into the car. The scent hadn't lingered for very long, she wondered if her mind was playing tricks on her. It wouldn't be the first time.

She flipped her visor open. The edges on the corners of the photo she kept there were worn but image was as sharp and clear as the day she'd taken it. Mark's thick, dark hair was messy as usual, and his brown eyes smiled down at her with a familiarity the passing of time could not erase. To Mariah, he was goodness and sunshine and youth all at once, and always would be.

"Morning, Mark," she said, smiling.

She remembered every curve of his long, lean body, but it pained her that she could no longer remember the sound of his voice. She held his gaze a moment longer.

"Has it really been five years?" she asked him, her eyes lingering on his. A blast of a car horn followed by the ringing of her cell phone was the only, jarring reply. The sounds startled her, nearly caused her to swerve out of her lane.

"What the hell was that for?" she shouted at her mirror, watching the Audi back off. Traffic was moving fine but she pressed her foot down on the gas hard, angrily reaching for her phone. She didn't need to check the caller I.D. Mariah knew exactly who was calling her this early.

Technically, Susan Davis was her employee, but it didn't feel that way to Mariah. For one thing, Sue was more than twenty years her senior, and much more passionate about the business than Mariah ever was. Besides being a loyal friend, she was also the only reason Back Bay Décor was thriving. Mariah briefly considered not taking the call but decided against that strategy, knowing Sue would simply keep calling her until she picked up.

"Hi, Sue," Mariah said, bracing herself for the complaints she knew were coming. She'd promised Sue on Friday that she'd be in the shop early this morning, before Sue's presentation to a potential new client. "Beautiful morning, isn't it?"

"Where are you?" Sue demanded.

"Still on the turnpike, I'm afraid. I'm so sorry. Traffic is horrible."

"It's always horrible this time of day. You left your parents' house late, didn't you?" Sue snapped.

"I overslept," Mariah admitted. She wouldn't tell her about the Ambien. If she did, an entirely different conversation would ensue, and Mariah refused to go there.

"This was important to me, Mariah. You swore you'd be here bright and early today. This woman is about to spend a small fortune on her house. She wanted you. Not me."

"I had a rough night," Mariah said, feeling herself bristle. She loved Sue, but she didn't like being spoken to as if she were a child. "You know I don't like being at my parents' house."

"I do. Which is why I still can't believe you went," Sue replied.

"I did it for Jake," Mariah clarified. "You know how much I love that dog, and I hardly ever get to see him anymore."

"I know," Sue sighed. "Did you see your folks at least?"

Mariah knew what Sue was really asking was if she had seen her father. "Nope. Got there two hours after they left on Friday. Why?"

Mariah's interactions with her father the past five years had been limited. Other than the letters she received every few months, she rarely communicated with him directly. On the rare occurrence when they did see each other, the encounters were brief and uncomfortable. It was for that reason she and her mother usually met in Boston. They'd shop or lunch or spa, and rarely discuss him.

"Just wondering, that's all. You've seemed preoccupied lately, and I was wondering if it had anything to do with them."

The last time Sue brought up her father, she suggested that Mariah call him after he'd left a desperate sounding message on their office phone. Mariah had stormed out of the room and slammed the door so hard, a painting in the showroom actually fell off the wall.

"Why not just ask me how Jake is?" Mariah asked.

"You know I'm not an animal person," Sue said. "But, fine. How is the dog that's so special, he couldn't be boarded?"

"He's too old to stick in a kennel!" Mariah said, defensively. "Jesus, will you get off my back? I've got a lunatic tailgating me, I'm barely awake…" *And I'm talking to Mark's photo. I nearly just drove my car off the freaking road, that's how well it's going!*

"Fine," Sue said. "But it's just like I said last week. Your head doesn't seem to be in the game anymore, and it worries me."

14

"Well, stop worrying," Mariah said. "We're doing fine, right?"

"We are. But we could be doing a lot better. I feel like I'm running this place on my own. At some point, we need to have a serious discussion about this. Soon, okay?"

"Sure," Mariah said. "I promise. I mean it, this time."

"Good. I'm holding you to it. Drive safely, *boss,*" Sue said, before hanging up.

"Will do," Mariah replied.

This wasn't the first time Sue had complained about Mariah's lack of interest in work. What made it all the worse was that Mariah knew Sue was right. Mariah had been checked out lately. Her heart wasn't in the business anymore. It hadn't been for a long while. She had been coasting along on Sue's hard work and talent almost from the very beginning, and they both knew it. Sue was the most sophisticated and talented person Mariah had ever met. While Mariah's interior decorating skills were the result of years of classes and practice, Sue's sense of style and creativity were innate. Her natural elegance left its mark on everything she touched, including her wardrobe. Mariah never had to buy a magazine to learn the latest fashion trends. All she had to do was look at Sue.

I'm lucky if I make it out the door with makeup on, she thought, absently scanning her face in the mirror.

The Audi was back on her tail.

"Fine, you win," she said, flipping on her blinker and shifting her car to the center lane. To her surprise, he also switched lanes and was once more directly behind her. The idea that she could be dealing with a potential psychopath crossed her mind, but she cautioned herself not to be paranoid.

When a familiar service station appeared in the distance, Mariah moved her car into the right lane. To her relief, the Audi remained where it was. But just as she was about to exit the turnpike, the driver shifted over to her lane and was once again directly behind her.

"You trying to intimidate me, buddy?" she asked, slowing down to a crawl in retaliation.

When the Audi swerved around her onto the dirt shoulder a few moments later, coming within inches of her side mirror, Mariah slammed her fist down on the horn. Her temper flared, and she stomped her foot on the gas, following the Audi into the station.

"Plenty of witnesses," she muttered, spotting how crowded the area was. "In case the guy really does turn out to be a psycho." Pulling into the open bay behind the Audi, she threw her car into park, contemplating her next move.

"Idiot," she hissed, watching a man emerge from the vehicle. Although the tall figure hardly looked like a serial killer, he barely spared a glance at her. For some reason, that infuriated her even more. She watched him reach into his back pocket for his wallet as he sauntered to the pump, still pretending not to notice her.

"Really?" she said. "Like you don't know it's me you just blew by?"

She'd had enough. Determined to give him a piece of her mind, she stepped from the car. The man turned and faced her the moment her heels hit the pavement. Mariah stared back, her fist on her hip, surprised that he seemed familiar. She tried to place him, wondering if he was a husband of one of her clients. The man narrowed his eyes on her briefly before reaching for the pump.

His height and build, Mariah slowly realized. *And the same shade of hair. Dark brown that bordered on black.*

It wasn't the first time someone reminded her of Mark. Her anger slowly dissolved. A familiar ache settled in her chest, and she turned back towards her car.

"Your front right tire looks a little low," the man called out to her.

It was not what Mariah was expecting to hear. She looked back at him but said nothing.

"Miss," he repeated, slowly approaching her, "you ought to get that checked out."

"Thank you," Mariah replied curtly over her shoulder, wondering why the man was walking towards her. Perhaps, he intended to apologize for driving like a moron?

"Leaving so soon?" he asked, rounding the front of her car. "Don't you need to fill up?"

"Are you kidding me?" she finally said, relieved to find his eyes were blue. There was a scattering of gray hair around his temples, too. Still, the physical similarities were uncanny. "Look," she began, hoping she didn't appear as rattled as she felt, "why don't you get back into that fancy little race car of yours and try not to kill someone today. Sound good?"

"That's it?" the man grinned. "That's all you got?"

Mariah stared at him; her eyes widening in disbelief. "Do you actually *want* me to tell you off?" she asked.

"Not particularly. But I have a hunch you'd feel a whole lot better if you did," he continued. "Personally, I'd much rather have a cup coffee with you."

"Excuse me?" she asked, blinking hard. "Do you admit you've been harassing me all morning on the highway?"

"I didn't mean to," he replied. "Honestly. Guess I'm a fast driver. I apologize."

"I don't accept your apology," she said, noting the flirtatious look in his eyes and the easy smile. "I'm fine with fast drivers. *I'm* a fast driver. You just drive like a complete idiot. Big difference."

"Let me make it up to you then. One cup of coffee?" the man asked, taking a step closer.

Well, aren't you the charmer? Mariah thought. Eyeing his impeccably tailored, navy suit, she guessed a man who looked like him was a not accustomed to being turned down. She needed time to think.

"So, let me get this straight," she began. "One minute you're following me like a madman, honking at me for no reason, then you nearly take out my side mirror on the off-ramp. And now you want to have a cup of coffee with me?"

"I wasn't following you. I needed gas," he said, turning to his car. "See?" he said, motioning to the pump sticking out the side of his car.

"Fine," Mariah conceded, "but you did nearly run me off the exit."

"True," he said, nodding, "but in my defense, you did deliberately slow down to annoy me. What was I supposed to do?"

"You have a point," Mariah admitted, half smiling.

"Apology accepted," the man said.

"What? No, wait…excuse me, I'm not apologizing for slowing down," Mariah corrected him. "Nice try, slick."

"Fine. How about that coffee? You pick the time and the place."

"Sorry. I don't go out with strangers," she said, "especially ones who drive like pissed-off teenagers."

"Andrew Madden," he introduced himself, stepping closer to her. He extended his hand politely, and Mariah paused briefly before accepting it.

"Mariah Talbot," she said, liking the way his palm felt in hers. Her eyes wandered to the faded scar on his left cheekbone.

"Now we aren't strangers," he said, smiling. "Coffee?"

"I can't do that," she said.

"Why not?"

"I don't know anything about you," she said. *And you remind me of someone else.*

"I'm a lawyer, and I got the scar playing hockey in college."

Mariah felt her face grow warm. *Stop acting like a silly schoolgirl,* she told herself. She'd dated plenty of men since Mark died, so why was this one making her so flustered? He had the same frame as Mark. So what?

"Why don't you give me your card or something?" she finally said. "I'm on my way to work."

"And where's that?" he asked.

"Back Bay."

"Me too," he replied. He reached into his breast pocket and pulled out a business card. "You know that *café* on the corner of Newbury and Clarendon?" he asked, handing it to her.

"I do," she nodded, her eyes fixed on the card.

"Meet me there in about an hour?" he asked.

"I can't today. Too many appointments this morning," she lied. "Maybe I'll give you a call," she said, reaching for her car door.

"I hope you do, Mariah Talbot," he said, staring at her a moment longer before turning back to his car.

Mariah watched him pull out of the service plaza. Andrew might have reminded her of Mark physically, but their personalities were completely different. For one thing, Mark would never have been so bold. While she liked Andrew's sexy, easy confidence, her instincts told her there was nothing easy about him. Mariah wasn't looking for anything or anyone remotely complicated.

But still, she thought, tapping his business card on her steering wheel, *there's something about him. And it's just a cup of coffee.*

She reached for her phone, not caring that she was being impulsive. Andrew picked up on the first ring. "I'll be there in an hour," she said.

Chapter Two

Mariah eyed her reflection in the window next to the *café*, wishing she'd put on some make-up this morning. She'd been in such a rush, the only thing she'd managed to apply was a dab of lipstick. Her curly hair was looking a little wild, too, and she quickly dug through her purse for an elastic. When she found none, she gave up and turned away.

At least her outfit was nice, she thought. She was wearing the new white, gauzy skirt she'd recently purchased and a fitted black sleeveless top. When she spotted Andrew sitting at a table toward the back looking down at his cell phone, she paused for a moment and studied him. For the briefest moment, she considered not meeting him after all. She was still contemplating the notion when he suddenly looked up at her and smiled.

"Too late now," she mumbled, reaching for the door. She stepped inside and held his gaze, noting the way he stood and watched her navigate the crowded space to the table. It felt old-fashioned, and she liked that.

"You came," he said. Judging from his tone, it was clear he'd been a little uncertain if she'd actually appear. She liked that, too.

"I did," she said, hoping she didn't look or sound as nervous as she felt. As she settled into her seat, her attention momentarily shifted to the visibly unhappy, young girl seated at the table beside them across from a woman Mariah assumed to be the child's mother. She guessed the girl was around ten years old. Her arms were folded across her chest, and she was close to tears.

"I'm glad," Andrew said. "What can I get you?"

"Hmmm," she said, turning to scan the neat rows of carefully displayed muffins and scones behind the glass case. "Just a medium black coffee, thanks."

"Sure," he said. "Want anything to eat?" he asked over his shoulder as he headed towards the counter.

Mariah smiled, shaking her head. "No thanks."

She watched Andrew as he politely ordered their coffees, just before reaching into his pocket for his wallet. After paying, he stuffed a few dollars in the tip jar. The woman behind the counter beamed at him with appreciation, and Mariah couldn't help thinking it wasn't just the tip the lady was admiring.

"Drink your juice," the woman next to Mariah said to the girl. "The cold will feel good on your throat."

The girl's arms were still tightly folded across her chest, and she was staring at the tall glass of untouched orange juice. She wasn't being defiant, Mariah realized, she was frightened.

"If I drink it all, can I not go to the doctor?" the girl asked. "My throat barely hurts anymore, I swear."

"Please," the mother said, glancing down at her watch. "It's just a quick swab in the back of your throat. We really need to leave. Your appointment is in twenty minutes."

"But I threw up last time they did it, remember? Can't I just go to school?" The girl's voice cracked with emotion, and Mariah watched a single tear roll down her cheek.

"They're not so bad," Mariah said, leaning over. "Strep cultures, I mean. Sorry," she said, smiling apologetically at the mother. "I couldn't help but overhear you. These little tables are packed so closely to each other."

"I know," the woman replied, in a friendly tone.

"Just close your eyes and breathe out as hard as you can, and you'll hardly feel the tickle," Mariah continued. "My father taught me that trick when I was about your age."

"Thanks," the child replied, shyly. Although the girl mustered a weak smile, it was clear she remained unconvinced.

Andrew appeared beside Mariah with a mug of coffee in each hand; carefully lowering them down onto the table. "What did I miss?" he asked, catching the last of the exchange.

"Nothing," Mariah replied, reaching for the handle. "This smells amazing," she said, lifting the hot mug cautiously to her lips. "Thank you, Andrew. I love the coffee here."

"You're welcome," he said, just as the girl pushed her chair back from the table. The juice toppled over, splattering everywhere. Her mother quickly reached for the glass before it crashed onto the floor, but not before the bright, orange liquid splashed onto Mariah's skirt.

"I'm so sorry!" the woman apologized, rising from her seat. She grabbed a napkin and started blotting the table and floor before noticing the stain. "Your skirt," she said. "Oh, no, I am so very sorry," she repeated.

"It's fine, really," Mariah said, looking at the girl who had now begun to cry.

"I'll grab some more napkins," Andrew said, standing up. "Hold on."

"It's these wobbly old tables," Mariah explained, hoping to put her at ease. "It wasn't your fault at all. It's an old skirt anyway," she lied. "I've been looking for an excuse to skip work today and go shopping, so I should be thanking *you*."

At that, the girl paused and looked at Mariah. "I guess you're welcome then?" she said.

"Do you need these?" Andrew said, handing Mariah a stack of napkins.

"Nope. It's all fixed," Mariah said, shaking her head. "Good luck at the doctor's office," she told the mother and daughter as they headed out of the *café*. The child was still looking at Mariah and gave her a tiny wave before she stepped outside onto the street.

"What was all of that about?" Andrew asked.

"Nothing, really. She's about to have her throat swabbed, and she's nervous," she explained. "That's all."

"I *hated* those!" Andrew said. "They always made me gag."

"So, you're a lawyer *and* a big baby?" Mariah laughed.

"I guess, I am," he admitted. "And you're great with kids, aren't you?" he said in return.

"I am," she said, shifting uncomfortably in her chair. She and Mark both loved kids. It was something they'd had in common right from the beginning. "I was the best babysitter on my block."

"I believe it," Andrew smiled. "And where was that?"

"I grew up in Wayland. What about you?"

"Right here, in Boston."

"Really?" Mariah said, genuinely interested. "That must have been wonderful."

"It still is. I get to walk to work. What about you? Where do you live now?"

"Brookline," she replied.

"And what do you do, Mariah Talbot?" he asked. "I mean, aside from an illustrious former babysitting career, that is."

"I own an interior decorating company," she said, reaching for her coffee.

"No kidding," Andrew said, raising an eyebrow. "That sounds exciting. Hard work, I'm sure, but fun."

"It's not fun at all, actually. In fact, I really dislike it," she replied, before she could stop herself. "Wow," she said, covering her mouth with her hand. "I can't believe I actually admitted that out loud."

"It's okay," Andrew said, amused. "Your secret's safe with me."

"Good to know," Mariah laughed.

During her senior year of college, when Mariah had informed her parents that she planned to open a decorating business post-graduation, they hadn't been overwhelmingly supportive. They had both wanted her to pursue a career as an artist. Particularly her father. In fact, her father had confidently predicted that Mariah wouldn't be happy doing anything else. But Mariah had followed through on her plan anyway. It was hard, even now, to admit to herself that her father had been right.

"People tend to open up to me. It's the lawyer thing," Andrew said. "What made you go into that line of work?"

"Money," Mariah said, flatly. "I thought I could make money while still doing something creative that involved colors and textures. Does that make any sense? I didn't want to be the cliché starving artist."

"Ah, so you are actually an artist at heart," he said, leaning back in his chair. "I can picture it."

"Not really," she said. "I mean, I was an art major in college, but I also studied design and took a few business classes. I've been running my own company for five years now," she stated.

"But if you hate it, why don't you do something else?" he asked.

"Easier said than done," she said, wishing to change the subject. All this talk about herself was making her uncomfortable. Especially since she'd made it a habit not to talk about her personal life. It was always a slippery slope. "Besides," she said, trying to make light of the conversation, "I don't know much of anything else, I'm afraid." Mariah watched Andrew study her closely over the rim of his coffee mug intently before speaking.

"Sure you do," he said. "It's just scary starting over. If you could pick anything else, right now, what would it be?"

Mariah paused, considering the question. "I'd love to design gardens," she said. "And of course paint the occasional masterpiece on the side," she added, with a laugh.

She decided that she was done talking about herself. "So why were you driving towards Boston this morning if you live here?" she asked.

"Client breakfast in Framingham. Total waste of time until you cut me off," he explained.

"Did I really?" she said, her eyes widening with embarrassment.

"Yes, you did," he nodded.

"So that was it," she said. "Well, I'm not going to apologize because I have no recollection of that."

"I'm not sure I believe that but since we're starting fresh, I'll give you the benefit of the doubt," Andrew said. "What about you?"

"I spent the last weekend in Wayland dog sitting for my parents," she said, checking the time. "I actually can't stay too much longer, I'm afraid."

"You're your own boss, right?"

"I am. Why?"

"Can't you give yourself the day off?" he asked, holding her gaze.

"I'm afraid not," she said. "The woman I work with is already unhappy with me." *But I wish I could more than you know.*

"When can I see you again?" Andrew asked.

She took a long, last sip of her coffee before replying. She did want to see him again. She had to. There was something about Andrew that intrigued her, and it had little to do with his obvious good looks and charm. She hadn't felt such an intense physical attraction to a man since Mark. *Just one date,* she told herself.

"How about tonight?" she asked, noting the surprise in his eyes.

"Where?" Andrew said. "Any place you like."

"Hmmm," Mariah said, considering her options. She wanted to be alone with him, not stuck in some crowded restaurant. "Do you like to cook?"

"Sometimes," he said. If the question had caught him off guard, he certainly hadn't shown it.

"Feel like cooking me dinner before I head home to Brookline after work this evening?" she asked.

"Absolutely," he said.

Chapter Three

"Well, look who *finally* came to work! How did I possibly get here before you?" Sue asked, watching Mariah stroll through the showroom.

"I stopped for coffee and ran into a friend," Mariah explained, satisfied she didn't exactly lie. She kicked off her shoes as soon as she entered their small office in the back. The room was separated from the shop by a half wall that was painted a soft misty blue. Sleek contemporary chairs flanked the rococo desk they shared, and stacks of wallpaper books lay scattered about. An array of fabric swatches were pinned to the corkboard on the wall behind them. Mariah eyed the work orders in Sue's hands. "How'd it go?" she asked.

"We got it!" Sue exclaimed, high-fiving Mariah. "This is going to be great for us. Four stories, Beacon Hill."

"You see?" Mariah said. "You didn't need me after all."

"Apparently not," Sue said, beaming proudly.

"What's the client like?" Mariah asked, wishing she could feel as excited as Sue.

"Her name is Candace Trainor, and unfortunately, she's kind of like me; twenty-five years and two husbands ago," Sue laughed. "Everything *must* be perfect. But I can handle that, no problem."

"Ah," Mariah replied, nodding. "Well then, she should keep us busy for quite a long while. Nice dress, by the way," Mariah added, eyeing Sue's smart navy shift. It complemented the strand of glowing white pearls she wore around her neck and the chic little patent leather flats on her feet. "Is it new?"

"New-ish," Sue said, in a curious tone. "Why?"

"I might need to do a little shopping myself today," Mariah said. "I had a little incident at the café earlier," she said, motioning to the bright orange stain on her skirt. There was no way she was going to Andrew's place tonight in the same clothes she was wearing now. Ironically, she realized that the girl in the café *had* done her a favor.

"How the hell did that happen?" Sue asked. "You just bought that skirt, didn't you? That's never coming out, you know."

"A little girl at the table next to me knocked over her glass," Mariah explained. "No big deal," she said. She wondered how the girl fared at her doctor visit. "She was a really cute kid. I felt badly for her."

"Ugh," Sue said, shaking her head. "That's exactly why I never sit at tables near children. And don't get me started on kids on planes. I'd rather have a colonoscopy than be seated anywhere near one."

"Just stop, will you?" Mariah laughed. "Geez, you're awful."

"I'm not awful, I'm honest," Sue corrected her, still eyeing the stain. "It's not like you're meeting any clients today. You can still get through the day with it, can't you?"

"Not really," Mariah began.

"Why not? Got a hot date or something?"

"As a matter of fact…"

"Seriously?" Sue said, grinning widely. "Who?"

"No one you know," Mariah answered, reaching for the work orders again.

"Your 'friend' at the coffee shop?" Sue pressed.

"Please stop, will you? I'll tell you all about him another time." If she told Sue she'd been basically picked up at a service station on the Massachusetts Turnpike, she'd never hear the end of it. "Let's see what your big fancy client wants done. Show me the orders?"

"Are you kidding me? Now you're interested in work when you've got some secret stud you're not telling me about? When are you seeing him again?"

"Tonight. And yes, something like that," Mariah admitted, smiling, pulling the papers from Sue's hands. "Three bedrooms, a living room and a library?" she said flipping through the orders. "Fabulous."

"Fine. I'll drop it for now," Sue said, rolling her eyes. "Whatever. Why don't you go over to Saks? Buy yourself a new dress or something."

"I can't afford Saks," Mariah said flatly.

"Yes, you can. You just hate spending money. It's that wretched hippie in you."

"Hold on a sec," Mariah paused. "Two minutes ago, you were annoyed at me for coming in late. Now you are kicking me out of my own office?"

"You mean *our* office?" Sue corrected her.

25

"I'm sorry. *Our* office," Mariah repeated, forgetting for a moment what a touchy subject this was lately.

"That's better. And yes, I am," Sue said.

"Why?" Mariah asked.

"Because I don't know who the heck this mystery man is, but I haven't seen you blush over some guy since, well, not since…"

The smile faded from Mariah's face.

"I'm sorry, Mariah. I have such a big mouth," Sue murmured apologetically. "I didn't mean to bring up the past."

"It's fine, Sue. Really," Mariah said. "You know on second thought, I think I will take a stroll and do a little shopping, if you don't mind," she announced, stepping back into her shoes. "It's such a gorgeous day to walk around Boston anyway."

"Want some company?" Sue asked. "All this paperwork can wait till tomorrow, you know."

"No, thanks. I always spend more money when we shop together," she said. But the truth was, she wanted to be alone. "Plus, I know how much you enjoy placing those orders. Especially after a good pitch," Mariah added.

"I do love spending other people's money," Sue admitted, grinning. "You sure you're ok?"

"Of course, I am. Really, please stop," Mariah said, waving her off. She knew the last person on earth who would ever intentionally hurt her was Sue.

"Good. Then can I at least make one suggestion before you see Mr. Wonderful this evening?" Sue asked, lowering her gaze to Mariah's hands and frowning.

"Sure, but I'm afraid to even ask," Mariah said, bracing herself.

"Will you please get yourself a decent manicure?"

Chapter Four

Mariah strolled down Marlborough Street admiring the row of antique brownstones. The brick sidewalk buckled in areas, and she was so focused on the amazing architecture she nearly lost her footing, twice. The thought of showing up on Andrew's doorstep with scraped knees like some tomboy almost made her laugh. It certainly wasn't the sexy entrance she envisioned.

The maple trees lining the street were perfectly pruned, she noted, absently brushing her hand over the trunk of one as she passed by. It had been a few years since she walked around the quaint Back Bay neighborhood, and she had forgotten how beautiful this part of town was. Most of the homes had gardens tastefully enclosed with decorative wrought iron gates. This was quintessential Boston, she thought, wondering what it must be like to live in one of these exquisite homes. How she would love working in those gardens, too. She glanced at her nails and smiled.

Sue had been right about the manicure. Mariah had enjoyed doing a bit of work in her mother's garden over the weekend and hadn't bothered wearing gloves. Nothing felt as good to her as getting her hands in the earth. It was a passion she shared with her mother. In fact, some of the best conversations she had experienced with her mother had occurred when they were working in the dirt, side by side. It was their common ground; their sanctuary. Even now, Mariah remembered the day they planted the morning glories under her bedroom window when she was a young girl. Mariah had been having a rough couple of weeks in school, and while her mother couldn't fix the problem of the few rotten apples in her daughter's class, she could ease her daughter's anxiety working side-by-side with her in the garden. It worked. Mariah had watched the flowers grow rampantly that first summer. Years later, no matter what the cause of her restless night's sleep had been, or the source of her latest teenage drama, the reliable purple flower always cheered her in the morning.

That was their magic, her mother used to tell her.

When she approached Andrew's building, she was delighted to find a perfectly shaped miniature Japanese maple tree anchoring a cleverly designed garden. The minimalist tenor of the expertly selected plantings was understated but far from simple. Mariah was impressed. Miniature boxwoods lined the steps, drawing the eye upwards to the massive oak door. A weathered bronze doorknocker, in the form of a lion's head, was mounted at eye level.

It suits him, she thought, ringing the buzzer. She heard his footsteps almost instantly.

"You're wearing an apron," she pointed out when he answered the door.

"You changed your outfit, too," Andrew replied, smiling appreciatively at her dress. "Couldn't get the stain out of the skirt?"

"I didn't bother to try," she admitted, looking down at the simple black jersey dress she bought this morning. On her way out of the trendy little boutique she'd purchased it at on Charles Street, she'd spied a rich green silk scarf. Although it cost almost as much as the dress, she'd splurged on that, too.

"You look beautiful," Andrew said. "Come in."

"Thank you," Mariah replied, stepping inside. "Mmm," she said. "Something smells amazing. Red sauce?"

"It is," he said. "And not from a jar, either."

"Pretty impressive," she said, following him.

"Don't get your hopes up too high," he warned.

"It will be great," she assured him, looking down the well-appointed hallway. There was an intricately carved spindle staircase to her left, and the walls were a soft gray. The molding around the ceiling was beautifully detailed and painted a pearly white. "This place is beautiful," she said. "Is everything original?"

"Most of it," Andrew replied. "I'm glad you like it. For a minute, I was worried you might tell me I needed a decorator."

"I'll reserve that opinion until I see the rest of it. The entire building is yours?" she asked, glancing up the stairs.

"It is," he said, leading her to the kitchen.

"Oh my," she commented, raising an eyebrow as she followed him down the hallway. "Wait," she paused, peeking into an open door off the hallway. "Is this your library?" she asked, stepping inside. The entire room was paneled in mahogany and the bookshelves were overflowing. "I love the weathered patina. You can't duplicate this," she said, turning to face him.

28

"I agree," he said, watching her intently.

An ivory marble fireplace with heavily carved sides flanked the opposite wall. There was a large copper bin full of firewood beside the hearth. "Does it work?" she asked, eyeing the empty grate.

"It does. Not that I use it much," he confessed.

"That's a shame," she said turning to face him. "It's a great room."

"I'm glad you like it," he said, softly. "Come on," he added, holding the door open for her, "before a fire breaks out in the kitchen."

The black and white kitchen was both functional and spacious with modern stainless-steel appliances and a simple white marble island. An oversized curved window on the far wall side of the room caught Mariah's attention. "That is stunning," she announced. "This room must get lots of natural light in the morning."

"It does," he replied, reaching for wine glasses.

"I almost forgot," she said, pulling a bottle of red wine from her bag. "I hope it's a good one," she added. "I don't know much about wine. Need a hand with those?" she asked, eyeing the bubbling pots on the stove.

"No, thanks. That's a nice bottle," he said, taking it from her hands. "Thank you. Take a seat while I pour."

Mariah watched him struggle briefly with the cork. She looked around the kitchen again. It was nearly perfect, she thought, but something was missing.

"You need some plants in here," she announced. "Something green."

"Oh?" he said, scanning the kitchen briefly before turning his attention to her. "Do you count?" he asked, eyeing the rich green scarf hanging loosely around her neck.

"I do not," Mariah smiled, stroking the soft silky material; pleased he'd noticed it.

"Plants, huh? You must really have a green thumb," Andrew said, pouring the wine.

"I do," she said. "I love gardening. I love the outdoors in general."

"I'm not surprised."

"Really?" she asked, eyeing him curiously. "Why is that?"

"You look like someone who belongs outdoors. Maybe it's the hair. You look like a fairy," he smiled. "Jesus, did that sound incredibly corny?"

"It did," she nodded, looking down at her hands.

"Sorry," he said, handing her a glass. "I didn't mean to embarrass you."

"You didn't," Mariah replied. *Someone else used to say the same thing.*

"Cheers," he said, tapping his glass against hers. "Here's to the Massachusetts Turnpike," he added with a laugh. "Maybe you could recommend a few," he said after taking a long first sip.

"A few what?" Mariah asked, confused.

"Plants. As long as they're the kind that won't die when I forget to water them."

"That could prove to be a challenge," Mariah said, taking a sip.

"I could always buy a bunch of those fake plastic ones," Andrew said.

"Don't you dare," she said, cringing. "I despise fake plants."

"Noted," he laughed. "Then tell me your life story," he said, briefly turning his back to her to check on dinner. He removed a lid from one of the pots and lowered the heat. "Just the basics, like where you went to school, stuff like that."

"I'm not very interesting, I'm afraid," she explained, leaning back in her seat and enjoying the view. When she detected a faint whiff of something burning, she debated saying something.

"Shit," Andrew mumbled under his breath, moving another pot from the stove.

"What about you?" Mariah asked, changing the subject. "I don't think I've ever met anyone living in Boston *from* Boston," she said. "That must have been exciting."

"It was great," he nodded.

"What made you want to be a lawyer?"

"It runs in the family," he explained. "My father practices, too."

"Ah...I see. Your father wanted you to carry on the family tradition?" When she caught the surprised look in his expression, she hoped she hadn't overstepped.

"Something like that."

"Well, do you like it at least?" she asked, curiously.

"Usually," he said, shrugging his shoulders. "It wasn't what I envisioned when I was younger."

"Which was?"

"You're going to laugh," he warned her.

"Try me," Mariah said.

"Fine," he sighed. "I wanted to play professional hockey."

"What's so funny about that? What held you back?" she asked.

"A few injuries...nothing too serious. By the end of college, I felt pressured to do something more conventional, anyway."

"I completely understand," Mariah said, knowing exactly what that felt like. Only in her case, the pressure hadn't come from her parents. It had come from Mark.

"Were you any good?" Mariah asked. "At hockey, I mean?"

"Maybe," he admitted.

"Well, look at it this way," she said, smiling. "A hockey career could have ruined those perfect teeth of yours."

"True," he laughed. "Too bad I didn't quit before it did this," he said, tapping the scar on his face.

"Ouch," she said, eyeing the long faded line.

"Slap shot to the face," he explained. "Twenty-or-so stitches."

"That must have been incredibly painful," she said. "Did your brother play, too?"

"Nope," Andrew replied. "He's a history professor over at Boston College," Andrew announced proudly.

"How interesting!" Mariah said. "I wish I had taken more history classes in college."

"Me, too," he said. "My brother, Tom, is one of the happiest guys I know," he added.

"And your father?" Mariah asked. "He didn't mind your brother's chosen career?"

"He did," Andrew said, "but by the time Tom informed him of his intent, I was already in law school. You might say I eased their disappointment a bit."

"You were a good big brother," Mariah said.

"Nah," he said, shaking his head. "Tom would have pursued his Ph.D. regardless," Andrew explained. "It's all he ever talked about since we were kids. Wanting to teach. We used to read like crazy. I think we read the complete Arthurian legends by the time I was ten or eleven."

"What a wonderful memory," Mariah said, imagining what Andrew was like as a boy.

"What were some of your favorite memories?" Andrew asked.

"Hmm," she said, thinking of her childhood for the second time that day. "I had a pretty rich fantasy life," she admitted. "It was pretty good, actually. We had lots of pets, all the time. Lots of strays mixed in there, too."

"Your parents didn't mind?"

"Nope," she said. "Once, I even brought home a baby squirrel I found behind our shed. I was able to keep it hidden from them for two whole days before it slipped out of my closet and found its way into my parent's bedroom in the middle of the night. I can still remember the sound of my mother's scream. And my poor father," she added, grinning. "It took him forever to calm her down. He let me keep the squirrel for a while, too, by the way."

"Oh, so you were that kind of kid," Andrew said. "A real Daddy's girl."

"Sort of," she admitted. She didn't want to recall how wonderful her father had been when she was young, and how she had adored him.

"You okay?" Andrew asked.

"I'm fine. I'm think I'm just hungry all of a sudden. It's been a long day."

"I forgot," he said, opening the refrigerator. "I put this together for us. Hope you aren't a vegan, or something," he said, placing a charcuterie tray in front of her.

"I was for about five minutes in college," she said, laughing. "That looks delicious," she said, reaching for the plate.

"Tell me about your dog," Andrew asked.

"Jake is wonderful," Mariah said, before taking a bite into a piece of cheese. "He's getting on though, nearly twelve years old now."

"That means your parents got him when you were..."

"I think I was fifteen...trying to figure out my age?" she asked, sweetly. "I'm twenty-seven. What about you?"

"I'm thirty," he said. "Don't let the few gray hairs fool you into thinking I'm older. It's another thing that runs in the family, I'm afraid."

Mariah eyed the hair around his temples. "It suits you," she said. "I also love cats. Does that scare you?"

"Not unless you're about to tell me that you have ten of them?"

"Not even one," she said, shaking her head. "I did have a big orange cat when I was a girl, though. Her name was Pinky. I adored her."

"So why don't you have a cat now?" Andrew asked.

"My apartment doesn't allow them. I think the water's boiling," she said, nodding to the pot. *And something burned.*

"You should move then," he said, reaching for the box of pasta. He dumped the contents into the water and checked his watch before turning to face her. "Find a place that allows them."

"First you tell me to quit my job, and now you're telling me to move out of my building. And I've known you, what, approximately ten hours?" Mariah said. "Who knows what you'll be telling me to do in a month."

"That depends," he said turning to her. "Are you seeing anyone?" he asked.

She regarded him carefully before responding. "No one special at the moment. You?" she asked.

"Just you," he said, pausing to face her.

"Oh really?" she said. "Pretty confident, aren't we?"

"Maybe a little," he replied tentatively. "Who's the 'no one special' guy?"

"Someone I date on and off. It's casual," she explained.

"I don't do casual, Mariah. You should know that about me right now," he replied.

Something shifted in Andrew's eyes, and Mariah placed her wine glass gently down on the counter before slowly rising from her chair. "I gathered that the moment we met," she said, coming to stand beside him. "Let me see what you're doing. I hate overcooked pasta," she said, reaching for the wooden spoon resting on the counter, "almost as much as I detest fake plastic plants. You burned the bottom of the sauce, didn't you?"

"Sorry," he said, turning to face her. "I was distracted. You had your nails done."

"I did," she admitted, turning all both the burners off. The mood in the room had shifted. "I'm surprised you noticed."

"They look nice," he added. "I'm a details kind of guy. Can't help it."

"That's a good thing," Mariah said. She glanced down at her dress. "The dress is new, too," she added softly. "Just in case there's a tag showing or something."

"Not that I can see," he said, lowering his voice.

"Good," Mariah said. "That would have been embarrassing. I like watching you cook, by the way," she added, reaching her hands around his back to untie the apron. When it fell to the floor, she slid her arms up his back and wrapped them around his neck. "Even though you completely screwed up dinner."

"I did," he agreed, his voice barely above a whisper now.

"We could always order a pizza later. Maybe make a fire and have a picnic on the floor in your study?"

"I couldn't believe my luck when you agreed to meet me," he confessed, placing his hands on the sides of her waist.

"I surprised myself, actually," she admitted.

"And I've never seen eyes like yours before," he said. "I couldn't tell if they were brown or green, this morning."

"They're both."

"I see," he said, pulling her closer. "I imagined touching your hair the moment we met."

"Then touch it," she said, closing her eyes, as he covered her lips with his own.

The kiss was soft and gentle at first, and Mariah could feel her body melting into his. He fit her perfectly, she realized, pressing against him. In that moment, she knew exactly why she had been so drawn to Andrew.

For the first time in years, she felt completely at peace.

Chapter Five

Mariah sat at her desk at Back Bay Décor, rereading her father's letter for the third time that afternoon. She'd been staring at the envelope for days, debating whether to open the note before her big weekend away with Andrew. It had been eight weeks since they'd started dating, and barely a night had passed in all that time that they hadn't been together.

She was glad she'd changed her mind about the letter.

Dear Mariah,

Guess what I came across today when I was digging through the attic? That old snow globe I gave you when you were a little girl. The one with the tiny plastic cabin in it surrounded by pine trees. You'd had a bad day at school and came home crying as I recall. It was right before Christmas, but Santa decided to come early to cheer you up, and it worked. You were fascinated with it, do you remember? I hadn't seen it in years, and it brought back such fond memories.

Anyway, you told me you are tired of me apologizing, so I will not apologize again. We both know the past cannot be undone. Since the accident, I have prayed each day not only for your forgiveness, but that you would one day find love again.

Your mother tells me that you have found someone very special, that you've been seeing for a few months. Is this true? If so, my prayers have been answered. I hope he treats you with the love and care you deserve.

Love always,
Dad.

For the first time in years, Mariah thought about calling her father. She wanted to tell him how wonderful Andrew was, and that she *was* in love again.

She'd reached for her phone more than once today, but each time, she couldn't quite manage to dial her old phone number.

"Coward," she mumbled. *Monday morning,* she told herself. *After Andrew knows everything. I'll call my father then.*

Staring at a blank piece of paper on her desk, she absently reached for it and began writing a letter to Andrew. It made no sense, she knew, but it felt good. The words poured out of her. She was so engrossed with the letter; she hadn't even heard Sue walk into the shop.

"For the love of God, will you tell me why you are still here, Mariah?" Sue asked.

Mariah was so startled; she nearly fell out of her seat. "You nearly gave me a heart attack!"

"Did you not hear me walk in?" Sue asked, peering over Mariah's shoulder.

"I was wrapping something up before I leave," she explained, hastily stuffing the note into an envelope. Mariah picked up her pen and scribbled Andrew's name on it before shoving the letter under a stack of work orders she had meant to file earlier in the day.

"What is going on?" Sue asked, regarding Mariah suspiciously. "You taking out a personal ad or something? Have you given Mr. Wonderful the boot?"

"Personal stuff," Mariah said.

"What has it been now…two months since you got picked up at a gas station?" Sue laughed, taking her seat. "I love it!"

"Yes, I know it was such a great source of amusement for you, Sue. For the record, I so regret telling you how we met," Mariah said, rising from her chair and reaching for her scarf.

"Aw, come on," Sue said, cracking a smile. "You've got to admit, it's a hell of a story. And why is he not driving you if you must go to that God-forsaken wilderness?"

"I've already explained it to you," Mariah said, rolling her eyes. "Work. He had to go to Hartford last minute, and it makes no sense to drive all the way back to Boston just to pick me up."

"Typical lawyer. Career always comes first," Sue snickered.

Mariah wound the scarf around her neck and grabbed her purse. "And it's New Hampshire, not the tundra," she corrected her.

"That's your opinion, my dear," Sue said, standing up to rearrange the drape of the scarf on Mariah. "Take your umbrella, too."

"It's not going to rain, but fine," Mariah said, just to make her happy.

"That looks better now," Sue said, taking a step back and admiring her work.

"Thanks," Mariah smiled. Ordinarily, Sue fussing over her appearance would annoy her. But not today. In a few short hours, she would be meeting Andrew at a cabin tucked away in Franconia, New Hampshire. "Ever notice how people love to complain about lawyers until they actually need one?"

"Not me, hon. But I will say that after my two divorces, the only ones who got richer were the attorneys. If I had been foolish enough to have had kids, I would have forced them to go to law school."

"Please, stop," Mariah said, shaking her head. She pictured the overnight bag she had carefully packed last evening, waiting for her in trunk of her car. Specifically, the sexy champagne colored nightgown she had splurged on for their weekend. Andrew was going to love it, she thought, feeling herself grow warm.

"Hello? Mariah? Are you even listening to me? You are truly smitten, you know that?" Sue said, smirking. "Dear lord, are you...*blushing*?"

"Of course not," Mariah said, looking away.

"Uh-huh," Sue said. "If you're so hot to trot to go, why are you still hanging around?"

"I already told you. I needed to write something down," she repeated again. "And..."

"And what?" Sue pressed.

"And I was also hoping Carlos would call before I left," she confessed. "I'm still upset about what happened at the installation today. I regret the day we ever took Candace on as a client."

"Look," Sue said, sighing. "I know you and Carlos are close, and I get it. He's been with you since day one. But you really baby him, Mariah. Candace shot her mouth off at him, so what? He's a big boy. He'll get over it."

"She threatened to call immigration on him, Sue," Mariah clarified. "That's a little more than just shooting her mouth off, don't you think?"

"Might I remind you of the commission we've made working for her? Not to mention the referrals that keep pouring in, thanks to her. People spending that much money on drapes and upholstery expect to be treated like royalty. You know that. Carlos screwed up a sofa, and she got pissed. Case closed."

"He offered to correct the issue immediately. Apparently, that wasn't good enough for her," Mariah replied, grabbing her coat.

"You and I need to agree to disagree when it comes to him, okay? You coddle him, and I don't. We'll finish this discussion on Monday. Now *go!*"

Mariah checked the time. It was already after four o'clock. If she didn't make it out of Boston now, the traffic was going to be terrible. "Fine," Mariah said. "Until Monday then. There are a few other things I need to talk to you about as well, actually."

"Oh?" Sue said, smiling optimistically. "Ready to make this a real partnership?"

"Without getting into details just yet, something along those lines. I think you'll be pleased," Mariah said, before Sue pursued the topic any further. "If you hear from Carlos, promise me you'll tell him to call me? I'll have a much better weekend if he checks in with me."

"Absolutely. Button up your coat, it's chilly out there," she warned her.

"I know, I love this time of year," Mariah said. It had been a long time since she'd felt this excited to get out of the city. "I can't wait to see the foliage. I bet the trees look spectacular. I'll bring us back a pumpkin for window."

"Oh, please don't," Sue said, crinkling her nose. "The storefront looks perfect just the way it is."

"Stop taking yourself so seriously," Mariah said, laughing. "And all of this stuff, too," she added, motioning to the pieces of decor cluttering the tables around them. The furniture and accessories were all incredibly sophisticated and current and, in Mariah's opinion, boring. "It wouldn't hurt to interject a little whimsy," she winked.

"Fine," Sue said, dramatically. "If you insist. Just make sure it's the perfect shade of Hermes orange."

"Got it," Mariah said, turning to leave.

"Hey," Sue said, before Mariah walked out. "You know how happy I am for you, right? I mean, all my bitching about men…it's just bluster. Andrew sounds amazing, and I can't wait to meet him."

"I know," Mariah said. "And he is. I never thought, well, this is all just very unexpected. For the first time in so long, I feel…I feel like I have something to live for. Does that sound crazy?"

"It doesn't sound crazy at all," Sue said, smiling. "You deserve this, Mariah. Don't listen to bitter old divorcees like me. Follow your heart."

"Thanks, Sue. For everything."

The two women gave each other a quick hug.

"You're one of the strongest young ladies I have ever known," she whispered into Mariah's ear. "Now get out of here, and have a fabulous weekend, and come Monday morning, I expect all the juicy details."

"Ha!" Mariah said, before walking out the door. "Believe me, that's *not* going to happen."

Chapter Six

After the third and final attempt to enter the address of the cabin in Franconia into her car's G.P.S., Mariah gave up. She was about to call Andrew to ask for help when her cell phone rang. It was Carlos.

"Are you okay?" Mariah asked, answering quickly.

"Long day, Mariah. But I'm fine," he said, in a tired voice.

"Do you know how worried I've been about you?"

"I'm sorry, Mariah, I—"

"Look," she interrupted, "Candace Trainor is a complete nightmare, and I regret the day we started working with her."

"I forgot that she changed her mind about the tufting, six weeks ago, when I picked up the couch. I tried to make her understand that we would correct it, but she wouldn't listen. She just started yelling crazy things," he explained. "So, I just left."

"I'm so sorry, Carlos. I heard she threatened to call immigration on you. Is that true?" Mariah asked.

"Yes," he said, laughing, "I told her I was a legal citizen of this country and would be happy to show her my paperwork. But that only made her scream louder."

"She's a nasty, miserable woman," Mariah said. "Can you imagine being married to someone like that?"

"No. But I don't care about the way she spoke to me. I care about the business. I spent the day trying to find the fabric in stock somewhere, but I came up empty. It's going to be another six weeks now. She is going to have another fit when she hears," Carlos said, sighing deeply.

"I don't give a damn about the couch or Candace Trainor anymore, Carlos. I don't want to be doing this the rest of my life. I want to do something I really love," she confessed. It felt good to finally say what she'd been feeling for so long. "I'm telling Sue on Monday that I'm ready to quit."

"Can't say I'm surprised to hear this, Mariah," Carlos said. "You're sure?"

"I am. I don't want to go into details just yet, though. Can we talk Monday? The three of us?"

"Of course. This has something to do with Andrew, doesn't it?" Carlos asked.

"I was feeling like this before I met him, but now, well, yes. Being with him makes me want to be happy again. I don't want to waste any more time. Fabrics and wallpaper and overpriced furniture...it's not what I want to be doing anymore. It never was, you know. I miss painting. Miss spending time outdoors and getting my hands dirty. You didn't know me before Mark," she explained. "I convinced myself that I needed to do something real after college. Something that I could make money doing. But I was wrong."

"You've grown up, that's all. And you're still so young. You can do anything with your life that you want," Carlos said.

"Thank you, my friend. If it wasn't for you and Sue, I wouldn't have made it through those years. I owe you both so much. I know this job hasn't been easy for you, either."

It was no secret to Mariah that Sue and Carlos didn't get along. They rarely saw things eye to eye, and even though Sue was well-intentioned, Mariah was fully aware of just how overbearing she could be. She needed to know that Sue wouldn't make Carlos' life miserable after she handed the business over to them. Therefore, the only solution Mariah could think of was to have papers drawn up the following week, making Sue and Carlos equal partners. The company was doing exceptionally well, but Mariah wanted no buy-out or compensation in any way. She simply wished to make a clean break.

"You owe us nothing. We only want what is best for you," Carlos said.

"I know you do, and I appreciate that. After Mark, I sort of stopped feeling anything. It was a choice I made. I don't want to be that way, anymore," Mariah explained.

"This Andrew, he makes you that happy?" Carlos asked.

"He does," Mariah said without hesitation. She knew beyond a doubt that for the second time in her life, she was in love. Not only could she envision a happy life with Andrew, it was now what she wanted more than anything else. She'd even allowed herself to dream about having children again.

"And you love him?" Carlos asked.

"I do," Mariah said.

"But he still doesn't know about Mark?"

"Not yet. He knows there was someone. That's all. But I wrote him a letter, just today, telling him everything," Mariah explained.

"What? You are seeing him this weekend, but you wrote him a letter?" Carlos asked. "This doesn't make sense."

"I know, I know," she stammered. "I can barely understand it myself. My father wrote me again. I wanted to call him, but I didn't. Andrew needs to hear everything first. Then I can tell my father and tell him everything."

"Okay," Carlos replied. "*That* I understand. But a letter, Mariah? Why not just tell him this weekend?"

"I am. I guess I just wrote it to get my head straight or something…it's scary, you know."

"What?" Carlos asked.

"Falling in love again. I didn't want to love anyone again. And I don't want Andrew to feel like he's competing with a ghost."

"I think there's more going on here then you realize," Carlos mumbled.

"Like what?"

"Let's talk about it when you get back," Carlos suggested.

"No," Mariah said. "Let's talk about it now. Please tell me what you think. Your opinion means everything to me."

"I don't want to upset you," Carlos began.

"You won't," she pressed.

"Fine. It's been five years since Mark died. No one expects you to stop loving the memory of him," Carlos began.

"And?"

"How many times a day do you still talk to him?" Carlos asked.

Mariah glanced at the visor overhead.

"You think I don't know that you do that?" he continued. "I've heard you, Mariah. Many, many times. Sue has, too. Sometimes I'm not sure if you even are aware that you do it."

She wasn't. Not really, anyway. "So?" she asked. "It's just a habit."

"I think it's a little more than that. Maybe, you don't want to let him go, completely? Is that why you haven't told Andrew?" Carlos asked, after a moment's pause.

"I have let Mark go," Mariah insisted. "I've been dating the past three years, haven't I?"

"Yes, but only to keep from being so lonely. You never cared deeply about any of them. You said so yourself…you didn't want to feel anything. But now you do, and you haven't shared the most important part of your life with him. Instead, you wrote him a letter?"

"Point taken. I guess I'm more screwed up than I thought." She wanted to end the conversation.

"No, you're not," Carlos said. "You're just scared. I didn't mean to upset you. You just need to tell Andrew everything. And don't think about me, or Candace Trainor or anyone but yourself this weekend," he said.

"That I can do," she said. "You didn't upset me. And I will have a great weekend, I promise. I'd better get off the phone, the traffic is starting to pick up. Love you, Carlos."

"Be careful, Mariah. I will see you on Monday. I love you, too," he said, hanging up.

Mariah stared out over the steering wheel, knowing there was much more she was struggling with than Carlos could possibly understand. Change was in the air. She was about to walk away from a business that was Mark's vision. She couldn't help feeling that somehow, even beyond the grave, she was disappointing him.

Mariah hadn't liked the concept of starting a decorating business fresh out of college. Mark had had a connection in Boston real estate who was eager to rent the tired old storefront to someone young and energetic enough to give it a fresh makeover. Since Mariah had majored in art and Mark in business, the notion of a decorating business of some kind wasn't entirely insane.

"I don't know," Mariah had said to Mark, their senior year in college. "I mean, I understand it makes sense, I guess. But the business side of it just isn't me. I guess I shouldn't have scoffed at the idea of taking those marketing classes, after all."

"Lucky for you, you know an incredibly talented guy who did take those classes. He also happens to be in love with you and really wants to move to Boston. Just think of the potential. You worked for that decorator last summer back home and loved it, remember?"

"I did," she had admitted. "But that was only because she allowed me to sell my paintings in her shop. They were all sold, by the way," she proudly added.

"You can do the same thing in Boston. Only now, it will be *our* shop," he explained, excitedly.

"I don't know why we can't stay here. We both love Vermont so much," Mariah groaned.

"And we'll come back some day. Who knows, we might even be able to buy a little summer place right on Lake Champlain. How awesome would that be? You could set up an art studio and even teach kids in the area."

"Why can't we do that now?"

"We need to make money, Mariah. And we need to experience living somewhere else. This will be an adventure. Besides, you miss your parents, don't you? Wouldn't you like to be able to visit them more often?"

"I would," she agreed.

Everything Mark had said made perfect sense. Especially the part about living closer to her parents. Neither of them could have predicted at the time that when they finally opened the business a few months later, Mariah and Mark would barely be on speaking terms with them.

Carlos was the first person they hired. He'd been working as a tailor at a shop in Back Bay. The two men had met when Mark needed to purchase a new suit for work. They'd struck up a conversation, and Mark had learned that Carlos' original line of work was upholstery. Carlos was eager to return to it and apparently, loved the idea of helping out a young couple.

After hanging a little sign that read, "Back Bay Décor Opening Soon!" in the front window of an empty storefront on Boylston Street, the three of them toasted the occasion by drinking champagne from paper cups.

"I'm sorry your parents aren't here, Mariah," Mark had said, knowing Mariah wasn't as happy as she was pretending to be.

"It's their choice, not mine," she replied. "This is going to be wonderful. I'm excited. Really!"

The truth was, she'd been terrified. She'd taken a few basic design courses and easily obtained her decorating license, but beyond that, felt lost. Her only ray of hope had been Carlos. It was clear he knew the ropes. He'd worked for several decorators in the past and was more than eager to share his expertise with her. Mariah had viewed him as a godsend.

"You know that your mother wanted to be here. Your father is still making things difficult," Mark said, reaching for her hand.

"It's been two months, Mark. She could have found a way if she wanted. And if he thinks I'm going to forget the way he treated us when he finally comes to his senses, he has another thing coming. Please let's not ruin the moment, okay?" she said. "This is a big day for the three of us."

"You're right," Mark nodded, raising his cup. "I'm so proud of you, Mariah. I know you're going to be a huge success. Here's to my beautiful, talented wife," he started to say, just as someone opened the door. A woman none of them recognized strolled inside.

Susan Davis had been wearing a fashionable Missoni sweater and a strand of black pearls around her neck. Her soft pink lipstick matched her nails, and her classic pageboy hairstyle framed her face perfectly. After scanning the space, she approached Mariah.

"I'd like to speak to your boss," she had stated.

"I guess I am the boss," Mariah had explained, looking back and forth between Mark and Carlos. Sue had raised an eyebrow and looked Mariah up and down, clearly disappointed. Mariah had been wearing a long peasant skirt and a tank top, she recalled. There were Birkenstocks sandals on her feet.

"How old are you?" Sue asked.

"Twenty-one," Mariah replied, nervously.

"Good lord, you're a child. But that's fine," she continued, waving the minor detail off. "My name is Susan Davis, but I prefer being called Sue. I'm recently divorced, I'm local, and if I don't do something creative soon, I'm either going to gain twenty pounds or remarry someone as utterly useless as my first two husbands."

"I really don't know what to say," Mariah said, turning to Mark for help. The woman looked more like a socialite than someone in need of a job.

"I'm a natural at decorating," Sue added. "Been decorating my friend's homes for years. Free of charge. The cape, Nantucket, the vineyard...I've done it all. It's a gift. May I have some of that?" she asked, motioning to the bottle.

Mariah remembered how Mark had just stood there, pouring Sue a cup of champagne with an amused expression on his face.

"This isn't chilled," Sue said after taking a sip. "How the hell can you drink champagne at room temperature?" she asked, grimacing.

Mark, Mariah and Carlos had just stared at her.

"Look, Sue," Mariah said. "You seem very capable, and I don't doubt your abilities, but I don't have it in my budget to hire anyone right now. We've poured everything we had into the lease."

"Well then, who is he?" Sue asked, pointing to Carlos.

"His name is Carlos, and he will be doing our upholstery."

"And the tall guy with the dreamy eyes?" Sue continued, turning to Mark, who beamed at the compliment.

"That would be my husband, Mark," Mariah informed her.

"I'll work for free then, just until you're established. When we start getting clients, you'll start paying me. What do you say?"

Mariah looked at Mark, then at Carlos who shook his head *no.*

"Why don't you come back in a few months?" Mariah suggested. "If we're still in business and haven't lost all our life savings, we'll take it from there."

"I'd rather not," Sue said, folding her arms across her chest. "Starting at the beginning from the ground up is the only way this will work. Besides," she added, scrunching her nose as she surveyed the space, "it's clear you could use my help now."

Mariah looked around the room, eyeing the peeling paint and stained carpeting. "We just signed the lease this morning," she explained.

"Well, the first thing we should do is rip out this disgusting rug," Sue proceeded to announce. "And after that, we should tackle the paint. The water stains can't just be painted over, you know. We need to sand them all down first. There's an odor in here, too, so I'm hoping we don't find mold under this thing," she continued, tapping her well-heeled foot down on the carpet.

Mark had grinned, nodding with approval. Carlos had slumped his shoulders in defeat.

"Well, then what can I say? Welcome to Back Bay Décor," Mariah finally said, extending her hand.

"Thank you," Sue replied, gripping it tightly. "Let's finish the warm champagne and get right to work then, shall we? The location is outstanding, but the condition of this place is truly abominable. I certainly hope you got a good deal on the rent."

***

Less than three months later, Mark was dead. The first time Sue knocked on her door after the funeral, Mariah had assumed it was her mother and reluctantly dragged herself out of bed. She hadn't showered in days and was wearing one of Mark's favorite old T-shirts under her bathrobe. Even though she and Sue had worked together a few months at that point, Mariah was more than a little surprised to find her marching into her apartment when she opened the door.

Since the day Sue began working for her, Sue had all but taken over. Not only was it clear that she viewed Mariah as some young kid with no clue as to what she was doing, which was accurate of course, but she also openly treated her like one. That was what had annoyed the hell out of Mariah the most. But she was a fast learner. It wasn't long before she caught the hang of things and even briefly considered letting Sue go. The only one who had disagreed at the time was Mark.

"It's the age difference, Mariah," he'd explained one day after Sue had completely redecorated the showroom after Mariah had worked on it for hours. "That's all. You know that old saying? Don't bite your nose to spite your face? Keep her around. She knows what she's doing."

"But she acts like *she's* the boss. I don't like it."

"Then stand up to her and prove her wrong," he said. "Don't forget, you're hardly paying her a salary. It's a win-win for you. Think about how much you're learning from her."

Of course, Mark had been right. But Mariah was still barely able to make eye contact with Sue when she'd barged into her apartment carrying a bag of groceries. In true Sue fashion, she'd walked past Mariah without saying a word, but there was no mistaking the look of disappointment on her face. Mariah had watched her mutely from across the room as she systematically tossed out old leftovers from her refrigerator before restocking it.

"How did you get into the building?" Mariah had managed to ask; her brain still in a fog.

"The manager let me in after I explained I was your assistant. Nice man, awful wife," Sue said, ignoring Mariah's vacant expression.

"Is that so?" Mariah said before turning back to her bedroom and slamming the door close behind her.

When Sue showed up again the following week, Mariah refused to open the door. But when the banging wouldn't stop, she eventually gave in.

"Everything is going well at the store," Sue explained, brushing by her. "In fact, you'll be pleased to hear we got two new clients this week. One is doing bedroom window treatments and the other is just re-covering dining room chairs but it's progress, don't you think? Oh, and one of the customers asked if your painting was for sale. I'm telling you, you could make a small fortune if you started painting again. You should see the overpriced crap out there. You're way more talented."

"How did you get in my building again?" Mariah asked in an icy tone, ignoring Sue's comments.

"Didn't I mention?" Sue explained, facing her. "I had a key made so I wouldn't need to bother anyone."

"You have no right to invade my privacy. Please leave. *Now*," Mariah demanded. "I mean it."

"I will once I finish emptying and reloading your refrigerator," Sue said, turning her back on her.

"I don't need you, Sue. I don't need anybody. And I'm not hungry," Mariah shouted, shoving the bag of groceries off the counter, and onto the floor.

"I can see that," Sue said, sarcastically. "You look like a skeleton. And a filthy one at that. When's the last time you washed your hair?"

"That's none of your business," Mariah screamed back. "Get the fuck out of here!"

"I spoke to your mother. She calls me every day, worried about you. Says you won't answer the phone."

"That's right," Mariah shouted. "At least she respects my boundaries, unlike you! How dare you have my key copied? You have some hell of a nerve. I'm going back to bed," she yelled over her shoulder. "You'd better be gone by the time I wake up, or I'm calling the cops."

"Fine," Sue barked back, following her into her bedroom. Mariah tried slamming the door on her, but Sue kicked it open with her foot. The curtains were drawn and the lights were off. Sue flipped them on and gasped at the sight of Mark's clothes strewn about the room. They were on the bed, the floor, and even on Mariah's pillow. "Oh no," she said, covering her mouth in horror. "Mariah, what are you doing?"

"Get out!" Mariah shouted, over and over.

But Sue ignored her. "You need help. Please, Mariah, let me get your mother over here."

"I'll never forgive you if you do that!" Mariah shrieked. Tears streamed down her face as she reached for Mark's University of Vermont T-shirt, pressing it to her face. "I can still smell him. I smell him on everything," she said, sobbing as she slid to the floor. "Please, leave. I need to sleep."

Sue never left her side. Instead, she knelt beside Mariah and gently rubbed her back while she cried.

"Why are you doing this?" Mariah whispered through her tears. "The business is over. Don't you get that? I don't want it anymore. I'm terminating the lease the first chance I get."

"How do you think Mark would feel seeing you like this, Mariah? Back Bay Décor was his dream, too. I will never forget the proud look on his face the first day I met you."

"He was proud," Mariah softly agreed. "He wanted us to be happy, successful. He had so many dreams for us," she added, eyeing the delicately etched gold band on her finger. "Did I ever tell you about the day he proposed to me? He was wearing this shirt," she said, holding it up.

"It's a beautiful ring," Sue said, reaching for the shirt. "We should put the shirt in a drawer, Mariah."

"It's Victorian," Mariah continued, slipping the band off and smiling weakly at the engraving inside. "It's got a beautiful inscription, too. There was this great old antiques shop in Burlington, Vermont, that we used to go to. We never bought anything, but it was always fun to browse. Then one day, he bought me this ring."

"He was a wonderful man. Let me see that," Sue said, reaching for the ring. "*Amor Vincit Omnia.* Love conquers all. He picked the perfect ring for you. I'm not surprised. I liked him the moment we met."

"He didn't want to wait. He wanted to get married on campus, where we met before we moved here to Boston."

"Very romantic. Why don't we get you into the shower?"

"I don't want to take a shower. I don't want to do anything. It's my father's fault," she sobbed. "He was furious with us. That's where Mark was going, you know, when he had the accident. To talk to my dad. He wanted to make amends."

"Don't think about this now," Sue said, gently, stroking Mariah's arm. "Let's get you off the floor. You're shaking, Mariah."

Mariah snatched the ring from Sue's hand and placed it back on her finger, ignoring her. "Some fucking drunk driver hit him straight on. Mark didn't have a chance, and the other guy walked away with a few bruises. It's not fair."

"I know, honey. I know," Sue said. "It's not. I am so sorry, Mariah."

Mariah remained perfectly still, staring at the band on her finger.

"I never want to see my father's face again as long as I live."

Chapter Seven

Katherine Talbot paused in her garden, pulling her left glove back to check the watch on her wrist. She calculated that Mariah was well on her way to New Hampshire by now and smiled despite the ache in her back. Since her daughter had started dating Andrew, she had noted remarkable changes in Mariah's personality; namely, the change in her daughter's voice. She was happier than she'd sounded in years. She also started to talk about the future, which was something Mariah hadn't done in years. Katherine's prayers had been answered. There was no doubt in her mind that Mariah was in love again. As she smoothed out the thick layer of mulch her husband Joseph had dumped in her garden bed this morning, she heard him call out to her from the front door.

"All finished?" he asked. "It's nearly five o'clock."

Katherine leaned back on her heels, surveying her work. "I think so. I forgot the pepper on the kitchen counter. Just need to grab it before I call it a day."

"I've got it," he said, making his way towards her.

"Wonderful," she smiled, ignoring the frown on his face. She had a strong hunch as to why her husband looked grumpy. "Nearly a hundred bulbs planted, all yellow and red this time. Should be a beautiful spring show if the squirrels don't dig them up," she said. Katherine imagined Mariah strolling the property with her in the spring when everything would be in bloom. *Things will be better by then,* she told herself.

"Here," he said, handing her a small glass jar. "It would be wonderful if this stuff really works, wouldn't it?"

"The garden club ladies swear by it," Katherine said, unscrewing the top. "Fingers crossed." After carefully sprinkling the cayenne pepper evenly over the mulch bed, she turned her attention back to her husband before her eyes briefly wandered to the front door of their home.

"He's inside," Joseph said, reading her thoughts. "Sleeping on the couch."

"When he was younger, it was *his* job to keep the squirrels away, remember?" Katherine recalled. She wanted to say that she also remembered a time when Jake would bark incessantly at the front door if Joseph walked the property without him, but she kept that to herself. The last thing Joseph needed to think about was Jake leaving them someday.

"I do," Joseph nodded. "Except the one Mariah smuggled into the house that time, remember?" he asked, as a wide grin spread across his face.

"Unfortunately, I do," Katherine said. She loved to see her husband smile. "Nearly gave me a heart attack as I recall."

"Feels like yesterday, doesn't it?" Joseph asked.

"It does," Katherine agreed.

"I guess Jake is starting to slow down," Joseph said. "But he still has a lot of good years left in him."

"Of course, he does," Katherine agreed. "It's just his arthritis. I can relate," she said, reaching for Joseph's outstretched hand. "I'm fine," she said, catching her husband's concerned expression when she slowly stood up. "Just rusty."

"Aren't we all," Joseph smiled. "Mariah didn't call."

"I'm sorry," Katherine sighed, kissing him gently on the cheek. "Is that why you've been sitting inside all day? Waiting for the phone to ring?"

"I'm still working on cleaning out the attic," he said. "So, technically, I wasn't just waiting for the phone to ring."

Katherine brushed the mulch from her pants. She loved her husband as dearly as she loved her daughter. The rift in their family had taken a toll on all of them. In the past, she would simply not interfere with either of them. It was the only way she could keep her sanity. That, and gardening. But looking into her husband's disappointed eyes, she broke her own rule for the first time in a long while. "She didn't read your letter," Katherine confessed. "I'm sorry."

"What?" Joseph said, surprised. "How do you know that?"

"Because she called me when she received it a few days ago and told me she wasn't going to open it until Monday."

"I don't understand…"

"Neither do I, really. Something about not wanting anything to ruin her weekend with Andrew."

"Well, I guess that's her prerogative," Joseph said, looking away. But not before his wife caught the flash of hurt in his eyes.

"You look tired, Joseph," she said. "I don't like those dark smudges under your eyes. Maybe all this work in the attic has been too much for you. I can always get someone over here to help move those old trunks, you know."

"I don't need help," he insisted. "I'm just about done, anyway. I couldn't find the owl decoy down in the garage, so I went back up there looking for it. No luck," he explained, shaking his head.

"Find anything else?" she asked, knowing there was more. Not only had they not used that decoy in years, Katherine hadn't asked him to dig it out for her. She knew *exactly* what her husband was doing up in their attic. He was nosing through Mariah's old things because he missed her.

"Just some more of Mariah's stuff," he admitted. "Her easel is still up there, and some of her old brushes. Maybe she'll get back to painting one day."

"Maybe," Katherine agreed, smiling hopefully. "Andrew sounds like a wonderful man, you know. Mariah hasn't been this happy in years."

"Are you sure she's really in loves this guy?" Joseph asked. "I know there have been, well, there have been men in her life since Mark. What makes you think this guy's the one?"

"I just do," Katherine said, reaching for his hand.

Joseph smiled up at the darkening sky. "The days are getting shorter," he said.

"They are. And better," Katherine added, optimistically.

She knew they were both thinking the same thing. If Mariah could fall in love again, then perhaps, she could also learn to forgive them.

"Our Mariah's in love again," Joseph whispered, squeezing Katherine's hand tighter. "Then our prayers have finally been answered."

Chapter Eight

"Hello, Andrew," Mariah said, answering her cell phone.

"What's wrong?" he asked. "You don't sound right."

"I'm fine," she said. "I just need a cup of coffee," she added, wishing she hadn't sounded so tired.

"You are such an addict," he said, laughing. "Where are you?"

"Just crossed into New Hampshire," she replied, eyeing the traffic. It was already starting to grow dark.

"Great, how's the ride so far?" he asked.

"Not too bad. I think I made it out of Boston in the nick of time. How was Hartford?"

"Exasperating. The meeting our client professed couldn't wait until Monday lasted less than thirty minutes. Shitty timing. I hate that we're not driving together," he said. "It's not what I envisioned. Pisses me off."

"It's not a big deal and besides, now if I get bored with you, I can just leave any time I want," she said jokingly. "See how nicely this all worked out?"

"You bored with me? Ha! Not a chance," he said. "There are a few snow showers in the forecast, so be careful."

"I'm not the one who drives like a madman," she replied. "But thanks for the heads-up. Promise you won't speed? Or follow some other woman into a service center?"

"I promise."

"I'm serious, Andrew. I know how you get when you're in a rush. Don't drive like an idiot."

"You worry about me?" he asked.

"Of course, I do," Mariah said. "Why? Am I smothering you or something?"

"On the contrary, it feels nice. I can get used to this. Someone keeping me in check."

"Oh really?" Mariah said, laughing. "Should I apply for the job, counselor?"

"You've already got the job. That is, if you want it. Maybe forever?"

Mariah paused a moment. "I *do,*" she said.

"I do, too."

A scene flashed through her mind like an old movie. She was standing on the quad at the University of Vermont, wearing a long vintage white dress. Mark was holding her hand. *I do, too,* she'd said to him, beaming.

"I promised Sue I'd bring a pumpkin back to the office, by the way," forcing the memory away. "She was thrilled."

"When am I finally going to meet this, Sue?" Andrew asked. "She sounds like a real piece of work."

"Soon, I promise. I warned you that she detests lawyers."

"I'll win her over," he said confidently.

"I do not doubt that for a minute. She's got a great eye."

"So you've told me. What does your G.P.S. say? Mine says I'll arrive by 7:30 tonight."

"Mine wouldn't accept the address. But it looks like, from where I am now to Franconia should only take two hours, so I'll probably beat you," she calculated.

"What do you mean you can't enter the address?" he asked.

"I tried three times. It won't recognize Black River Road. I figured I'd call you when I got closer or just stop somewhere. No big deal."

"I'll text you directions from the Franconia exit, okay? I don't know how dark these country roads are going to be," he cautioned her. "It looks like the cabin is not too far from the exit, actually. You shouldn't have any problem finding it."

"Stop worrying. I'm used to country roads," she said, sensing his concern. "All those years going to college in Vermont, remember? I've got this."

"Hello? Mariah, are you still there?" Andrew asked. "You cut out for a second."

"Yup, I'm here."

"Damn, I'm getting a call," Andrew said. "I need to take this. I'll call you back, okay?"

"Drive carefully. I love you," she added.

"Wait, what did you say?"

"I said drive carefully."

"What was that other thing though?"

"Don't you have another call?" she reminded him.

"I love you, too, Mariah."

Chapter Nine

After an unexpected forty-minute work-related call, Andrew tried calling Mariah back. When the call went directly to voicemail, he sent her a text.

ANDREW: Take exit 37 off of 93 North in Franconia. Make a right off the ramp and Black River Road is about a mile and a half down. Turn left and the cabin is the third house on your right. Let me know you got this.

"She loves me," he murmured, reaching into the breast pocket of his jacket. He withdrew the small red leather box he'd been carrying close to his heart all day. He flipped the top open to see it again, imagining how the diamond ring, and nothing else, would look on Mariah, tonight. The classic platinum setting was understated and elegant, but the diamond sparkled with fire. He couldn't have selected a better ring to suit Mariah's personality. The only one he'd shared his intentions with was with his brother, Tom. Naturally, Tom had cautioned him against proposing to a woman he'd only known for two months, but Andrew hadn't paid any attention to him. In fact, he'd expected it.

"I know her," Andrew had explained. "I don't need more time. Wait until you meet her. She's unlike any other woman I've known. Smart, sincere…grounded. And gorgeous. Did I mention that already?"

"Sounds too good to be true," his brother laughed. "I'm happy for you, big brother. When do I get to meet her?"

"Next week, I promise. When the ring is on her finger."

As long as he lived, Andrew would never forget the moment he first laid eyes on Mariah Talbot. He'd been in a hurry to get back to Boston when she'd cut him off in her car that morning. He'd been on his cell phone at the time, trying to convince one of his partners not to leave the firm while simultaneously riding Mariah's bumper, hoping to get her to switch lanes. He'd been more than a little bit aggravated. Although he regretted his behavior, he was grateful that he'd been driving so closely to her. There was a moment when she'd drifted out of her lane for no apparent reason. If he hadn't slammed his fist on his horn to get her attention, she might have sideswiped the car beside her. He'd never asked her about that moment, mostly because he felt certain Mariah would have an entirely different take on it but also, part of him had blamed himself for her near accident.

Yes, his stunt on the ramp was a reckless one. But he was glad he'd done it. When she'd first stormed out of her car, he'd braced himself for a well-deserved tongue-lashing. The last thing he expected was for her to freeze on the spot the moment they locked eyes on each other. But then again, so had he. She'd taken his breath away. Her hair had been loose and wild, whipping around her face in the early morning breeze. Even from a distance, he could see the fury in her eyes. When she had suddenly turned back to her car, he knew he had to say something quickly before she got in her car and drove away. The low tire was the first thing that came to mind. It wasn't the most impressive line he'd ever used, but it worked. In the eight weeks they'd been together since that morning, they'd rarely spent a night apart.

It didn't mean he knew everything about her, however. There was something in her past that she wasn't telling him. He knew that she hadn't been interested in a serious relationship after their first night together. He'd watched Mariah slip out of bed in the early morning hours and quietly get dressed. The room was dimly lit, and she hadn't realized he'd been staring at her until she stepped towards the door.

"Don't leave, Mariah," he'd asked her. "Please?"

Mariah had turned to face him but remained silent. Her hand still rested on the doorknob.

"Mariah?" he repeated, sitting up. Even in the poor light, he could see the hesitation in her eyes.

"I've been hurt," was all she said. Her voice was soft and low.

"I'm sorry."

"You deserve someone who can give you more, Andrew," she said.

Andrew rose quickly before she uttered another word. He wrapped his arms around her tightly and whispered into her ear that he would never hurt her. They stood in silence until Mariah slipped her hand into his and lead him back to bed. He vowed that morning that he wouldn't push her into discussing her past. He'd assumed it was a relationship that had ended badly. The notion of some guy hurting Mariah infuriated him. It wasn't long before he also discovered that Mariah didn't like to talk about her family.

"Everybody has issues with their families," he'd said to her one evening, while she lay in his arms. "My parents were no picnic either. They hated that I was serious about hockey. It didn't fit in with their plans for me to go to law school."

"Is that why you really gave it up?" she asked.

"My mother got breast cancer when I was in college," Andrew explained. "She pulled through, but it was a tough battle. One day, when she was particularly low, she mentioned that it was her dream to see me follow in my father's footsteps. Talk about pressure."

"How incredibly unfair," Mariah said.

"Don't feel sorry for me, Mariah. I'm not unhappy with my professional life. Turns out, I'm pretty good at it, too. It's just not the career I would have chosen for myself."

"I understand. My mother is wonderful." Her voice had been tentative, he recalled. "My father...well, I can never forgive him for what he did," was all she said before pressing her body closer to his.

"What did he do to you?" he whispered, drawing her close. He was certain that time, she'd open up to him.

"I can't," she said. "I'm not ready."

"You can tell me when you are." It had taken every ounce of willpower not to coax her into revealing more.

"Okay," she said, nuzzling closer to him. "I'm happy now. That's all that matters, right? *You* make me happy, Andrew. I never thought I could feel like this again."

"I've never felt this before," he said.

He couldn't erase whatever had happened to her in the past, but he could certainly make sure no one would hurt her in the future. She'd slept soundly in his arms that night until the sound of rain woke them both. The room was pitch dark when Mariah asked if he minded opening the window a crack. When he returned to bed, he pressed his face into the back of her head, kissing her.

"I can smell the rain in your hair," he said.

"That's not possible," she laughed. "But I love that you think you do."

"Do you now? Hmmm...what else do you love about me?" he asked, as she slowly turned in his arms to face him. They held each other's gaze before Mariah spoke.

"Just about everything," she admitted.

That was the moment he knew he was going to marry her.

Only another hour or so, Andrew thought, reaching for his phone to try her again.

Chapter Ten

Mariah looked at her phone, disappointed there was no message from Andrew. She sighed, frustrated with the lousy cell reception and tightened her grip on the wheel, glancing at her left hand. Her ring finger was bare, but she had a strong hunch that things were about to change.

"What would you think of me, Mark?" she asked, "if I married someone else, I mean?"

Her thoughts wandered to the day she'd slipped Mark's ring off forever, three years ago. It was right after some college friends had visited her in Boston. They'd insisted on getting together for drinks, even though Mariah hadn't wanted to. It was exhausting for her, having to act as if she was doing just fine all the time. But it was easier than telling everyone the truth. That she was in hell. She had perfected the art of appearing stable, at least, which made the people around her feel more relaxed. It wasn't their fault, she knew. After all, what was one supposed to ask a grieving widow? Have you emptied out his side of the closet? Or worse, have you slept with anyone yet?

They'd arranged to meet at a trattoria in the North End. She'd put on makeup, concealing the bags under her eyes and dug out a pretty dress she had forgotten she owned. The moment Mariah stepped into the noisy restaurant, she panicked. It was crowded, and her gaze darted around the room nervously in search of her friends. When she failed to spot them, she turned to leave just as she heard her name being called from a table near the back. She planted a smile on her face as she approached them. The last time they'd been together was at Mark's funeral.

"You look good," Tina had said, eyeing her up and down. "Doesn't she, Karen?"

"She does look good," Karen had replied, nodding enthusiastically.

Mariah could have written the entire script. When anyone who knew about her story bumped into her, there was the inevitable awkward comment of how 'good' she looked. It was never 'great' or 'fabulous' or 'amazing'. That would have sounded way too phony. 'Good' was good enough.

"Thanks," Mariah had said, hoping to appear relaxed. "It was great to hear from you. How long are you two in town for?"

"Not long at all," Tina explained, motioning for the waiter. "What are we drinking?"

"Martinis?" Karen suggested, grinning mischievously.

"Fine," Mariah nodded, seeming to delight her friends. "So how are you, Karen? Do you like living in New York?"

"I love it. Such an amazing city. You should come visit."

"Maybe someday," Mariah replied, knowing she never would. "I'm so busy with work. It's nuts."

"That's good, right? Being busy?" Tina asked.

"It is," Mariah nodded. She wanted to tell them to relax. Tell them she was still the same Mariah they'd went to school with. Instead, she sipped on her drink.

"How's business?" Karen piped in.

"Pretty good, although I can't say I'm loving it."

"Of course, you are," Tina said. "You were always so artistic, so creative. How could you not love decorating people's homes?"

"I do," she tried to explain, "most of the time anyway. The majority of the people I work for don't care about creativity. They just want what's 'in' now."

The first round of martinis went down quickly and still no one mentioned Mark. Instead, they ordered another round of drinks and talked about their careers and current boyfriends. Neither of them asked Mariah how she was *really* doing. The longer Mariah sat there, drinking, the more their avoiding the subject angered her. It wasn't long before she'd started scanning the room, planning an exit strategy.

A man standing by the bar caught Mariah's eye and smiled at her. She smiled back. When he walked over to their table a few minutes later, saying the waiter had personally sent him to check on the three lovely ladies in the back, they'd all laughed. He was considerably older than they were and very attractive. It was the first time Mariah had heard herself laugh in years and the sound had felt foreign to her.

Karen had insisted he sit down. At first, Mariah hadn't felt comfortable with some strange guy crashing their evening but after speaking with him some more, she found she actually enjoyed his company. The man was a diehard Red Sox fan, and of course, Tina and Karen loved the Yankees. The bantering was brutal, but entertaining. It had been so long since she'd felt anything but pain and suddenly, something deep within her stirred. She didn't want to be disappointed in her friends anymore. Didn't want to be terrified of leaving her apartment, of talking to people. She wanted to laugh again. To be happy.

"Aren't we going to order something?" Mariah had finally asked, downing the last of her third drink.

"Actually," Karen said looking at her watch. "We've been talking so much we've lost track of time. Tina and I both have early morning flights to catch," she said with a wink. "But you should stay, Mariah."

"But we haven't even eaten?" Mariah said, confused.

"I can order us something," the man quickly offered.

Mariah opened her mouth to respond but the man rose from his seat, addressing Tina and Karen. "I've got this," he said, when they'd reached into their purses for their wallets. "Even if you *are* fans of the Evil Empire. It was a pleasure meeting you, regardless."

"Stay," Tina insisted, kissing Mariah goodbye. "And have fun," she whispered into her ear.

How Mariah had ended up in the man's apartment later that night was still a blur. Her head was pounding when she woke up, naked, under a thin sheet, beside a man she barely knew. She was ashamed and embarrassed, and her only thought was to get as far away from this place, this stranger, as fast as she could. Easing her body off the mattress and praying he wouldn't wake up, the first thing she spotted was her bra on the nightstand. She'd cringed, picking it up before she tip-toed across the room. She had almost made it out the bedroom door when he spoke.

"Morning," he'd said.

Mariah quickly slipped her dress on, turning her back on him. "Morning," she'd replied.

"Everything okay?" he had asked.

"Of course," she said.

"It's Sunday. Do you have to leave so early? I can go get us some breakfast if you like."

"Thanks, but I need to go. This is the North End, right?" she asked, looking out his bedroom window as she zipped her dress. Her hands were shaking so terribly, she could barely complete the task.

"Yup," he said, yawning as he stretched his arms overhead. "Best espresso in Boston. How about I go and get us some?"

Mariah had ignored the question and stepped into her shoes, asking him where her purse was instead.

"I'm pretty sure you left it in the kitchen. So, you married?" he asked matter-of-factly when she turned to leave.

Mariah had frozen on the spot at his question, unable to move. "Why do you ask?" she said, her back still to the bed.

"The ring," he said. "Wasn't sure if you wore it to keep guys like me away, or if you were really married," he joked.

Her stomach heaved. Certain she was going to be sick right there on his floor, she covered her mouth with her hands before racing out of the room.

"Because I don't have a problem with that, you know. If you're married, I mean," he called out to her.

By the time she stepped out onto the sidewalk, she was choking back tears. She spotted a narrow alley between two buildings across the street and quickly made her way towards it, ducking inside just before bending over and emptying the contents of her stomach onto the pavement. She leaned a hand against the building to steady herself, but her knees buckled, and she fell on them hard, scraping them. The stinging pain had unleashed the torrent of sobs she had been holding back.

Was his name Dominic or Danny? She thought frantically, covering her face with her hands. Mariah couldn't believe that her "friends" had left her with him.

Scenes from the evening flashed through her head. They'd left the tavern after sharing a pizza, holding hands in search of a *café*. Mariah recalled liking the way it felt to hold someone's hand again. Along the way, he'd managed to convince her to go to his apartment for coffee instead. When he had rummaged through his cupboards confessing that he was out of coffee, they'd both laughed. Mariah was still laughing when he'd started kissing her. The shock of being touched by someone other than Mark had stunned her, but it wasn't long before she'd begun kissing him back.

64

Pushing herself up from the pavement, she dug through her purse knowing there was only one person she could call.

"I'm sorry to be calling you so early on a Sunday morning, Carlos," she said. "I'm in the North End, and I need a ride home. Can you come get me?"

"Where are you?"

She walked to the edge of the alley to get her bearings. "I'm on the corner of Fleet and North Street," she shakily replied, looking up at the street signs before ducking back into the alley. At that moment, two elderly women dressed for church walked past her; the top of their heads covered in black lace. They'd frowned in her direction before turning away. Mariah looked down at her bloody knees and cringed. Vomit covered the front of her dress. The pain in her burning knees was nothing compared to the shame and humiliation she felt in her heart. She wished she were dead.

"I'm on my way," Carlos said, hanging up.

Mariah sank down to the pavement, recalling the man's question if she was married. She looked at the gold band on her hand, slipping it off, and tracing the inscription she knew by heart with the tip of her trembling finger.

"*Amor Vincit Omnia,*" she whispered. The day Mark had slipped the antique band of gold on her finger had been one of the happiest days in her life. The sun had been streaming down on them at their favorite spot in the woods, as if declaring them the most special couple on the planet. Their life together was supposed to be perfect. A fairytale.

"We were wrong, Mark," she said, tilting her head up to the sky. There were no trees around her then. No scent of balsam hanging in the air or the sounds of birdsong overhead. The alley had been littered with garbage, and the only thing she'd smelled was the wretched scent of her own vomit. After her behavior that night, one thing was clear. The girl that Mark had proposed to in the woods all those years ago didn't exist anymore.

It felt as if she had lost him all over again.

Chapter Eleven

When she took the exit for Tilton, New Hampshire, Mariah was relieved to find a quaint looking diner right off the ramp. It was getting dark, and she still hadn't been able to get through to Andrew. She decided that she'd grab a quick cup of coffee and hopefully, find a good old fashioned pay phone. After pulling into the parking lot, she dug into her purse for her wallet, catching a glimpse at the letter from her father at the bottom of her bag.

"Progress, Mark," she mumbled, withdrawing it from her purse. The first year after Mark's death, she'd thrown her father's unread letters directly into the trash. But as the time went by, she began to read them. When this one arrived at her office a few days ago, her first reaction had been not to open it until after her weekend with Andrew. She didn't want anything to taint her trip. She was glad she'd changed her mind.

Mariah's wedding had taken place on campus, the day before her graduation from the University of Vermont. Mark had arranged the ceremony with the school's chaplain without her knowing. When he'd finally revealed his plan, which he had hoped Mariah would find romantic, her initial reaction had been the exact opposite. All she could think of was how devastated her parents would be. But when Mark explained that the ceremony was just for them and that they would do it all over again in front of their parents in a church back home, Mariah had agreed. It had all happened so fast and it hadn't been long before she got caught up in the excitement. She and her friends had found a long vintage white dress at one of her favorite thrift shops in downtown Burlington and Mark had picked her an enormous bouquet of lilacs. Mariah had worn a chain of daisies in her hair. They had been surrounded with friends when they exchanged their "I do's," on the very campus where they'd fallen in love.

What she and Mark hadn't counted on, unfortunately, were her parents strolling across the quad the next very day, being congratulated on their daughter's wedding. By the time her father had found her standing in her graduation gown, he'd been livid. Mariah had tried to explain the situation, but her father had been too busy shouting at her to listen. He'd made an awful scene and stormed back to their hotel room, refusing even to watch the commencement ceremony. Her poor mother had been caught in the middle all those years ago, and still was. Mariah knew that needed to change, too.

"You wanted us to make up with my father, Mark. I promise, I will. It's time," Mariah said, stepping from her car.

It was freezing outside, and she buttoned up her coat as she rushed towards the diner. She could see her breath in the cold air as the first few snowflakes of the season swirled around her, lightening her mood. She laughed, ironically, thinking how it reminded her of her old snow globe.

Chapter Twelve

Andrew wondered where Mariah was, and why she wasn't answering her phone. He tried not to worry, reminding himself of how spotty cell reception was in this part of New Hampshire. But it was nearly eight o'clock and beginning to snow. The lack of lights along the highway was also concerning.

Spotting the turn for the cabin, he felt a wave of disappointment when he didn't see Mariah's car in the driveway. He reached for his cell phone and called her again. Still no answer.

The cabin was just as charming as it had looked online. It was surrounded by hundreds of pine trees lightly dusted with snow and an old-fashioned well stood in the front yard. Someone had placed a pumpkin in the pail, suspended over the opening, and he smiled, knowing Mariah would like that. Andrew grinned, recalling how just a few days ago, Mariah had been delighted to find the storefront windows on Newbury Street being decorated for Halloween.

"We should dress up this year," she had suggested, slipping her arm through his. "What do you think?"

"Don't tell me you're one of those people who starts decorating for Halloween a month in advance?" he'd replied.

"And what if I am?" she laughed.

"I might have known," he said, kissing her on the cheek. "And if you want me to dress up, I will. But I can't say I'll enjoy it."

"Don't tell me you are one of those boring old fuddy-duddies who takes himself too seriously to wear a costume?"

"As a matter of fact, I am," he admitted. But for her, he would make an exception.

"Well, that is going to have to change. In fact, I think I'm also going to carve a few pumpkins for your stoop. What do you think of that?"

"I think I'd like that," he replied.

He couldn't remember the last time he'd carved a pumpkin. Probably it had been when he was a kid with his brother. As long as he was with Mariah, however, he'd do anything. No woman had ever made him this happy in his entire life.

"Does that get me out of having to wear something, though?" he continued.

"Nope. Don't you have any of your old hockey jerseys laying around?" she asked.

"I do. Why?"

"Perfect. We'll throw a little ketchup on it and *voila!* Instant costume!" Mariah announced.

"And what will you be?" he asked her.

"Hmmm…" she replied, rubbing her palms together, as if she were about to cast a spell. "Something equally terrifying. I think I'll be a ghost this year."

"Ha!" he snorted. "There is no such thing as ghosts. How about a gypsy?" he suggested instead, running his hands through her long hair. "A beautiful sexy gypsy with a crystal ball. That's how I see you."

"Oh yeah?" she said. "And what would the crystal ball tell us?"

"That we should get out of Boston for a weekend. Maybe take a ride up north somewhere? Would you like that, do you think?"

"I would love that," she answered, excitedly.

"I'll make it happen then," he promised.

And he had. Reaching for his overnight bag on the seat beside him, he stepped from the car. When he heard a car approaching, he paused, looking back to the road, certain it was Mariah. But when no car passed, he turned away, disappointed.

"Come on, Mariah," he said, making his way to the door. "Where the heck are you?"

The listing agent said the cabin would be unlocked, and it was. He stepped inside onto the wide pine floors, immediately pleased with the cozy atmosphere. A comfortable looking brown, suede sofa sat between two plump chairs, before a giant fireplace. The mossy green and clay tones of the furniture were perfectly suited to the ceiling's exposed wood beams. Thick, wooly blankets were draped over the sides of the sofa, their fringed bottoms touching the floor. Aside from the temperature, everything was picture-perfect. He dropped his bag to the floor and searched for the thermostat.

"Fifty-five degrees?" he murmured. "No wonder it's freezing in here."

After raising the heat, he eyed the mound of ash in the fireplace. There was an empty bucket alongside the hearth, and after he removed his coat, he immediately set himself to work. In less than twenty minutes, he had an impressive fire going, and he beamed at it proudly. Still, he wished he could ignore the feeling that something was wrong. He reached for his phone to try Mariah again. When the call went directly to voicemail, he checked the time before tossing it onto the sofa out of frustration.

"Okay, you're not that late," he said after calculating the time again that it took to drive from Boston to Franconia in his head. He reached for the bottle of champagne in his bag and was about to rummage through the cupboards for an ice bucket when his phone finally rang.

"There she is," he said, relieved, rushing towards the couch. "It's about time."

Chapter Thirteen

Mariah felt oddly unsettled as she turned off the exit for Franconia. Her stomach was beginning to ache, and she wondered if was because of the winding roads or the strong coffee she had had at the diner, or both. The snow was falling more steadily now, and it was dark out. She hadn't heard from Andrew and still had no idea how to find the cabin. When a service station appeared just around the bend, she couldn't believe her luck. Immediately after pulling in, a young man who could not have been more than eighteen years old, approached her car. He wore a navy peacoat, and his jeans were cuffed at the bottom. His kind expression set Mariah immediately at ease, and she smiled, lowering her car window.

"Looks like something out of a Norman Rockwell painting," she muttered under her breath, as he headed over.

"Well, hello there," the young man said, greeting her warmly.

"Hello," Mariah replied. "I don't need gas. I'm actually a bit lost."

The young man nodded, seeming to understand. When he failed to speak, Mariah continued.

"Could you direct me to Black River Road? My G.P.S. is giving me some trouble today."

"You headed to the cabin, then?" he asked.

"Why, yes. But...well, how did you know that?" she asked curiously.

"It's a popular destination in the Franconia Notch," he explained. "And besides, you've got Massachusetts plates," he stated. "We get lots of visitors from there."

"Of course," Mariah said, satisfied with the explanation. "That makes perfect sense. It's been quite a long drive," she sighed, "and I'm a bit tired."

"Sounds like you're due for a bit of R&R then," he said.

Mariah nodded, detecting a flash of concern in the young man's expression. "I'm fine," she explained. "Really. Just tired and a little dizzy from the winding roads."

"Understandable," he said. "Black River Road is less than a mile from here. You'll want to take a right out of the station," he instructed her, pointing down the road. "Keep driving until you hit a fork, then turn left. The cabin is about a quarter mile down on the right. You won't miss it, I promise."

"Well, that sounds simple enough. Thank you…"

"Gideon," he said. "My name is Gideon."

"That's an interesting name. Is it Irish?" Mariah asked.

"It's a Biblical name, actually."

"Well, it's lovely," she remarked. "And unusual. Certainly not a name you hear every day."

"Are you sure you're okay? I don't mind leading you down there. I'm not expecting much business tonight," he explained.

"That's thoughtful, but I'm all set. I truly appreciate the offer though." It occurred to her she should give him a few dollars for his help.

"That's not necessary," he said, as she reached for her purse. "I'm just doing my job. Really. Better get to the cabin before it gets much darker. These roads are tricky at night."

"Will do then," she said, feeling like there was something more he wanted to tell her. "Thanks again." When she checked her side mirror as she pulled out of the lot, he was still watching her. "Do I seem that helpless?" she murmured.

The directions he gave her were perfect, and in no time, she found Black River Road. Turning up the driveway, her first impression was that the cabin looked like something from a fairy tale. Old-fashioned lanterns lined the driveway, and hundreds of pine trees, dusted with snow, surrounded the tiny log cabin. Her only disappointment was not seeing Andrew's car out front. Knowing what a fast driver he was, she was surprised she reached the cabin before him.

The heavy scent of balsam was the first thing Mariah noticed after stepping out of her car. She closed her eyes, inhaling the familiar fragrance and for a moment, was transported to another time and place. She didn't feel the cold. Instead, she felt the warmth of Mark's hand in hers, their arms swinging back and forth in an easy, familiar rhythm.

"Stop!" she said, opening her eyes. The fantasy had felt so real; she almost expected Mark to be standing at her side. This was not how she envisioned her weekend starting.

"I shouldn't have been talking so much about Mark today," she scolded herself, recalling her earlier conversation with Carlos. "No wonder I'm imagining things." She stared at the cabin a moment longer before moving.

"Monday," Mariah said, shaking the bizarre incident off. "Everything will be different come Monday," she assured herself.

She thought she heard laughter coming from the woods and looked towards the tree line beyond the cabin, wondering if there were kids playing somewhere. She paused a moment longer listening intently, but the sounds had stopped. "Great. Am I starting to hear things now, too?"

She hastily made her way to the cabin. When she finally stepped inside, she immediately felt relaxed. There were logs burning in the hearth, and she wondered if Andrew *had* arrived earlier. Perhaps he had gone out in search of supplies?

But a quick scan of the room found no telltale signs of his having been there. She decided the owner of the cabin must have lit the fire in anticipation of their arrival. Colorful braided rugs covered the old pine floors, and an inviting blue and white striped sofa stood in the center of the room. There was even an old patchwork quilt draped over the armrest.

"Excellent touch," she said, nodding appreciatively.

When she spied an easel in the corner, she approached it slowly. A blank canvas was propped on top and jars overflowing with paintbrushes of all shapes and sizes rested on the table alongside it. There were also dozens of unopened tubes of paints.

"This has to be Andrew's doing," she said, running her fingertips along the fine bristles. She imagined him secretly purchasing all these supplies. Had he sent them to the owner of the cabin earlier in the week, she wondered? The thought warmed her heart, even as the ache in her stomach grew. She tried to ignore the growing pain until the logs crackled loudly, startling her more than they should. The pain intensified and she flinched, reaching for her chest.

"What has gotten into you tonight?" she said, willing herself to calm down. She rubbed her stomach, wishing the pain would go away.

"Focus on something else," she told herself, her eyes drifting to the mantle. A large glass vase overflowing with fresh lilacs caught her attention. How had she missed those?

"That's not possible," she said. "Lilacs aren't in season."

The discomfort was growing worse, and it now hurt to breathe. Squeezing her eyes shut, she covered her face with the palms of her hands, praying she wasn't having a panic attack.

You're going to be just fine, came a familiar voice.

"I remember what you sound like!" she cried, as visions of herself wearing a long white dress, dancing on the grass with Mark, filled her head.

When the fire crackled sharply again, another vision emerged. She saw the face of a man she recognized but didn't know. His skin was an unhealthy shade of gray, and he was sweating. Mariah stood there terrified, watching as his eyes roamed up and down the length of her body. She smelled the alcohol on his breath. She knew, without looking, that there was a gun in his hand.

"No, no, no," she yelled, as a searing pain tore through her back. She fell to the floor, screaming the name "Scotty," without knowing why.

"This isn't real," she said, squeezing her eyes closed, panic gripping her. "I'm hallucinating." She curled herself into a ball praying for Andrew to walk through the door. "It's a fever," she told herself. "It has to be."

When she felt something soft rub up against her back, she slowly turned around. There was nothing there. She scanned the room, thinking an animal was hiding somewhere, pausing when a table she hadn't noticed before came into view. A familiar item rested on top.

"It can't be," she said, as the object came into focus. Her legs were shaking when she stood, but she made it to the table without falling. With trembling hands, she picked up the snow globe her father had given her when she was a little girl and turned it upside down. The name "Mariah Talbot" was neatly written in cursive on the underside, just as she knew it would be.

"What's happening?" she whispered, choking back tears. When something rubbed against her again, she lowered her gaze to a pair of glowing amber eyes.

"Pinky?" she said, as her eyes widened in disbelief. "Is that really you?"

Mariah scooped her old orange cat up into her arms and buried her face in her fur. "I know this is impossible, but you feel so real," she whispered, as the pain in her body lessened. But the moment of reprieve was shattered in an instant. A boy's scream, followed by the sound of two gunshots bounced off the walls. Pinky jumped down and Mariah dropped to the floor and covered her ears, knowing exactly what the sounds meant.

"It didn't happen," she said over and over. "It didn't happen," she continued to say, her voice traveling off.

But it did, it did, it did...

The pain returned. This time, it pierced her heart. She placed her hands on the front of her silk blouse and felt the dampness spread, knowing the sweet metallic scent she inhaled was the smell of her own blood.

"It didn't happen," she continued to say, even as she inspected the warm red liquid on her shaking fingertips. Tears streamed down her cheeks onto her blouse, darkening the growing stains.

"It *did* happen, Mariah," came a voice behind her.

Mariah turned, recognizing the young man immediately.

"Gideon? How did you get in here?"

"I'm here to help," he calmly explained.

"I do need help. I need to get to a hospital," she cried, looking down at her blouse. But the red stains were no longer there. Neither was the pain. "I don't understand...I think I've been hallucinating or something..."

"You haven't been hallucinating, you've been remembering," he told her.

"How do you know my name?" she asked, eyeing him warily. "And how did you get in this cabin? I need to call a friend who is on his way," she said, looking around the room for her purse.

My purse, she thought, frantically. *I left my phone in my purse in the car!*

"There is no car, Mariah," he said, reading her thoughts. "Your purse is gone, too."

"Get away from me," she begged. "*Please!*"

"Do you remember the diner?" Gideon asked, sitting down on the floor opposite her.

"No," she insisted, backing away from him, squeezing her eyes shut.

"Try harder," he asked, calmly.

"Where is Scotty?" Mariah screamed, looking around the room.

"The diner, Mariah. Remember the diner? You parked your car and went inside for coffee. It had just started to snow."

"I remember," she said, breathing deeply.

"Remember what happened next?" he asked.

"No," she said, shaking her head violently. "I don't want to," she cried.

"Please," Gideon said.

"Help me," Mariah said, finally meeting his gaze, "I'm so cold."

"You're going to be okay," he said, reaching for the quilt hanging off the couch. He placed it carefully around her shoulders before sitting back down beside her. "What do you remember?"

"There was a little boy," she began. "Scotty. The kids at the table opposite were making fun of him. I was furious...that's when someone grabbed me," she said. "He pushed me onto the floor. The man with the gun. Oh my god," she whispered, looking him straight in the eye.

"What happened, Mariah?" Gideon pressed.

"He killed me."

Chapter Fourteen

I walked into the diner and ordered a cup of coffee at the register. I was about to ask about a pay phone when I noticed a little boy sitting alone in a booth. I didn't get the sense that anyone was with him, which struck me as odd, given his young age. There were colored pencils strewn on top of the table, and he was sketching something. A group of older kids were in the booth across from him. They were making fun of him, calling him a 'Grandma's boy', and taunting him with other words I couldn't quite make out. The boy ignored them at first and kept looking past me towards the kitchen, as if he were hoping to catch a glimpse of someone. I caught his eye and smiled at him. He returned the smile briefly, before returning to his drawing.

When one of the boys threw a French fry at him, I heard him yell at them to leave him alone. That's when I snapped. Just as I started to make my way towards his booth to set those kids straight, someone grabbed me from behind.

"Get on the floor!" a man screamed, twisting my arm. I landed hard on my knees and cried out, confused. When I looked up, I saw a man standing over me, pointing a gun at my face. He had a wild, crazy look in his eyes and demanded that everyone raise their hands, or he was going to start shooting. The boy in the booth stood up and started to scream.

"No one talk or move!" the man yelled, looking at the boy. "Sit back down, kid."

But the child ignored him and tried to run past him to a waitress behind me. She had yelled at the boy to listen to the gunman, but it was too late.

"What the fuck do you think you're doing?" the man screamed at the boy before kicking him to the floor.

"You bastard!" I yelled, crawling over the kid. I wrapped my arms around the boy and told him to stay quiet. He was sobbing, and I held him tightly. "I'm not going to let you go," I kept saying.

"You have a death wish, lady?" the man asked just before kicking me, too.

77

"He's just a kid!" I shouted.

"Shut him up if you know what's good for him."

"He's my grandson, Scotty," the waitress screamed. "Please don't hurt him!"

I looked into the boy's frightened brown eyes. "Scotty is a great name," I whispered. "It's a brave name. You just act brave, okay?"

"I'll try," he said. "Please, don't leave me."

"I won't. I promise."

I watched the gunman open the register, frantically stuffing bills into his coat pockets. He kept waving his gun around the whole time.

"You already took everything," one of the patrons yelled. "Why don't you go before anyone else gets hurt?"

Scotty started shaking, and my fear was that he was going into shock.

"What grade are you in?" I asked him.

"Fourth," he said. "Is my grandmother going to be okay?"

"Of course," I said, praying it wasn't a lie. "Is your mom here, too?"

"I don't have a mother anymore," he said. "She left me."

"I said to keep that kid quiet," the man yelled.

"Scotty, you stay with the nice lady now, you hear me?" his grandmother called out. "The man is going to leave soon."

The waitress and I locked eyes on each other just before she averted her attention to a man in a booth who was nodding cautiously back at her. She mouthed, "He has a gun," to me, and I covered Scotty's body with my own. I watched as the man in the booth slowly lowered his raised arms.

"What are you doing?" the gunman screamed at the man, charging across the room towards the waitress. "Raise those fucking arms back up, asshole," the man said, pointing the gun directly at the old woman's head. The man in the booth obeyed him immediately.

That's when Scotty broke free from under me.

"Don't hurt my grandma," he screamed, scrambling towards her. Scotty tripped but bounced back up and the gunman laughed.

"Maybe I'll shoot you instead," he said, pointing the gun at Scotty's face.

"You going to shoot a kid?" I cried, standing up, putting myself between them. I looked into the man's vacant eyes and knew there was no way I could convince him to leave the diner before someone got killed. I thought of my father, and how I wished I had called him today. The gunman's gaze fixed on someone behind be and I slowly turned around. It was that same customer. Only this time, he was pointing a gun in our direction.

"I'm a police officer," he stated. "Get out of here now before anyone gets hurt."

That's when I heard the first shot. I was still staring at the officer when I felt something rip through my back, into my chest before I fell to the floor. A second shot rang out and I watched the gunman fall to the floor alongside me, dead. Blood gushed from a hole in his forehead, and I squeezed my eyes shut not wanting that to be the last thing I ever saw.

"Is he dead?" someone asked, rushing towards us.

When I opened my eyes, people were moving all around me. I craned my neck to look for Scotty. His grandmother was on her knees with her arms wrapped tightly around him, shielding him from the scene. She looked over at me, crying. The officer was leaning over me now, pressing down on my chest, and yelling at me to keep my eyes open.

"Hold on, lady, please!" he screamed. "There's an ambulance on the way."

But as hard as I tried, I couldn't. My final thought before closing my eyes was that Andrew was waiting for me.

Chapter Fifteen

Andrew's grin vanished the instant an unknown New Hampshire phone number appeared on his caller I.D. Had Mariah lost her phone, he wondered? Was she stuck somewhere?

"Yes?" he answered, hoping to hear Mariah's voice.

"This is the New Hampshire State Police. To whom am I speaking?" came a firm, male voice.

"Excuse me?" *The police?* A sick feeling washed over him. He glanced out the window and noticed it was still snowing. Had Mariah been in some kind of accident?

"This is Andrew Madden. Can I help you?" he asked tightly.

"Mr. Madden, we are contacting you because there has been an incident involving a woman that we have reason to believe you know. We are in possession of her mobile device and noticed several missed calls from this number."

"You mean Mariah's phone? Is she there?" he asked.

"Mr. Madden, we need to contact her next of kin," the officer explained, after a slight pause.

"What's happening?" he demanded. "Please tell me."

The officer explained there had been an armed robbery at a diner in Tilton earlier and a female, believed to be Mariah Talbot, had been killed.

"No," Andrew insisted, shaking his head. "Mariah was not at any diner today. This is a mistake."

"Sir, I realize this is a shock, but we need to locate her next of kin. We would greatly appreciate your help."

"Are you saying she's dead?" he shouted into the phone. "What are you talking about? It's not possible!"

"Sir, what is your relationship to the victim?"

"I'm her fiancé," he yelled. "There has to be a mistake," he repeated, bracing his hand on the back of the sofa. His mind was spinning, and he stared at the fire he had just made moments ago. "It can't be," he kept saying over and over. "It can't be."

"I'm sorry, sir. Pending a positive identification, all I can tell you is a woman carrying a driver's license identifying her as Mariah Talbot was pronounced dead at the scene."

"Where is she now?" he asked, still unconvinced the woman was Mariah.

"Her remains have been transported to Plymouth Hospital where they will be autopsied after an official identification by her next of kin."

"He *remains*? Fuck you!" he shouted.

"We need your help, Mr. Madden," the officer said more forcefully. "Please help us."

"Wayland," he heard himself say. "Her parents live in Wayland, Massachusetts," he said, hanging up.

Andrew remained frozen on the spot, unable to move his legs until he felt something heavy in his hand. It was the bottle of champagne. He'd been holding it during the entire phone call. He forced his fingers open, watching the bottle drop to the floor and roll a few feet away before coming to a stop. Andrew stared at it blankly, unable to fathom what he had just heard.

"No," he said, shaking his head. There was no way Mariah was dead. Clearly, a terrible mistake had occurred. He looked around the cabin one last time before heading for the door.

"I'm coming, Mariah," he said, stepping out into the night.

Chapter Sixteen

When the Wayland police knocked on the door of the Talbot home at approximately ten p.m., Katherine and Joseph had just turned off their bedroom lights.

"Who could it possibly be at this hour?" Joseph said, quickly rising from the bed. Jake was barking downstairs as Joseph hurried to the bedroom window, pulling the curtains aside. "It's the police," he said.

"Oh, please, no," Katherine said. She pushed the quilt aside and stood up quickly.

"I'll go see what they want. You stay here, Katherine," Joseph said, shakily.

"Absolutely not. Did you hear me, Joseph?" she asked, as she watched him walk towards the door. "Stop," she said. "Put on your robe."

"Oh, right. Yes," he nodded, pausing. "My robe…"

A chill swept over her. There could only be one reason the police were here. Something had happened to Mariah. "This can't be happening again," she frantically whispered to herself, recalling a night five years ago. Jake had barked then, too.

The evening had started like any other. She and Joseph had just sat down to dinner when Mariah phoned, warning them that Mark was on his way to speak to Joseph.

"I have nothing to say to *that boy*," Joseph had grumbled, loud enough so that Mariah might hear him. Katherine was furious and covered the receiver with the palm of her hand. But it was too late. Mariah had heard.

"What did he just say?" Mariah had yelled back. "Did he just call Mark 'that boy'?"

"He didn't mean it," explained, glowering at her husband. Joseph put down his fork, folded his arms across his chest, and stared at his wife.

"I wish you had come with him, Mariah," Katherine said into the phone.

"I begged him not to go, Mom," Mariah replied. "Dad is the one who should come *here,* asking for our forgiveness; not the other way around."

"You can't go on like this," Katherine said, sighing. "The two of you, I mean. I'm glad Mark is coming over, and I assure you your father will behave with the utmost respect," she continued, daring her husband with her eyes that he'd better do *exactly* that. "We need to be a family again. It's time to put this unpleasantness behind us," she added, before hanging up. Instead of sitting back down at the table, she reached into the cupboard for another plate.

"What are you doing?" Joseph asked.

"What does it look like I'm doing?"

"It looks like you're setting another place setting for…" he hadn't finished his sentence before pushing himself from the table.

"You sit right back down, Joseph Talbot, or I swear, I will pack my bags and leave this house tonight."

In all their years of marriage, she had never threatened to leave him until that day.

"Fine," he said, impatiently, looking at his watch. "I'll listen to what he has to say, but he can't undo what's been done, Katherine. You know that as well as I."

"Good lord, Joseph!" Katherine screamed. "And what is this great injustice that cannot be undone? That Mariah didn't walk down the aisle of our church, clinging to your arm in a proper gown and veil?"

"It's not just that," he said, shaking his head.

"Or that you missed your father-daughter dance? Our daughter is happy, can't you see that?"

"Is it a crime for me to have wanted a traditional wedding for our only child? Can you honestly sit here and tell me you were fine driving up there for her graduation, only to learn the kids got married without us?" he snapped back.

Katherine covered her face with her hands, exasperated. "Of course, I wish we had been there," she admitted. "But that's not what happened. So, what are we to do now, Joseph? She is our only child. This rift isn't too big to mend. Do you really want to alienate them from our lives?" she asked, searching her husband's face for an answer.

"I do not," he admitted.

"Good. Let's cover our dishes and wait for Mark, okay? And we are both going to accept him into this house with love, Joseph," Katherine warned.

"I'll do my best," Joseph muttered.

But Mark never arrived. Nor had he called. It wasn't until several hours later when Mariah banged on their door, her eyes swollen with tears and shock, had they learned what happened.

"You killed him, Dad!" she'd screamed, when her father opened the door. Katherine watched her daughter as she pounded her fists onto Joseph's chest, shrieking that she never wanted to speak to him again, and that he was not to show his face at Mark's funeral. Joseph had just stood there, frozen in horror.

"Because of you, he's dead!" she kept saying, over and over, until collapsing into her mother's arms.

Katherine squeezed her eyes shut, willing the awful memory away. When she opened them, Joseph was staring at her intently. The color had drained from his face, and she knew he'd been reliving the same nightmare.

"Please stay here, Katherine," he begged her, as the knocking continued.

"Not a chance," she stated, defiantly. She followed her husband down the stairs, where Jake was standing at attention by the door. "Good boy," she said, in a shaking voice. "Go in your bed, now."

But Jake remained by the door.

"It's Wayland Police, Mr. Talbot," came a voice from outside.

Katherine locked her gaze on Joseph and reached for his hand, clasping it tightly before he opened the door. "Be strong," she said, taking a deep breath.

Two uniformed police officers, framed by the night, stood on their steps; their hats in their hands. There were no flashing lights in the driveway, no sense of urgency in their telling stares. There was only sadness.

"May we come in?" the older officer asked.

Katherine glanced at her husband, who had already begun to cry. "It's okay, Joseph," she said, gripping his hand tighter.

She knew their beloved Mariah was gone before the officers even stepped inside.

Chapter Seventeen

"Where's Mark?" Mariah asked Gideon. "I *feel* him."

"He's close," Gideon answered. "But he's not here."

"Really?" she said, looking around the room. "Because I could swear that he was."

"He's not," Gideon said, averting his eyes.

Mariah could sense that there was something Gideon wasn't saying. "He doesn't want to see me, does he? Because I wasn't faithful to him after he died?"

"Of course not," Gideon said. "You mustn't think that."

"I want to see him. *Now*," Mariah demanded, staring at the lilacs. "Those are from him, aren't they?"

"They are."

"How could he leave those here for me but not be here? He picked a bunch for me on our wedding day," she said. "It was our flower."

"He told me that," Gideon admitted. "You need to think clearly about what I am required to explain to you, Mariah."

"Excuse me?" she said.

"You still have the ability to impact those you left behind."

"I didn't leave anyone," she said, bitterly. "I was taken."

"Yes," he agreed. "Nevertheless, once you acknowledge that information and still wish to pass over, you can. Then, and only then, is when you will see Mark," he said, glancing at the flowers. "That's what you want, right?"

"Of course, it is, but I don't understand...I can impact people? How?" she said, puzzled.

"You have options," Gideon explained.

"Options?" she snapped impatiently. "Am I not dead? Are you not an angel or something?"

"You are, yes. And I'm whatever you want to call me," he added. "First and foremost, I'm here to help you. To explain that while you are dead, this is only the beginning of your journey. You can walk through that door right now, to Mark, but that means severing all ties to those you left behind. Or," he said, taking a seat on the sofa, "you can return to the world as you knew it for one final look. Either way, you no longer possess a human form."

"I'm not understanding," she said, still confused. "Like a…a ghost, you mean?"

"Exactly."

"Why on earth would I want to be some, some creepy ghost?" she stammered.

"I couldn't agree with you more," Gideon said, nodding. "However, you'd have, well, certain capabilities…the ability to influence people, should that be your desire. In your case, I strongly recommend you don't."

As the full meaning of Gideon's words began to sink in, Mariah let out an ironical laugh.

"What's so funny?" he asked.

"Andrew said he didn't believe in ghosts," Mariah said.

"Oh," Gideon said, understanding.

"I still can't believe this is happening," she mumbled, covering her face with her hands. "And what do you mean, in *your case*?"

"You didn't have a chance to say good-bye," he explained. "There was no lingering illness, no bedside farewells. Those are usually the ones that move on quickly. I know this is difficult to hear… it was your time, but you weren't ready."

"Exactly," Mariah shouted, frustrated. "Then tell me why you are against it?"

"Because it's dangerous," Gideon said, holding her gaze. "Do you hear what I'm saying?"

"I'm listening, Gideon."

"You could get lost. Not find your way back here," Gideon said, choosing his words carefully. "Not find your way back to Mark."

"But all I want is to be with Mark," Mariah said, eyeing the door, sensing Mark was just outside. "How could I possibly not find my way back?"

"Because the longer you remain among the living, the more likely you are to lose sight of your purpose. Things become muddled there. I've seen it

86

happen so many times," he explained. "So many lost souls," he added, coming to stand beside her. "It's easy to lose your focus…things get, well, foggy. Do you understand?"

"I think so," she replied, as the full meaning of his words sank in.

"Good," Gideon said.

Mariah stared at the cabin door. "Will they be okay?" she asked, thinking of all the people she loved that she would never see again. Not just Andrew and her parents, but Sue and Carlos, too.

"It's a process," Gideon replied truthfully. "I don't have all the answers, Mariah. But I can say without a doubt that the passing of time helps."

She averted her eyes from the door. "My poor father," she said as she started to pace the room. "I waited too long. I was such an idiot."

"Remember that he has your mother. She's strong, like you," Gideon assured her.

"Yes, but for how long? Do you realize what my mother has been through?" she asked, turning to face him.

Gideon stared at her but remained silent.

"The boy at the diner, Scotty, is he okay?" Mariah continued.

"He survived the shooting," Gideon said.

"That's not what I mean," Mariah said impatiently. "There was something different about him."

"He was shy before the incident, but now…" Gideon replied, his voice trailing off.

"Now what?" Mariah pressed. "Look, you've made yourself clear. You think it's a bad idea for me to go back. But if it's your job to give me the facts, then give me all of them."

"He was already withdrawn," Gideon admitted, reluctantly. "Now he has witnessed a traumatic event. It will take him a long time to put what happened in the diner behind him."

"Well, is he getting help? Will he overcome this?" she asked, recalling the terror in the boy's eyes. "The poor boy…he watched me die."

"He's getting help," was all Gideon said.

"Wait, what am I thinking," she said, running her hands through her hair. "I want to be with Mark. And not because you think I'd get lost as you say, but because I need to be with him. You have no idea how much I have missed him. It wasn't fair what happened to us."

"Then open the door," Gideon said.

Mariah placed her hand on the doorknob and took a deep breath. How many nights had she cried herself to sleep, missing Mark? Her life had been shattered the day he died. To think she could see him now, just by stepping outside, was all she'd ever dreamed of.

It's not complicated, she told herself. *He's right there!*

She couldn't do it. Slowly, she removed her hand from the brass knob and pressed her forehead against the door, closing her eyes. "I have so many regrets," she said, thinking of her father. "If I don't go back, he's never going to forgive himself. I don't have a choice."

"Is that your decision then?" Gideon asked.

"I guess it is," she said, stepping back, as her eyes filled with tears. "Mark," she said, anxiously. "He'll wait for me, right?"

"Yes," Gideon said.

"I won't get lost," she said. "You don't know me, Gideon. Once I have something in my head…"

"I hope you're right," he interrupted her. "For both your sakes. Here," he added, bending over to pick up Pinky. He handed the cat to Mariah. "Take her with you."

Mariah held Pinky close to her chest. The thought of her not being alone comforted her. "I can bring her?" she asked, relieved.

"You can. I'm on your side, Mariah, even if I don't agree with your decision. Pinky may even come in handy. Most people won't sense you unless you want them to. But that's not the same for animals," he warned.

"Why not?"

"I'm not sure," he said, stroking Pinky's head. "It's just the way it is."

"I'll keep a close eye on her," Mariah said. "I promise."

"Are you ready then?" he asked.

Mariah wanted to ask him how it all worked. How she was going 'back', and where she would find herself when she left his side. Instead, she took a deep breath and looked around the cabin, eyeing the lilacs on the mantle one last time.

Please be here when I get back, Mark.

"I'm ready," she nodded, as Gideon placed his hands on her. Her last thought before the room went dark was that she hoped she'd made the right decision.

Chapter Eighteen

Andrew parked his car outside Plymouth Hospital, ignoring the 'Ambulance Only' sign. A man wearing surgical scrubs and smoking a cigarette called out to him.

"You can't park there, buddy!"

"The keys are in it," Andrew snapped, brushing past him. "Move it yourself or tow it. I don't care." His heart was pounding, and his legs were still shaking as he approached the front desk, scanning the people in the waiting area. A woman rocked a sleeping girl in her arms, her lips hovering over the child's ear, singing in a low voice. Across from her sat a man, holding his bandaged arm, staring blankly at the television overhead.

"Can I help you, sir?" the receptionist asked, looking up at him politely.

"Has a Mariah Talbot been admitted?" Andrew demanded. "Mariah Talbot," he enunciated more clearly when the woman didn't immediately respond. "Is she here?"

"Just a moment, please," she replied, turning away and reaching for the phone.

Andrew watched her dial quickly, then whisper something into the receiver. She hung up the phone and turned back to face him, with an uncomfortable expression in her eyes.

"I'm getting that information," she informed him in a calm, professional tone. "Is there anything else I can do for you at the moment? Would you like to take a seat?"

"No, I would not like a fucking seat," he replied coldly. "Who's in charge here?"

A woman, who appeared to be in her late sixties, entered the waiting room from an office down the hallway. She was wearing a pale blue suit and a chain around her neck with a simple, gold cross. She glanced at the woman behind the desk and nodded before turning her attention to Andrew.

"May I ask your relationship to Mariah Talbot?" the woman asked.

"I'm her fiancé. Andrew Madden."

"I'm Margaret Howe," the woman said. "Why don't we talk in my office?"

"Fine," Andrew said, following her down the hall. He wanted to scream that he didn't want to hear what he knew she was about to tell him.

When he stepped inside the tiny room, she motioned for him to take the seat opposite her. Andrew watched her with guarded eyes as she cleared her throat and calmly folded her hands on her desk. A cheaply framed poster depicting a soaring eagle against a backdrop of snow-capped mountains hung on the wall behind her. Below it read the quote,

Those who hope in the Lord will renew their strength.

They will soar on wings like eagles.

Isaiah 40:31.

Andrew clenched his jaw reading the verse, fighting the urge to pull the frame from the wall and smash it into a million pieces.

"Would you like a glass of water?" Margaret asked.

Andrew shook his head.

"Mr Madden," she began. "Mariah Talbot was recently brought in, deceased upon arrival from a single gunshot wound. According to the paramedics who were on the scene, within moments of the incident, she died instantly and with minimal suffering. We are all deeply sorry for your loss."

Andrew looked down at the floor. It was cheap hospital linoleum marred with dozens of scuffmarks. He thought of the people who had sat here before him, the ones who had caused those jagged black lines. *This isn't happening,* he thought. Things like this happened to other people. He wasn't supposed to be one of them.

"How do they know?" he said stiffly.

"I'm sorry?" the woman asked, confused.

"How do they know it was instant, with 'minimal suffering' as you phrased it?"

"Would you like to meet with a grief counselor, or perhaps speak with our chaplain?" she offered, rising from her seat.

"No. I'd like you to sit back down and answer my question," he said, glaring at her.

She hesitated, looking at the door briefly before sitting back down. "The bullet penetrated her heart," she admitted softly. "She wasn't alive for more than a minute or so."

Andrew pictured Mariah on some restaurant floor surrounded by strangers as her life slipped away. She knew she was dying, he realized.

"So it wasn't *that* instant, was it?" he said coolly. "I want to see her. Now."

"I'm sorry. Until her parents arrive, I'm afraid that's not possible."

"Why the hell not? I'm her fiancé," he shouted, pounding his fist onto the desk.

"Please control yourself," she warned him. "I understand your pain and again, I am deeply sorry for your loss. But unfortunately, until her parents arrive, no one is permitted to see her. It's hospital policy. The Massachusetts police are escorting her parents as we speak. Of course, once they arrive, you may view the body with their permission. You are welcome to wait here."

"Mariah," Andrew corrected her, running his hands through his hair. "Her name is Mariah. And I apologize."

"I'm sorry, too," she said, lowering her voice. "For *Mariah*."

"Fine. I'll wait here."

"Can I bring you anything?" the woman offered once more before stepping from the room. Again, Andrew shook his head no.

After the door closed, he pushed back his chair and rested his elbows on his knees, covering his face with his palms, recalling the last conversation he had with Mariah. "It's my fault," he whispered, looking back at the poster.

He knew he would never forget this room. Not the smell, or the harsh fluorescent lighting, or the sterile furniture. He imagined Mariah's body, ice cold, on a metal table somewhere in the bowels of the hospital. She wasn't supposed to be there, he told himself. She was supposed to be laughing in his arms, wearing the ring and planning their future. He was going to be sick. He stood quickly, eyeing the wastepaper basket but before he could reach it, he slammed his fist into the wall.

The bullet penetrated her heart, the woman had said.

How could he possibly face her parents? Explain that he was the one meeting their daughter. That because of him, Mariah was dead.

"You're a fucking coward," he said, turning to the door.

91

Chapter Nineteen

Sue fumbled for her keys in the rain outside Back Bay Décor. Her head was uncovered, and she wore no make-up. After stepping inside, she flipped on the lights and stared at the room, ordering herself not to cry. It was eerily still, and for the first time in all her years working there, she felt like a trespasser.

When Carlos had called her late Friday evening, she had just returned from a wonderful dinner out with friends. In fact, she'd initially considered not answering the phone when she saw his name on the caller I.D. Her poached lobster salad had paired beautifully with the Grand Krug they had selected, and she wasn't in the mood to have Carlos taint the evening by discussing the Trainor debacle. Remembering she had given her word to Mariah; she changed her mind and took the call. The moment she heard him crying on the other end, she knew whatever he was calling her about had nothing to do with work.

"The police found my number on Mariah's phone," he'd said. "Turn on the news," he'd instructed her, sobbing.

Sue quickly turned on the television, sinking down to the floor in shock as she listened to the story unfold. She didn't cry or scream or make a sound. Instead, she stared at the television screen long after the breaking news segment about a Boston woman being shot and killed in some diner in New Hampshire had ended. When she finally stood up and entered the bathroom, she slowly unbuttoned her blouse and stepped out of her skirt. Before she could reach for the faucet, her body shuttered violently as she proceeded to vomit her lobster dinner onto the marble floor.

Ninety-six hours later, she still couldn't believe that Mariah was gone. Entering the door marked 'Private' in the back of the shop, Sue glanced at her desk, half expecting to find Mariah there, buried up to her nose in fabric samples. Everything looked exactly as it had four days ago.

"Focus," she said. After a long deep breath, she lifted the stack of work orders and began flipping through them, prioritizing what could be canceled and what needed to be honored. After making several phone calls, she reached into her bag to retrieve the letter that she composed the previous evening.

Dear Back Bay Décor Clients,

It is with great sadness I inform you of the recent loss of Mariah Talbot, proprietor of Back Bay Décor. As a result, the shop will be temporarily closed.

All custom orders currently in production will be completed and installed as scheduled. However, orders not yet in production will be cancelled, and those deposits will be refunded within the next two to four weeks. Please feel free to call me with any questions or concerns.

Thank you for your patience and support,
Susan Davis.

"Now for the hard part," Sue whispered, reaching for touchpad of Mariah's computer. The moment she tapped it, a screenshot of Andrew appeared on the monitor. He was grinning broadly and holding a glass of wine at a sidewalk *café.*

"Don't cry," Sue said, holding back tears, as one screensaver faded into the next. So many of them were Mariah and Andrew, smiling and laughing and looking so much in love. When the bell attached to the street door entrance rang, she cursed herself for not having locked the door.

"Damn it," she said, regretting she hadn't been more attentive. The last thing she wanted to do was talk to anyone about Mariah. She was barely able to keep herself composed, let alone discuss her death. She also knew full well that tragedies such as these often drew unnatural interest and speculation. She would not allow what happened to Mariah to be exploited for anyone's morbid curiosity.

Bracing herself for an uncomfortable confrontation, she breathed a quick sigh of relief when she looked up and found it was only Carlos. She rushed out to meet him and found his appearance startling. Besides looking uncharacteristically disheveled, his eyes were bloodshot, and his hair was uncombed.

"I came in to put a note in the window," she blurted out.

"What can I do?" he asked.

"I'm not sure, but we'll need to figure out a plan soon. I've placed a call to Mariah's accountant and to her attorney," she said, wishing she had greeted him kindlier.

Standing there, it occurred to Sue that in all the years they worked together, she and Carlos had never been in the office together without Mariah. Mariah was always the buffer between them, settling their arguments and disagreements. Now it was just the two of them. An uncomfortable silence fell between them, and she wondered if Carlos was thinking the same thing.

"How is Irma?" Sue asked.

"She hasn't stopped crying. We loved her like she was our own daughter," he said, wiping away fresh tears.

"I know you did. They say she saved that boy's life."

"It doesn't surprise me," he nodded, smiling weakly. "Mariah was selfless."

"She was," Sue said. *And I loved her too, you know.*

"And brave," Carlos added.

Sue looked around the room, awkwardly, then back at Carlos. "I haven't heard from Andrew. Have you?"

"No, but I wasn't expecting to, I can't imagine what he must be going through. I guess we'll meet him tomorrow?"

"I assume so," Sue said. The idea of meeting Andrew for the first time under these circumstances was surreal. How many times had she told Mariah she wanted to give him the 'once over' and make sure he was good enough for her?

Now, she would be meeting him at Mariah's wake.

"So, there's nothing I can do?" Carlos said, looking around the shop.

"Nothing I can think of," Sue said. "But it means a lot to me that you came in today," she added.

Before she knew it, Sue wrapped her arms around him and hugged him. She felt his shoulders tremble when he started to cry, hugging her back. They stood there in silence for a moment, not speaking until Sue finally pulled away.

"Well, if you think of anything…" Carlos mumbled, dabbing his eyes with his handkerchief.

"Go home, Carlos. Get some rest. Tomorrow is going to be a long day," Sue said, looking away.

"It will," he agreed. "It's so strange being here without her, isn't it? I keep expecting her to walk in."

"Me, too," she admitted.

Carlos placed his hand over Sue's for the briefest instant before turning to leave.

"See you tomorrow, Carlos," Sue said, as he stepped out onto the street.

"Tomorrow," he repeated.

Carlos loved you, Mariah, she thought, as she watched him disappear from view. Sue had always known that Carlos and Mariah shared a special bond, right from the beginning. It occurred to her now, as she locked the door behind him, that perhaps she was always a little envious of that fact. Is that why she was always a short with him, she wondered?

She placed the letter in the front window and walked back into the office. Mariah's umbrella still hung from the coat rack, and she stared at it.

"You forgot to take your umbrella," she said, as the tears she'd been holding back streamed down her face. She sat back down at the desk and reached for a tissue. This time when she tapped the keypad, a giant image of a perfect orange pumpkin filled the screen.

"Well, would you look at that," she said, still crying. "Hermes orange, as per my request."

She leaned back in Mariah's chair and turned to look at the umbrella again. Somehow, the room felt lighter than it had just moments ago.

"Mariah, you know that I detest crying," she said, setting herself to work. "It causes wrinkles."

Chapter Twenty

Gideon remained on the couch long after Mariah and Pinky left the cabin, staring into the fire. "Are you still here?" he asked, not bothering to turn around.

"I told you she'd go back, didn't I?" came a male voice from behind him.

"You did," Gideon said, turning to face Mark, who was wearing a comfortable looking hoodie over a pair of faded jeans. He didn't look pleased. "And for the record," Gideon added, "I don't like lying."

"You didn't lie, you—"

"White lies are still *lies*," Gideon interrupted.

"*Omitted,* is what I was about to say. If she couldn't see me, I wasn't here. Right?" Mark said, raising an eyebrow.

Gideon shrugged his shoulders and said nothing.

"Game of chess?" Mark asked, plopping himself down on the couch.

"Fine," Gideon said as a chessboard materialized on the ottoman. "She felt you. It didn't matter."

"If she'd seen me, she wouldn't have been able to think clearly. Even I couldn't cross that line. It wouldn't have been fair to her."

"Please," Gideon said, dismissively as he placed the pieces onto the board. "Since when do you play fair? The lilacs?" he said, pointing to the mantle. "Admit it. You thought they'd sway her, didn't you?"

"I had hoped they would," he confessed.

Gideon frowned. "I tried my best, Mark. I'm sorry."

"I know. I'm not worried, just frustrated. She'll come back to me, I know it. I just need to be patient a little while longer," he said.

"What about Andrew?" Gideon asked after a slight pause.

"What about him?" Mark said, scowling.

They each made their first moves in silence.

"She has deep feelings for him," Gideon said, after a while. "You're not worried she'll stay...forever?"

"Not a bit," Mark said, tilting his chin up confidently as he captured one of Gideon's pawns.

Gideon remained unconvinced. "How can you be so sure?"

"Because," Mark explained, eyeing the board intently, "whenever she was with him," he said, making his next move, "she still thought of me."

"No thanks to you," Gideon mumbled.

Mark had never left Mariah's world. Not completely, anyway. Gideon had visited him from time to time just to keep an eye on him, but he'd never worried about Mark finding his way back for the simple reason that Mariah was the only woman he'd ever loved. This wasn't the case with Mariah, and they both knew it.

"Now, Scotty, he might take a while," Mark said, sighing.

"I agree," Gideon said, knowing that despite his show of confidence, Mark was just as concerned as he was.

"Mariah loved kids," Mark added. "She warned me when we started getting serious that she wanted a big family, and that if I didn't feel the same way, I'd better let her know."

"And did you?" Gideon asked.

"Of course," Mark said, softly. "I told her I felt the same exact way."

"I'm sorry," Gideon said.

"About what?" Mark asked.

"I'm sorry that you never got the chance," Gideon said, his eyes still fixed on the chessboard.

"Me, too. You may need to help her along, you know," Mark said, gruffly.

"I don't like to interfere," Gideon said. "Mingling among the living is always a delicate dance. One simple act can trigger a ripple effect and before you know it, the trajectories of people's lives are changed forever."

"Bullshit," Mark snorted, thinking of all the times Gideon had done just that with him.

They played in silence the rest of the game.

"Checkmate," Gideon finally said.

"That was too quick," Mark said, frowning hard at the board. "I was distracted."

"Another game then?" Gideon suggested, pleasantly.

"Why not," Mark said. "This might take a while anyway."

Chapter Twenty-One

The first person that Andrew encountered at the wake was an expressionless man in a dull black suit standing next to an easel bearing Mariah's name. When Andrew approached, the man nodded towards the guest book and offered him a pen.

"Would you like to sign in?" the man somberly asked.

"No," Andrew said.

Tom wanted to be at his brother's side today, but Andrew had refused the offer. It was bad enough that he had not waited in the hospital to meet Mariah's parents, he explained. For Tom, another stranger, to appear at her wake felt completely inappropriate. Tom had strongly disagreed, but in the end he respected Andrew's wishes.

The usher motioned for Andrew to proceed through another set of doors. Andrew entered the crowded space, pausing for a moment while his eyes focused on the coffin at the far end of the room. He hadn't realized he'd been holding his breath until he heard himself exhale. It was draped in hundreds of tiny pink roses and beside it was a woman strongly resembling Mariah. Shame washed over him, and he looked away.

The room was stuffy, and the heavy scent of flowers was nauseating. Andrew lingered in the back where dozens of photographs of Mariah were scattered about. To his surprise, the first one that caught his eye almost made him smile. Mariah could not have been more than fifteen years old and was holding a large orange cat. He recalled her telling him about her cat on their very first date. In another photo, she was older, standing in what looked like an open field in the woods. Her hair was long and loose around her shoulders, and she was wearing a sundress.

Like a fairy, he'd said to her once. *You belonged outside.*

He thought of the few times she'd tended the garden in front of his home. He used to tease her that she was more interested in his small patch of property than the house itself. Just last week, he'd watch her from the front stoop, hunched over the shrubs, ripping out weeds he hadn't even known existed.

"You need to fire your gardener," she had told him, pulling out a fistful of clover. "Do you see this?" she'd continued, sitting back on her heels and holding up her hand, as if she were handling some dangerous green invader.

"Looks pretty harmless to me," he'd replied, squinting at the unimpressive looking clump.

"Ha!" she snapped, shaking her head. "This 'harmless' little interloper will take over the whole bed if you don't pull it out by the roots," she explained. "Look at the way it's spreading like wildfire under your boxwoods."

"I'll take your word for it. You just about done?" he asked, debating whether to tell her about the streak of dirt on her forehead.

"Almost," she said.

"We should plan a weekend out of the city like we talked about. Would you like that?" he asked.

"I would love that," she replied, smiling.

"Vermont?" he suggested.

"No," she said, pushing herself up. "Someplace else."

As long as he lived, he would regret the day he ever mentioned New Hampshire.

"Mariah," he whispered, wishing he could relive that day as he stared at her coffin.

"She was beautiful, wasn't she?" someone said behind him, in a thickly accented voice.

"She was," Andrew replied, turning to the face the man who had come to stand beside him. The man's short, brown, and curly hair was neatly cut and speckled with gray. Looking into the man's broken eyes, Andrew realized he had to be the man Mariah had so often spoke of.

"You must be Carlos," Andrew said.

"I am," Carlos said, extending his hand. "And you're Andrew?"

"I am," Andrew said.

"I've seen your picture," Carlos explained.

"Oh, right," Andrew said, nodding.

"She loved nature. Loved to be outside," Carlos said, pointing to a picture of Mariah on the beach.

"She did," Andrew nodded.

"I like this one," Carlos said, pointing to a more recent photograph of Mariah sitting on a park bench. There was a giant weeping willow tree behind her and a pond.

"It that Boston Common?" Andrew asked, eyeing it more closely.

"It is. It was taken after she opened her business. When you're ready," he said, inching closer to him, "I'll introduce you to Mariah's family."

But Andrew was no longer listening to him. Another photograph had completely caught his attention. "This can't be," he whispered, staring at the image of Mariah in a long white dress with a chain of daisies in her hair. Her bare feet were peeking out from just below the hem. The young man next to her was beaming with pride, pointing to the gold band around Mariah's finger. Andrew felt the color drain from his face as he continued to stare at the image.

"She was going to tell you, Andrew," Carlos explained. "Come sit with me, and I will tell you everything," he said, placing his hand on Andrew's arm.

"When?" Andrew whispered, ignoring him.

"It was five years ago. Before they even graduated college," Carlos said, lowering his voice.

"So, this is the guy that broke her heart? Is he here?" Andrew said, scanning the room.

"No, you don't understand," Carlos said, shaking his head. "Please, Andrew, come sit."

"I don't want to sit down," he said, feeling his jaw tighten.

"His name was Mark," Carlos began. "You have no idea what Mariah went through. She was planning to tell you everything."

"She loved being barefoot," a woman interrupted. "Ever since she was a little girl. I can't tell you how many arguments we had over it."

"Yes," Carlos said, nodding nervously. "Even at the office. The first thing she always did was flip off her shoes."

Andrew turned to face the woman who had been sitting by the casket. She was wearing a simple dark suit and her wavy hair was pulled back neatly from her face. Her gaze lingered on Andrew before turning her attention to Carlos.

"Hello, Carlos," she smiled, embracing him. "Thank you for coming."

"There are no words, Katherine," Carlos stammered. "No words."

"How is Irma?" she asked softly.

Carlos turned to his wife who was sitting in a chair at the back of the room clutching rosary beads and praying.

"She loved her very much. We both did."

"I know. She loved you both, too," Katherine said, smiling sadly.

"This is Andrew," Carlos explained.

"Hello, Andrew," Katherine said, extending her hand.

Andrew stared at her, unable to speak. Not only did the woman sound like Mariah, but they also had the same eyes.

"Are you alright?" Katherine asked, leaning closer.

Andrew nodded mutely.

Carlos quickly excused himself, returning to his seat.

"Mariah was married?" Andrew finally said.

"She was," Katherine said, nodding.

"She never told me," Andrew said, his voice tight with emotion. He wanted to be angry with her for not telling him, but all he could think was how beautiful Mariah looked in the photograph.

"It wasn't for very long, I'm afraid. They went to college together. We can talk about it another time, if you like," Katherine offered.

"I'd like to talk about it now," he said.

"This is hardly the appropriate time, Andrew."

"Of course," Andrew said, looking away.

"Would you like to come back to the house after the service tomorrow?" Katherine asked. "We could talk then." When Andrew didn't answer, she placed her hand on his arm and lowered her voice, "this is a difficult time for all of us."

Andrew stared at the floor. "I...I'm not sure," he said. The room was stuffy, and the smell of so many flowers was making him sick. "I need a moment," he explained. "I think I'll step outside for some fresh air."

"I would go with you, but..."

Andrew followed her gaze to her husband who was sitting alone in the front row, opposite Mariah's coffin.

"There's no need to explain," he said.

"Please come to the house after the service, Andrew," Katherine repeated. "I would very much like for you to meet Joseph. I need to get back to him now."

Andrew watched Katherine return to her husband's side. He continued to stare as Katherine placed her arm around his shoulders and whispered something into his ear. Joseph slowly turned around and looked at Andrew.

The man looked broken, Andrew thought. Instead of approaching him and introducing himself and offering his condolences as he should, Andrew looked at Mariah's wedding photo one last time.

"How could you not have told me, Mariah?" he asked, feeling his eyes burn. The walls felt like they were closing in on him and he regretted his decision not to let Tom come with him today. Before turning away, he reached for the photograph of Mariah sitting in the park.

"You'll always be beautiful," he said, closing his eyes. For the briefest moment, he imagined the feel of her hair brushing against his cheek. The sensation felt so real; he opened his eyes half expecting her to be standing by his side, explaining this had all been a bad dream.

But this wasn't a dream, he reminded himself. He looked at her coffin one last time and whispered the words, *I love you,* in his head. Tucking the photograph under his arm, he rushed towards the door.

Chapter Twenty-Two

Sue sat in her B.M.W. outside the funeral home, unable to exit her car for nearly twenty minutes. Instead, she replayed her final moments with Mariah in her mind. *Did I tell her I loved her?* she tried to recall.

Mariah had been so excited for her romantic weekend with Andrew, and she'd been teasing her about it all day. Then there was that business with Candace Trainor and Carlos.

"Shit," Sue hissed, recalling how she had given Mariah a hard time about Carlos that afternoon. She would always regret that.

Every Boston station was covering the story and a news van was in the parking lot of the funeral parlor. "Go away and give the family their privacy," she said, eyeing the van with disgust. "Lousy vultures."

They were calling Mariah a hero, and although the boy she saved had never appeared on camera, his grandmother had. The woman had described how Mariah placed herself between the shooter and her grandson, convinced if it were not for Mariah's act of heroism, the boy would have been killed in her place.

A pick-up truck with New Hampshire plates pulled into the parking lot, immediately diverting Sue's attention. It hadn't occurred to her that some of the people who had been in the diner that night might show up. She instantly recognized the older woman who stepped from the vehicle from the news. The woman wore a simple black dress and a pair of sturdy looking shoes. Her short gray hair was neatly styled, and she wore no make-up. When she rounded the front of the truck to open the passenger door, Susan leaned forward in her seat, hoping to get a better look at her companion.

"You brought him?" she whispered, shocked to see a young boy with the woman. The news had only given the boy's age, not his name. He was tall and lanky for a ten-year old, Sue thought, and his faded khakis were at least two inches too short. His hair was neatly combed, and he wore an argyle vest over a bright white buttoned-down shirt.

Sue opened the car door without hesitation and rushed to meet them.

"Excuse me," she called to them, hoping they would wait for her to catch up. But the door to the news van opened as well, and Sue watched in horror as a reporter hurried towards them.

"Will you have some common decency and leave these people alone?" Sue snapped at him, putting herself between them.

"How did you know the victim?" the man asked, ignoring Sue completely.

Sue turned, placing her hand on the woman's shoulder, hurrying her towards the door. The little boy clung to his grandmother the whole time. As soon as they entered the funeral home, the reporter stood down.

"Well, at least he didn't try coming inside," the woman said.

"I'd have called the police if he did. I'm Sue Davis," she said, extending her hand. "I worked with Mariah."

"Theresa Bartlett, but everyone calls me Terry. And this is Scotty," Terry said, smiling down at her grandson.

Sue lowered her gaze, trying to make eye contact with the boy who remained staring down at his shoes. "It's very nice to meet you, Scotty," she said.

"Thanks," he said, not meeting her eyes.

She tried not to imagine what the Scotty had seen that night at the diner. Her only hope was that somehow, he had been shielded from the worst of it. She also couldn't help thinking if Scotty coming today was a good idea. But then again, she was the first to admit that she knew nothing about kids.

"Is he…is he getting help?" Sue asked Terry, in a low voice.

"He is," Terry said. "He wanted to come," she added. "I wasn't sure if he should…but the counselor thought it might actually help."

"That makes sense," Sue said, forcing a smile. "What grade are you in, Scotty?" she asked.

"Fourth," he said, still averting his gaze. "I should be in fifth," he explained, "but I stayed back a year."

"Well, I think it is amazing that you came here today. You are one brave boy. I've been sitting in my car for almost a half hour, willing myself to walk in here," Sue admitted, nervously. At that, Scotty slowly raised his eyes to hers.

"Then let's walk in together then, shall we?" Terry offered.

"Thank you," Sue said. "I think Mariah would have liked that. Believe it or not, this is my first wake. I've made it a habit of avoiding them my whole life," she admitted, as they approached the usher who was still standing outside the viewing room. Sue spotted a guest book on a pedestal. "Are we supposed to sign this?" she whispered.

"Yes," Terry said, just as a man rushed out the door, colliding head on with Scotty.

"Damn it," Andrew said, attempting to right the boy. But it was too late. Scotty hit the floor, hard. The picture frame that had been tucked under Andrew's arm shattered onto the ground. "You need to watch where you're going, kid," Andrew snapped.

Sue recognized Andrew instantly.

Scotty was sitting on his backside, wide-eyed, staring at Andrew, making no attempt to stand up.

"I'm so sorry," Terry apologized, immediately bending over to help Scotty off the floor. "Are you okay, honey?" she asked.

"I'm fine, Grandma," he mumbled.

The four of them glanced at the broken image of Mariah on the ground. Scotty looked away, returning his gaze to Andrew.

Terry was the first to speak. "Please let me help," she said, as Andrew angrily bent down to retrieve the broken pieces.

"I've got it," he replied tightly.

"It's *her*, Grandma," Scotty whispered.

Sue watched, utterly confused, as Scotty nudged his grandmother and pointed to Andrew. The photo of Mariah was still on the floor, not in Andrew's hands. She searched Andrew's darkening expression, trying to make sense of the moment. Sue was still watching Andrew the instant he realized who Scotty was. A shadow passed over Andrew's face.

"I'm Susan Davis," Sue quickly interjected. "I worked with Mariah."

"And I'm Theresa Bartlett," Terry added, extending her hand to Andrew, who ignored it.

"I'm leaving. I'm…I'm sorry," Andrew said, moving past them quickly.

"Wait," Sue called out. "There's a reporter out there. Can we talk for a minute?"

"This isn't a good time, Sue," Andrew said.

"Well, when then?" Sue asked, following him.

"When what?" Andrew asked, turning to face her.

"When can we talk?" Sue stammered, impatiently. She wasn't giving up.

Andrew said nothing. Although he was facing Sue, his focus returned to Scotty. Sue's eyes traveled back and forth between them. She watched, horrified, as Scotty unconsciously stepped backwards.

"Why don't we go inside?" Terry said, reaching for her grandson's hand. "You too, Sue."

But Sue made no motion to leave. "Will you be at the funeral tomorrow, Andrew? Do you know where the church is?" Sue asked.

"No," Andrew said, turning away.

"No, you won't be there? Or no, you don't know where the church is? It's just a few blocks from here. St. Elizabeth's. Maybe we could have coffee afterwards?" Sue asked.

"No, I don't intend to be at the funeral," he nearly shouted.

"Why not?" Sue blurted out angrily before she could control herself.

"That's my business, Sue," he said in a low, menacing tone. Sue watched him storm away, stupefied as to why he was behaving so terribly.

"This is the Andrew Mariah was so in love with?" Sue spat out.

"Come on," Terry urged her, clasping her hand. "He doesn't want to talk to you."

"But she *loved* you!" Sue screamed at Andrew's back.

Andrew's posture stiffened as he slowly turned. "Did she?" he asked, his eyes wet with tears. "I'm not so sure."

"Let's go together tomorrow, please?" Sue pleaded, taking a step closer to him. A sob escaped her throat as she watched him slowly shake his head *no*.

"Why?" she cried, trying to understand.

Andrew blinked hard, looking down at the floor, unable to meet Sue's gaze. "Because I can't watch them put her in the ground."

***

Scotty stood by the window in the crowded room where his grandmother had instructed him to wait. He'd watched intently as Andrew's car sped away, relieved that Mariah hadn't left with him. He didn't like that man.

"They didn't see you," he whispered to her.

"I know," Mariah replied.

"Why can *I* see you?" he asked.

"I'm not quite sure," Mariah admitted softly. "You're not afraid of me?"

"Why would I be?" he asked, slipping his hand into hers. "Please don't tell anyone I can see you. Especially my grandma. She worries too much."

"I won't tell," Mariah promised.

"Thank you," he said, moving closer to her. "That man you were with who just left…" he started to say.

"Andrew?"

"He's not nice. I don't like him."

"He's in pain. He didn't mean to knock you over. I'm sorry," Mariah said.

"It was fine," Scotty said.

"I can't stay," Mariah said, tugging her hand from his. But Scotty held on tighter.

"Please don't leave. Remember what you said? That you wouldn't leave me alone?" he asked, turning to look at her. She looked exactly how he remembered her. Only here, she wasn't afraid.

"I remember," Mariah said.

Scotty smiled, relieved. It felt good to talk to the woman who died. The last time he'd seen her, she'd been lying on the floor in a pool of blood. It was like something he would get in trouble for, for watching on television. But now, seeing her looking normal again made him happy. Almost like that day in the diner didn't really happen at all. Maybe the kids in school were right. Maybe there was something wrong with him.

"The kids at school think I'm strange," he said.

"You're not strange," Mariah said. "Don't listen to those bullies. They don't understand kids like you."

"What do you mean?"

"You're special, Scotty. And you have a wonderful imagination. You think those other kids could see me the way you can?" Mariah asked.

"Nope," he said, smiling. It was the first time he'd felt happy since he watched her die. "You're right."

"Of course, I am," she said. "And even if they did, they'd pee their pants!"

Scotty burst out laughing, quickly covering his mouth with his hand. But it was too late. He looked at his grandmother, who was staring at him with a bewildered expression on her face.

"Uh-oh," he mumbled, as he watched his grandmother approach. "We're in trouble."

Only then did he realize that Mariah was gone.

Part Two

Part Two

Chapter Twenty-Three

Katelyn McGraw ran her fingers through her hair, wishing she could make the two inches, recently hacked off, magically reappear. How she had let the stylist talk her into what she'd claimed would be a 'sophisticated transformation' she would never know. What she did know, however, was that it made her look even younger than she already did. The exact opposite of what she had hoped for. It was bad enough that she'd already been mistaken for an intern on more than one occasion at her new job at the firm of Olson and Matthews.

"Not much I can do about it now," she muttered, walking into her building. The massive space still managed to impress her each morning. Sunlight streamed through the glass windows, their rays reaching the perfectly positioned potted trees that flanked the entire length of the lobby.

It was early, and there were few people around. The firm was located on the thirty-third floor of the building, and many of the offices had sweeping views of Boston Common. But not hers. In fact, she didn't even have a private office. That was something she was determined to change. She'd been hired as a first-year associate, and her goal was simple: she'd arrive early each day and work her butt off for the next seven or eight years to make partner. If it meant barely having a social life, or any kind of life, so be it. It would all pay off in the end.

Bracing herself for her daily exchange with Kenny, she rounded the corner to the security desk as she pulled out her wallet from her purse. *Please don't try to make small talk this morning,* she inwardly prayed. She wasn't in the mood today. It was only her third month working at the firm, and the building's security guard already asked her out twice. Both times, she'd declined. Although he seemed to handle the rejection well, Kenny managed to make her feel awkward every time she saw him. *Great,* she thought, spotting him. He was staring at her with his usual big grin as she approached the desk.

"Morning, Katelyn," he said to her. "Nice haircut."

"Hi, Kenny," she replied. She ignored the comment about her hair and inserted her identification card into the electronic scanner. "Hi, Mike," she added, acknowledging the older guard. Katelyn guessed Mike to be in his sixties and liked the way he tipped his head ever so slightly when he greeted her each day.

"Morning, Ms. McGraw," Mike said. "Beautiful day, isn't it?"

"It's gorgeous," Katelyn agreed, smiling at him.

"Always one of the first to arrive," Kenny interjected.

"Got to beat the morning rush," Katelyn said, continuing down the hall towards the main elevators. She could feel his eyes following her the entire time.

The first time Kenny had asked her out, she had been completely caught off guard. She'd nervously laughed, something she'd hated herself for doing, explaining she was busy that evening. The second time she lied, saying that she was dating someone. Besides the fact that she had no intention of getting involved with anyone at work, she didn't have time to date. They were about the same age, and he was handsome enough, but something about him made her uncomfortable. She couldn't quite put her finger on exactly what that was. Between college and law school, she'd known many people who weren't particularly adept at taking social cues. Hopefully, she told herself, Kenny was harmless and fell into one of those categories. Pushing the button for the thirty-third floor, she stepped back from the elevator and checked her reflection in the mirrored doors.

"I look like the little Dutch boy," she said.

She did like the way her shorter hair made her earrings stand out, however. Running her fingertips over one smooth, pearl stud, she thought of her father. They'd been a gift from him on her fourteenth birthday, the year before he died. Katelyn never took them off. Her father had missed all her graduations, her proms, her acceptance to the Massachusetts Bar…all the milestones of her life. Not a day went by that she didn't think of him. If he could see her now, working at one of the best law firms in Boston, he'd be so proud of her. The thought made her smile.

The sound of someone approaching caused her to turn. The smile faded from her face as Andrew Madden came into view. "Good morning," she said. *Three months working here, and all the man ever does is scowl at me.*

"Morning," he replied curtly, looking down at his phone.

Wishing the doors would slide open, she turned her back on him. He was the only colleague of hers that made her nervous. Everyone else had welcomed her warmly, extending lunch invitations or including her at dinners after work. But not Andrew Madden. Since she'd first been introduced to him, he'd seemed perpetually annoyed with her. Much of her workload was assigned directly by him, too, and while he hadn't complained about her performance so far, he certainly hadn't commended it either. She stared down at her comfortable black flats, hoping someone else would appear. She also wished she'd worn heels today. She felt tiny next to him. Despite his brooding disposition, he was still one of the most handsome men she'd ever met. She'd caught herself wondering more than once about the type of women he dated and decided they were most definitely the tall, willowy type. The ones who looked like models and wore three-inch heels with ease, she thought, still staring at her sensible shoes. Sighing, she raised her eyes back to the doors. This time, she found him watching her, looking thoroughly annoyed. She returned his frown as they finally slid open.

"After you, *Katie*," he said in a low voice.

"Thank you," she replied curtly.

It wasn't uncommon for her mother or her friends to call her Katie, but no one in the office, apart from Andrew, ever used that name. At first, Katelyn didn't mind. She'd assumed it had simply been an innocent mistake on his part. Maybe he'd had a relative or friend with the same nickname? But she did mind now. It was the way he said it, as if she were a child. She turned to face him, deciding to say something about it, but he was still focused on his phone. Her gaze wandered to his face. There were dark smudges under his eyes, and she found herself wondering if he had had a poor night's sleep.

"Is there something you wished to say?" Andrew asked, his eyes still glued to his device.

"No," she stammered, feeling her cheeks burn with embarrassment. She wanted to kick herself for being such a coward. When the doors opened, she quickly brushed passed him, grateful she hadn't worn heels today. The image of her clumsily falling flat on her face in front of him would have compelled her to give the firm her two weeks' notice immediately.

Chapter Twenty-Four

Andrew Madden entered his corner office and closed the door behind him. For a moment, he just stood there, staring at the papers on his desk. The file he'd been reading yesterday was just as he'd left it. For the briefest moment, he imagined himself gathering the pages up and tossing them out the window.

"That would give everyone something new to talk about," he said dryly, slipping off his jacket. He barely glanced at the spectacular view of the park outside before taking his seat. He felt unsettled and agitated, as his eyes shifted to the closed door.

Does she think I have horns and a tail?

In the three months Katelyn McGraw had been with the firm, Andrew could not have been more pleased with her performance. She arrived early each morning, was one of the last to leave each evening, and consistently completed her work on time. The word around the office was that she didn't socialize much with the rest of the staff outside of work, which he also liked.

It had been more than two years since he'd lost Mariah. Despite the long leave of absence he had taken after the tragedy, his reentry at the firm had been a rocky one. Besides a regrettable work-related outburst, in which he'd reduced a paralegal to tears, he'd also become more demanding and less tolerant of errors of any kind. Rumors that he was involved with Mariah Talbot, "that decorator killed in New Hampshire," had started to circulate around the office almost immediately. The talk had quieted down the past year, but he was still regarded warily by many of his coworkers. The fact hadn't seemed to bother him, until now. It might explain why Katelyn was so apprehensive around him.

With the exception of his brother, Tom, Andrew had never spoken to anyone regarding Mariah. He planned to keep it that way. He scowled at the file staring back at him on his desk and thought of the calls and meetings he had scheduled today. He wished he could cancel them all and drive to the cape.

A walk on the beach on a brisk morning like this, far from the hustle and bustle of Boston, might be just what he needed to clear his head today.

Do it, he imagined Mariah saying. *The firm won't collapse if you play hooky, you know.*

"I can't," he murmured.

Work is what had kept him sane since Mariah's death, he reminded himself. That, and Tom. He'd always been close to his brother but since Mariah, he'd grown to appreciate their brotherly bond even more.

His thoughts wandered back to Katelyn and the way her wide blue eyes regarded him so warily. He had noticed her haircut right away, and he couldn't help thinking it perfectly suited her delicate bone structure. There was no denying that she was attractive. Or that he was lonely. That didn't mean he wanted her.

There'd been no other woman in his life since Mariah. He had come to terms with the fact that she hadn't been open with him about her past, but felt strongly that if they'd had more time, that would have changed. After all, a failed marriage was never easy to talk about. Perhaps the guy was a jerk, or she'd been too embarrassed to admit that she'd impulsively married the wrong person. Maybe he had hurt her so badly; it was simply impossible for her to ever trust anyone again. The thought of anyone harming his Mariah angered him, even now. The notion that Mariah had been the one that had screwed up the marriage crossed his mind from time to time, but he always dismissed the idea.

"Impossible," he said out loud. "You weren't capable of hurting anyone."

Chapter Twenty-Five

"Nice haircut, Katelyn."

Katelyn looked up from her laptop to find her coworker Grace standing over her desk. She was wearing a royal blue silk blouse tucked into pinstripe gray skirt, that fit her curves perfectly.

"Thanks, but I'm not liking it," Katelyn said, scrunching her nose.

"It suits you. Seriously," Grace said. "How was your weekend?"

"Good. Yours?"

"Not bad. Hung out with the usual gang. We missed you," Grace said, smiling. "Did you end up seeing Stephen?"

Katelyn eyed Grace's high heels, ignoring the question. "How can you possibly work in those all day?" she asked. "I mean, they're gorgeous, but don't they kill after a while?"

"Of course, they do," Grace said, laughing. "But they make my legs look great, don't they?" she added, pivoting her hip. "You know, we should go shopping again one of these days. That was fun the last month. Wasn't it?"

"It was," Katelyn nodded. She didn't want to appear dismissive, but she really didn't have time to chat this morning. "Lunch later?" Katelyn asked, eyeing her laptop, hoping Grace would take the hint.

"Sure," Grace said. "So, what did you do this weekend?" she continued, making no motion to leave just yet.

Katelyn knew she was stuck. "Nothing much, really. Just sort of hung around the apartment with Stephen."

Not discussing her private life was an old habit of Katelyn's, and one she knew could made her appear standoffish. It was unintentional and something she'd struggled with since her father had died. At first, it was simply a way to avoid sympathetic stares and whispers from her friends and neighbors, and even the occasional morbid questions regarding the particulars of his death. It had amazed her how insensitive some people could be. She'd grown up quickly, learning to insulate herself and her mother from appearing vulnerable.

Besides that, there was no way in hell she was ever going to admit to Grace that all she really did this weekend was she lay around her apartment binge watching Antiques Roadshow. Katelyn appreciated Grace's energy and liked going out with her occasionally, but the two of them were very different. A good time to Grace was spending the entire weekend bar hopping and meeting people, all which were perfectly normal given their ages. But it just wasn't Katelyn.

"Okay, I'd better get back to work," Grace finally said. "I dropped the ball on a few things Friday and need to power through them before I get started on today's crap."

"Anything I can help you with?" Katelyn asked.

"No, but thanks for asking," she said, flashing her a grateful smile. "Oh, before I forget, a bunch of us are going out this Thursday night to that new place that opened up across from Trident Books on Newbury Street. Wanna come?"

"I don't know. I'm always so pooped by the end of the day," Katelyn said, shrugging her shoulders.

"That's because you work too hard," Grace teased. "You have to find a balance in your life between work and fun. You having much fun lately?"

"Not really," she admitted.

Grace rolled her eyes. "It's just dinner and a few drinks, Katelyn. Or in your case, one drink. Not a rave. We haven't been out together in a while, either."

"I know," Katelyn said. "I really need to get back to this, Grace. I'll let you know, okay?"

"Whatever," Grace said. "No pressure."

"See you at lunch," Katelyn said.

Since the day Katelyn began at the firm, Grace had tried to include her in everything and for that, Katelyn was appreciative. *I should make more of an effort,* she thought, watching Grace walk away, just as something slammed down onto her desk.

"I sent you an e-mail asking you to come to my office ten minutes ago, *Katie,*" Andrew snapped. "Our docketing person is out sick today. You need to handle these."

"I'm sorry," she stammered, eyeing the stack of folders. "When do you need me to—"

"By the end of the day, please. Let me know when you're finished," he said over his shoulder as he stormed back to his office.

Her heart beat wildly in her chest. Not only had he startled her, he'd embarrassed her. She looked around, wondering who had witnessed the interaction. She then imagined removing one of her sensible, black shoes and hurling it directly at the back of his perfect head. For the life of her, she couldn't figure out why Andrew Madden despised her. She was sick to death of it and impulsively reached for her phone to text Grace.

KATELYN: You're right, I could use a fun night out.

GRACE: Awesome. I'll let everyone know!

Chapter Twenty-Six

Andrew stepped over the mail scattered on the floor of his foyer at the end of the day, not bothering to pick up any of it. Instead, he loosened his tie and walked directly into his study, pouring himself three generous fingers of scotch. The smooth amber liquid was all he had thought about on the chilly walk home. He tipped the glass to his lips, glad to put the day behind him.

When he'd left the office, Katelyn had still been sitting at her desk. He'd contemplated approaching her, telling her to go home and finish up in the morning, but ended up walking past her without saying a word. He'd treated her poorly today. He told himself that he would make sure she had an easier day tomorrow, and that he wouldn't give her anything extra to do.

He sat on the couch, eyeing the remnants of the charred log in the hearth. It had been over two years since the fireplace was lit, but he still couldn't bring himself to clean it out. He'd even instructed his cleaning service not to remove a single ash. The last time he'd built a fire in this room he'd been with Mariah. They'd shared a bottle of her favorite wine on the couch and talked about their weekend in New Hampshire.

"Do you think the leaves are past peak?" she had asked him, excitedly. She couldn't wait to escape Boston for a weekend.

"I'm not sure. But I tell you what," he'd replied, placing delicate kisses along her neck as he'd slowly unbuttoned her blouse, "I promise I'll keep driving until we find some spectacular shades."

"I like the sound of that. But let *me* do the driving, please," she'd said.

The next morning, he'd called her from work, explaining they needed to drive separately. He would regret that decision for the rest of his life. Sinking lower into the sofa, he stared at the near empty glass in his hands.

He knew she was watching him.

"Hello, Mariah," he said, looking up at the photograph on the mantle. Mariah smiled back at him from her bench in the park. He'd had the photograph professionally matted and reframed after her wake. He would never forget a moment of that nightmarish day. He'd replayed his encounter with Scotty over and over in his mind, each time wishing he'd shown the boy some kindness. But he'd been out of his mind with grief. Even now, he tightened his grip on the glass, trying not to picture Mariah surrounded by strangers as she bled to death. Downing the last of his drink, he closed his eyes, willing the scene from his mind but knowing it would haunt him forever.

And so would she.

He knew exactly what Mariah would say to him if she were sitting beside him.

No more drinking, Andrew. Go eat something, please?

"You're right," he whispered, wishing he could slip his hand in hers, just one more time. He imagined the sound of wood crackling in the fireplace and, for the briefest instant, felt the heat of the flames on his face. The sensation was so real, he opened his, half expecting to see a fire glowing in the hearth.

The tension he'd been carrying in his shoulders all day melted away, and he welcomed the numbness that had spread through his body. He glanced down at the empty glass contemplating another, knowing Mariah wouldn't approve.

"I'm sorry, Mariah. I'll eat something later. I promise," he said, raising his blurry gaze to her photo. Slowly, he rose from the couch. He carefully refilled his glass and slipped from the room, but not before brushing his fingertips over her face when he passed her.

"Night, Mariah," he said, closing the door behind him.

His glass was empty before he stumbled into bed.

Chapter Twenty-Seven

"I'm fine, Mom. I swear," Katelyn assured her mother when she returned to her apartment that evening. "It was just a really long day, and I'm tired."

"Well, you don't sound fine to me, Katie," her mother replied. "Why are they keeping you there so late?"

"They're not," she explained. "The more I get done one day, the less I have to do the next." *Until Andrew Madden comes along and slams another pile of someone else's work on my desk.*

"Fine. When are you coming home to visit?"

"Soon, I promise. I'll call you tomorrow, Mom. All I want to do is take a long hot shower and curl up in bed with Smokey," she added, eyeing the large gray cat that was rubbing up against her calves, reminding her he needed to be fed.

The last thing Katelyn would ever do is complain to her mother about her workload. She'd certainly never dump on her about Andrew Madden, either. Her mother had enough to worry about. She had never remarried or even dated anyone since her father died, and Katelyn knew she was lonely. That's why she made a point to call her each day. Katelyn had had very little free time in law school and now with her new job at the firm, even less. There were times she wondered how happier they both might have been if her mother had met someone.

"You're still young, Mom," Katelyn had said before leaving for college. "And you're beautiful and smart." It had been the truth, but Katelyn had had other motives for wanting her mother to seek companionship. Namely, the guilt she'd felt over accepting the scholarship to Georgetown University. While her mother had been proud of her, encouraging her to take it, they both had known what that meant. There would be no visiting Massachusetts from Washington DC on the weekends. Katelyn was essentially leaving her mother alone for the first time since her father died. She'd only applied to law schools in Boston, after her graduation. By then, Katelyn had finally come to terms with the fact that while she couldn't cure her mother's loneliness, she could make sure her mother would grow old comfortably. By Katelyn's calculations, she would be able to buy her mother a tiny condo on Cape Cod in a few short years. It had been a dream of her parents to have a place on the cape and Katelyn was determined to fulfill her father's wishes.

A demanding 'meow' jarred her back to the present.

"I know you're hungry," Katelyn said, bending over to pick up Smokey, who was still trying to get her attention. "What do you say we get in our jammies and lay on the couch?"

Smokey flicked his tail and jumped from her arms, sauntering over to his empty bowl.

"Fine," Katelyn mumbled. "I already apologized for being late tonight." As she emptied a can of food into his bowl, she heard a knock at the door. "That has to be your buddy," Katelyn said, knowing it could only be Stephen. Since moving into the building a few years ago they'd become close friends.

"Well, hello there, Ms. Career Woman," he greeted her, when she opened the door. "What the heck took you so long to get home tonight?"

His short blond hair was in its usual mess, and he looked more like a surfer dude than a tech-savvy programmer. He had a bottle of wine in one hand and a bag of pretzels in the other.

"Oh no," Katelyn said, eyeing the Boston Bruins jersey he was wearing. "I forgot we were watching the game tonight."

"That hurts," he said, strolling past her towards the kitchen. "Hurry up and get changed into something more comfortable while I crack this baby open."

Smokey rubbed up against Stephen's leg. "You're getting heavy, mister," he said, picking him up. "Time to put you on a diet."

"I heard that," Katelyn said on her way to the bedroom. "Take that back immediately."

"In Vino Veritas," he called to her, after pouring two healthy glasses of wine. He entered her bedroom, handing her a glass. "Drink some, quick. I can tell you need it."

"You could say that," she sighed, unbuttoning her blouse. She reached for the glass and took a giant sip before setting it down on the bureau. "All I want is get under the covers, to tell you the truth."

"I'll take a pass tonight," he said, plopping himself down on the bed.

"Ha!" she laughed, digging through drawer for a cozy sweater and a pair of jeans. "You and everyone else," she mumbled, stepping into the bathroom.

"What the heck are you talking about?" Stephen asked.

"Never mind," Katelyn said, slipping out of her clothes.

"Tell me," Stephen urged her. "Come on."

"I'm being stupid," she said. "It's just that attorney, Andrew Madden? He truly despises me. I just don't get it. I haven't made a single mistake since I joined the firm. All the other attorneys rave about my work. But not him, of course."

"Why do you care?" Stephen asked. "You know you're great at what you do."

"I don't," she said pulling on her jeans. Katelyn slipped the sweater over her head and scooped up her work clothes from the bathroom floor before reentering the bedroom.

"Um, apparently you do," he said, smirking.

"Just forget I mentioned it," Katelyn said, grabbing the glass off the dresser.

"You mention his name an awful lot. You like him, don't you?" Stephen laughed. "That's it!"

"That's ridiculous," Katelyn said, scoffing at the notion. Besides the fact she would never get involved with a colleague, it was clear the man detested her.

"You know that old expression? Don't shit where you eat?" he said, grinning.

"That is a disgusting phrase," Katelyn said, scowling. "And to be clear, all I've ever said is that the man is incredibly handsome."

"Whatever you say," Stephen said, raising his glass in a mock toast. "Can we watch the game now, or are we going to braid each other's hair?"

"Turn it on and order us a pizza," she said, heading to the closet. "I'll be right there."

As she placed her blouse and skirt on hangers, she scanned the rest of her wardrobe. Mostly everything she owned was black, gray, or white.

So drab, she thought, recalling Grace's gorgeous blue blouse today.

"I need to go shopping," she muttered, eyeing the expensive designer heels she'd splurged on a month ago. She and Grace had gone shopping over their lunch hour and Grace had talked her into buying them. Katelyn still hadn't worn them. What was she waiting for?

"They do make your legs look great," she heard herself say. "That doesn't mean I'm trying to look good for *him*," she told herself, deciding she would wear them tomorrow.

Chapter Twenty-Eight

"You're drinking too much, Andrew. It's not healthy."

Andrew stirred in his sleep, rolling onto his back. Something had woken him, and his eyes fluttered open, checking the time.

"Three a.m.," he groaned. He couldn't remember what he was dreaming about, only that it had something to do with Mariah. He scanned the bedside table, wishing for a bottle of water. There was none. He eyed the empty scotch glass and sighed.

"That's what you get for falling asleep drunk," he said.

He reached for his phone out of habit, checking his messages. "Shit," he said, noticing the missed calls from his brother. They'd talked about getting together to watch the Bruins last night. Andrew had completely forgotten. He'd have to call him today and explain. He groaned, knowing that Tom wasn't going to let him off easy.

"Great. Another person I need to apologize to," he said, getting up. His head was already starting to pound.

He slowly made his way downstairs for water and an aspirin, trying to piece together his dream. Mariah had been angry with him, but he couldn't remember why. He'd been so happy to see her, he hadn't paid much attention to what she was saying. That had also infuriated her, he recalled.

He opened the refrigerator and scanned its contents. The only semblance of a meal he could find was some leftover pizza, a few yogurts, and a carton of eggs. He reached for the eggs and checked the date stamped on the carton. They'd expired over a month ago.

"Disgusting," he murmured, tossing them into the trash. He vowed he would go grocery shopping tomorrow as he shoved a piece of cold pizza into his mouth. A sound from outside the kitchen caught his attention. He quietly slipped from the room to check the front door, finding it locked. Street noise,

127

he thought. The mail was still scattered on the floor, and when he bent down to gather it up, his head pounded in protest. He needed that aspirin.

"That was a mistake," he muttered. "I *do* drink too much," he said absently. Only when the words were out did he realize what he'd been dreaming. Mariah had been in his room, her fists on her hips, looking down at him disappointedly. He'd been so happy to see her that all he kept saying was how beautiful she looked, and how much he missed her. She'd responded by threatening to break every glass in the house.

His brother, Tom had been on his back about his drinking, too. On more than one occasion, he'd called to find Andrew too drunk to talk. Andrew would either hang up, not wishing to hear his younger brother berate him, or simply allow him to drone on. Sometimes, he'd even pour himself another drink out of spite. It was reckless and unhealthy, but he couldn't seem to stop himself.

Before making his way back to bed, he stepped into his study and placed the stack of mail on top of his desk. The bottle of scotch on his desk, which he'd only purchased a few days ago, was almost empty. He thought about emptying the remainder down the sink.

"That would make you happy, wouldn't it, Mariah?" he asked, glancing at the mantle, startled to find her picture lying flat. He walked towards it, vaguely recalling touching it earlier in the evening.

"What did I do?" he asked, picking it up carefully. The glass was cracked. The break ran diagonally across her face, creating a distorted image of her smile. Shame washed over him as he quickly pulled the frame apart, tossing the broken shards into the wastepaper basket.

"Shit," he mumbled, when the tip of his finger got nicked. He quickly pressed it to his lips, hoping he hadn't stained her photograph. He turned on the desk light to inspect it.

"Good," he said when he found no damage. He paused before turning away, eying the drawer handle. For the first time in over two years, he thought about tucking the photograph safely away.

Do it, Andrew…

"I can't," he whispered.

He propped the photograph back on the mantle on his way back upstairs, vowing he would try to be better.

Chapter Twenty-Nine

Mariah remained on the sofa with Pinky curled in her lap after Andrew left the study. She watched him slowly climb the stairs until he was out of sight, wishing she knew how to help him. It pained her to see him drunk all the time. She looked at the bottle of scotch on the desk and thought about tipping it over onto the floor. *He'd only go out and buy another.*

A feeling of hopelessness gripped her. What was she doing there? She was there to help Andrew, she reminded herself, not to hold him back. So why was a tiny part of her relieved when he couldn't slip her photo into the drawer? It made no sense.

"I need to figure out how to help him, Pinky," she said, stroking the cat's ears.

Pinky responded by jumping off Mariah's lap. She flicked her tail, exiting the library without looking back. Mariah knew exactly where she was going.

"Thanks for nothing," Mariah said, as the cat disappeared. She eyed her photograph, trying to remember the day the image was taken. Had she been hiking that day?

"No," she murmured. "We were at the Boston Public Gardens." She and Mark had just moved back to Massachusetts from Vermont. It had been one of the happiest times of her life.

So had her time been with Andrew. She smiled, brushing her palm over the couch. How many times had they curled up together in this very spot, she wondered? It had been Mariah's favorite room in the whole house. It still was. She could stay in this room forever, she thought.

"No," she said, shaking the crazy notion off, ashamed. Mark was waiting for her.

"It must have been hard for you to watch me fall in love with him, Mark," she said, knowing he could hear her. She tried not to imagine what Mark had felt, watching her from the other side. Her relationship with Andrew had been intense.

"And incredibly passionate," she added, smiling. "I'm a ghost. Not a saint," she said, just in case Mark heard that, too.

Andrew wasn't a saint either these days, she thought frowning. His drinking was becoming a real problem, and he was neglecting his health. Mariah hardly recognized the Andrew she once knew. His behavior at the office had worried her today. Other than right after her death, she'd never seen him so volatile.

"I'm not the only one feeling guilty," she murmured, recalling his harsh treatment towards Katelyn. Mariah knew why Andrew was so hard on the poor girl, even if he had no clue. Neither of them did. But the reason was crystal clear to Mariah. She just wished that Katelyn had stood up to him. That she had marched into Andrew's office demanding to be treated better, or else.

"That's what I would have done!" Mariah said, shaking her head. But it appeared to her that Katelyn didn't have it in her. Mariah found that immensely disappointing on many levels.

"This is the girl you fall in love with after me?" she asked, tilting her head back, knowing he was sleeping directly above her. Maybe that's why Mariah was pleased her picture still stood on the mantle.

"Katelyn McGraw," Mariah said, sinking deeper into the couch. Could she be wrong about her? She stared at the charred embers until they burned a bright orange, setting the room aglow, contemplating just that.

I'm going to need to keep an eye on her for a while.

Gideon's warning about staying too long sounded in her head. "I won't let that happen, Gideon," Mariah said, firmly. "There's just so much more I have to do."

Scotty needed her, too. And she still hadn't been able to connect with her parents the way she'd planned.

"So much more I need to do," she repeated, closing her eyes. When she opened them, she found herself standing at the foot of Andrew's bed. Pinky was curled up beside him, fast asleep.

"Traitor," she said, shaking her head. "We need to go, Pinky. Now," Mariah said, leaning over Andrew and scooping the cat up in her arms. Andrew moaned in his sleep.

"Not you, Andrew," she whispered into his ear. "You need to rest and to not be thinking of me."

But she smiled anyway, knowing that he was.

Chapter Thirty

"What do you think, Carlos?" Sue asked, optimistically, from her kitchen stool as she sipped her wine.

"I think it's too early to be drinking," Carlos replied, without looking at her. His concentration was fixed on the papers spread out on the granite island.

"Funny," she said. "But that's not what I meant."

"I know, I know," he said, nodding. "Let me finish, will you?"

"Fine," Sue said, standing up and nervously pacing the room.

"You're like a shark," Carlos muttered under his breath.

"You know I hate sitting for very long," Sue said, anxiously reaching for the small brass watering can beside the kitchen sink.

Mariah watched her hold it under the faucet before watering the bowl of succulents on the windowsill.

How many times did I beg you not to overwater those?

It was clear to Mariah that Carlos was enjoying seeing Sue this flustered. He was deliberately taking his time reading the same contract he'd already read through several times before. Mariah plopped down on the sofa, enjoying the show, thinking how nice it would be to have a glass of wine as well.

The apartment in the South End was just as she remembered it; beautifully decorated in warm, neutral tones with natural organic accents everywhere. Vintage glass apothecary jars filled with clumps of green moss and birch twigs sat on tables scattered all over the living room. She fondly recalled the day she and Sue had scoured the flower market together, arranging the glass containers. Mariah had teased her mercilessly that afternoon, telling her that if there was a way to kill sticks and moss, Sue would find a way.

"Those are nice," Carlos commented, briefly looking up from the paperwork, motioning to the arrangements.

Mariah froze, wondering if Carlos had read her thoughts or sensed her presence.

"Thank you," Sue said, eyeing the glass jars. Mariah detected the flicker of sadness in Sue's eyes and realized that she was thinking of that fun day, too.

"Well, you know me," she snorted when the emotion passed. "House plants and I do not agree. It's one of the few things Mariah disliked about me. You in or you out?"

Um...the few?

Carlos finally looked up from the paperwork. After weeks of discussion and meetings with their accountant, he was more than comfortable with the terms set forth in the agreement. He looked up at Sue and nodded. "I'm in," he said.

"Fabulous!" Sue said, clapping her hands. "Took you long enough."

"But like the contract says, this needs to be an equal partnership in every way, Sue," he warned her.

"We've been over this before. It will. Might I remind you, I have been keeping up the lease the past two years while you've been deciding whether to come on board? The office is a complete mess because I've barely had time to reorganize everything."

"I understand. But as of today, we split the rent, so all decisions from this point on, we make together."

"Then sign away," she nodded, handing him a pen. "Here, here, and here," Sue directed him, excitedly flipping the pages of the contract and pointing to the neon-colored tabs stuck to the signature lines.

"I know where to sign, Sue," Carlos sighed. "I'm not colorblind."

"Okay, okay," she said, raising her hands up defensively. "Just trying to be helpful, *partner*."

"About the name of the company," Carlos said.

"What about it?" Sue asked, eyeing him warily.

Mariah froze, waiting to hear what Carlos was about to say. Was he actually going to suggest changing the name?

"Back Bay Décor will never be renamed. Agreed?" Carlos asked.

Sue tilted her head and looked at him curiously. "Why would I ever rename our brand? That wouldn't be a smart business move, would it?"

"That's not why we are never changing the name," Carlos explained.

"Relax, Carlos. I would never dream of changing the name Mariah chose," she assured him. She opened her mouth to say something else but paused.

"What?" Carlos asked.

Sue hesitated before continuing. "Do you remember the day I walked into the shop? Before it had even opened?"

"How could I forget?" Carlos laughed. "You bullied Mariah into giving you a job."

"I did," she admitted, proudly. "I was desperate. I hadn't even known the shop was there, as a matter of fact. I was walking off my lunch. I've never shared this with anyone. Not even Mariah. I had just been out with a few friends at a café up the street, well, women I thought were my friends."

"And?" Carlos asked.

"I had excused myself to use the ladies' room about halfway through the meal, and when I returned to the table, I caught the end of a discussion they'd been having in my absence. They were planning our next outing when I heard my friend Gail, say 'Well, what else has Sue got in her life besides spending money and lunching? Of course, she'll be free that day.' They all burst out laughing."

"Women are brutal," Carlos said.

"We can be," Sue agreed. "But it was just the kick in the ass I needed, as it turns out. I decided right then and there I wasn't going to turn into some middle-aged woman who has nothing else better to do than to sit with 'friends' who talk about her the minute she walks away from the table. Boy, did that one sting."

Finally, Mariah thought. She'd witnessed this side of Sue many times, but Carlos never had. He needed to look past what he saw when he looked at Sue, Mariah used to tell him. The perfect hair and makeup and clothes…they were all part of her armor. The truth was, Sue had been one of the least fulfilled people Mariah had ever met. She'd joked about her failed marriages from the very beginning, but Mariah had known much of it was just an act. Sue had thrown her time, energy and soul into 'Back Bay Décor', and in the process, transformed herself.

It's done, Mariah thought, eyeing the signed contract. There was just one more thing they needed to do for her. They needed to find the letter.

"Shake, partner?" Carlos said, extending his hand to hers.

"I like the sound of that," she said, smiling. So, yes, we keep the name Back Bay Décor she reiterated. "Same colors, same logo. But I would I like to have the showroom repainted and some new carpet installed. We need a little change, don't you think?"

"I agree," Carlos said. "I'll get some estimates."

"See?" she said, grinning proudly. "Been partners for less than a minute and we're already agreeing. How about that?" she grinned, downing the last of her wine.

"Uh-huh," Carlos said. "Let's see how long this honeymoon lasts."

Mariah was wondering the exact same thing.

Chapter Thirty-One

"Isn't this place great?" Grace asked, scanning the crowded room with a bright pink drink in her hand.

"It is," Katelyn said, determined to have a good time. The trendy restaurant on Newbury Street they were at was packed. So far, they were the only two people from the office who'd arrived. "Who else is coming?" she asked.

"I'm not really sure. How's your drink?"

"Strong," Katelyn said, taking a sip. "But good." She didn't want to say that what she really wanted was some food. She'd worked through her lunch hour today and was starving.

"Lightweight," Grace teased. "Oh look," she said excitedly, pointing to the people that just walked in. "A bunch of them are here." She stood up and waved their coworkers over to their table.

"Is that Kenny?" Katelyn asked, surprised to see him part of the group.

"Yes," Grace said, settling back into her chair.

"Why is *he* here?" Katelyn asked, feeling her heart sink.

"Geez, Katelyn," Grace snorted. "I didn't realize you were a snob."

"I'm not a snob at all," she insisted. "It's just, well, I'm surprised."

"What for? Kenny's pretty cool, and I think he has a thing for me," Grace said, winking. "I mean, nothing has happened yet, but I definitely get the vibe that he's interested in me."

"He is? Really?" Katelyn said, wishing she hadn't sounded so surprised.

"Wow," Grace said, slightly insulted. "Is that so hard to imagine?"

"Of course not, that's not what I meant at all," she said, reaching for her glass and taking a giant sip. She wished she were home. When the group appeared at their table, she watched as Grace bounced up from her seat and quickly hugged everyone, including Kenny.

"We should try to find a bigger table," Katelyn proposed when Kenny sat down beside her. She pushed her chair away from his until she was nearly wedged up against the wall. "Or should we all just stand by the bar?"

"Well, look who showed up," Kenny said, ignoring the suggestion. "Hi there, Katelyn."

"Hi, Kenny," she said.

"I'm getting the first round," Grace announced. "Who wants to come with me?" Katelyn watched the way Grace directed the request to Kenny, who said nothing.

"I'll come with you," someone else said.

"I'll come, too," Katelyn said, starting to rise. But before she could make her escape, someone else agreed to go. Katelyn watched the group walk off, wondering how the hell she'd found herself stuck in this situation.

"What are we drinking?" Kenny asked her, moving his chair closer to hers.

"A berry martini of some kind, I think," she said, catching a strong whiff of his musky cologne. "Not sure what it's called. Grace got it for me."

"I'll get you the next one," he said, draping his arm on the back of her chair.

"Thanks, but I'm still nursing this one," she said, motioning to her glass. "I'm not staying very long. I have to be up early."

"Believe me, I know," Kenny smiled, leaning even closer. Katelyn felt his leg brush against hers and tried to put some space between them. "I think you have to be the most dedicated person in that office. You look really nice by the way," he added. Katelyn watched as his eyes roamed down her body appreciatively.

"I disagree," she said, feeling herself cringe.

"You don't think you look nice?" Kenny laughed incredulously. "You're really pretty Katelyn, trust me."

"No, I didn't mean about that. I mean about being the most dedicated person in the office. Everyone there works really hard," she corrected him.

"Not like you, I bet," he said, lowering his gaze to her mouth.

Gross! She wanted to scream. "Oops, getting a text," she lied, pulling out her phone. She was determined to get out of there.

"Uh-oh, got a hot date or something?" Kenny said, watching her tap into her phone.

"As a matter of fact, I do," she replied, sweetly. She angled her phone away from him, but not before catching the twisted look in his eyes. He wasn't just disappointed, he was angry. She quickly texted Stephen.

KATELYN: Where are you right now?

STEPHEN: Bar on Newbury. You?

KATELYN: That new restaurant across from Trident Bookshop.

STEPHEN: I'm a few blocks down. Why? All O.K.?

KATELYN: Guy from work weirding me out…am stuck.

STEPHEN: Just leave. Say you have a hot date with the hunk from your building.

KATELYN: Come get me. Complicated.

"Well, before you run off, the next one is on me, no argument," Kenny said. When Katelyn's only response was a tight smile, he continued to talk. "So how do you like work? They treat you okay?"

"They do actually," she said, folding her arms across her chest. "I like it a lot."

"A lot of uptight lawyers on that floor. Half of them have sticks up their asses if you ask me. Present company excluded, of course."

"I don't get that impression at all, actually. Everyone has been very welcoming," she said, reaching for her glass. She downed the rest of her drink and placed it back on the table. "I do not want another," she warned him, before he offered yet again.

"Got it. Half of them barely say hello in the morning," he continued to complain.

She'd had enough. "I need to go to the ladies' room. Do you mind?" she snapped. When he failed to move, her temper flared. "Seriously, Kenny?"

"Of course," he said, sliding his chair back. But instead of rising to get out of her way, he remained seated. "You can squeeze by, can't you? A small thing like you?"

"I can, but I choose not to. Please move, Kenny. *Now.*" If she hadn't finished her drink, she would have dumped the remainder on his head. To hell with Grace thinking she was a snob.

"Why are you so uptight?" he laughed. "You really do need another drink."

"Hey, Katelyn," a male voice said. "Yo, buddy, would you get out of my girlfriend's way?" Stephen asked, reaching for Katelyn's hand. Kenny's eyes darted back and forth between the two of them, and he quickly rose.

"Sorry," Kenny said, watching as Stephen bent down placing a firm kiss on Katelyn's lips.

"You ready to go?" Stephen asked Katelyn in a suggestive tone.

"I am, hon," Katelyn said. "Bye, Kenny," she said without looking back. "Tell Grace my boyfriend showed up, please," she added, wrapping her arm around Stephen's waist.

"Boy, has that guy got the hots for you," Stephen mumbled as they swiftly walked away. "Aren't your other coworkers going to wonder why you left?"

"I don't care anymore," Katelyn said. "He was the one I was telling you about, the security guard," she explained, reaching for the door and rushing outside.

"The dude has issues," Stephen said, following her.

"Apparently," she agreed, taking a long deep breath. The cool air felt good on her face. "This feels better," she said. "I think I'm a bit buzzed. Thank you for saving me by the way. It was very gallant, you know."

"My pleasure, darling. It's not often a guy like me gets to save a damsel in distress. Want to hang with us? The boys would love to see you," he added.

"I don't think so," she said. She wasn't feeling particularly upbeat and didn't feel like pretending otherwise. The evening had been a disaster, and all she wanted was to be alone. She spotted the bookstore across the street.

"Well, you shouldn't drive just yet," he warned her.

"Thanks, *Dad*," she laughed. "I Uber-ed into work today, actually. Thought I'd be too tipsy to drive home. Which is true. See? I know I'm a lightweight."

"Then I'll wait with you till your ride comes," Stephen said.

"I think I'll peruse the book shop, actually," she said. "Maybe grab a muffin and coffee or something, too."

"Was the kiss that bad?" he asked, pretending to be offended. "Books over me?"

"On the contrary. It was outstanding," Katelyn assured him, patting his arm.

"Want another one in case he's still watching?" he asked with a mischievous grin, inching closer to her.

"Sure," she said, looking back at the restaurant. In the off-chance Kenny was spying from the window, it just might put him off of her once and for all.

"Just no tongue this time, please," she said, wrapping her arms around his neck playfully.

"You got it," he said, pressing his lips on hers and patting her on her bottom. "Gotta run. I'll knock on your door if I don't get in too late tonight."

"Great. And I did not say you could touch my ass," she added, pulling away. "God, I hope he was watching. Tell everyone I said hello."

"I know but it's a nice ass. Wait till the guys hear I kissed a girl tonight!"

Chapter Thirty-Two

A pair of steely eyes *had* been watching Katelyn. The expression of distaste on Andrew's face had nothing to do with the kale salad he had convinced himself to order. He had never seen Katelyn look so relaxed and happy, kissing and clinging to some guy who groped her ass in the middle of the sidewalk.

So, it's not all men who make you nervous. Just me.

Katelyn was still glowing when she entered the bookshop. But her expression changed the moment she spotted him sitting in the window.

"Hello, Katie," he said politely, rising from his chair.

"Hello, Andrew," Katelyn said.

"Looking for any book in particular?" he asked.

"Not really. You?"

"Just having a bite to eat," he said. He thought about adding that he'd enjoyed the show but changed his mind.

"They have such delicious food here," she said, shifting uncomfortably. He followed her gaze to the food counter.

"They do."

"Well, have a nice evening," Katelyn said, turning away.

"You look hungry," he heard himself say. "Feel like grabbing a bite? I'm finished, but I'm going to get myself a cup of coffee."

"Um, sure," she said in a surprised tone. "Is there something you wished to discuss regarding work?" she asked, following him to the food counter.

"No," he said, casting her an annoyed glance. He tried to catch the server's eye to place his order, but the place was busy.

"Then I don't understand why you asked me to join you," she stated flatly.

Andrew was taken aback by the blunt comment, narrowing his eyes on hers. "What is that supposed to mean?"

"I'm sorry, Andrew," she said. "I didn't mean to be rude."

"Well, you were," he said. "I'm just being cordial, *Katie*. Nothing more. Did you think I was asking you on a date or something? Can't two colleagues share a cup of coffee and a muffin?"

"Why must you be so damn difficult?" she snapped. "For the record," she added, facing him squarely, "If either one of us is rude, it certainly isn't me. Ask anyone in the office, and I'm sure they'd agree. This night just keeps getting better and better," she hissed under her breath, turning away.

He watched her leave, debating whether to chase after her. He also thought she seemed a little drunk. Her outburst had surprised him, and he berated himself for having been such a damn jerk. After shoving a few dollars into the tip jar on the counter, he followed her outside.

"Hold up a moment," he said, calling out to her. She was walking briskly, and when he finally caught up to her, he reached for her arm. "I want to apologize," he started to explain, just as her phone fell from her hand, landing hard face-down, on the pavement.

"What the hell!" she screamed. "I can't believe you did that. That's a brand-new phone!"

"Well, if you hadn't behaved like a child stomping out of the store, this would never have happened," he said, bending over and picking it up. "Uh, oh. The screen shattered. It was my fault. I'll replace it for you first thing tomorrow."

"What did you say?" she said, ignoring the phone. "Did you call me a child?"

"I said you were behaving like one. Big difference," he clarified. Judging from her mortified expression, he knew he'd struck a nerve. Her eyes glistened with fury, and for an instant, he thought she was either going to cry or smack him; or perhaps do both.

"Why are you the only one at the office who calls me Katie?" she blurted out.

"I am?" he asked, surprised.

"You are," she stated.

"I honestly don't know," Andrew replied truthfully, still holding her broken phone.

"The only person who calls me Katie is my mother," Katelyn said, snatching it from his hands. "Well, this looks shot to hell, thanks to you. I was in the middle of requesting a ride home."

"Would you prefer I call you Katelyn, then?" Andrew asked.

"I would," she said.

"Fine. What is your address, *Katelyn*?" he asked, pulling out his phone.

"Why?"

"I'll request a ride for you. Or should I call your boyfriend instead?" he asked.

"My boyfriend?"

"I assume the guy pawing you across the street a while ago was a boyfriend?" he said sarcastically.

"He's just a friend," she said defensively.

"You kiss all your friends like that?" he retorted.

"It's complicated. Ninety-eight Needham Street in Newton," she replied, turning away from him while he entered her address. "Is there a car close by?"

"There is," he nodded. "Just a few minutes away."

"Great."

Andrew had never seen Katelyn this rattled. She was always so composed in the office, so difficult to read. She'd started to pace up and down the sidewalk, avoiding him completely. "I'll wait with you until it arrives," he said, knowing he should apologize.

"You don't have to," she said.

"I know I don't," he said, sighing. "But I am. *Period*. I'm not leaving you here until your ride shows. My home is a short walk from here, anyway."

"Whatever," she said under her breath.

They stood next to each other in silence as they watched the steady stream of cars pass by. "I think this is it," Andrew finally said when a sedan maneuvered its way to the curb.

"Thank you, Andrew," Katelyn said, turning to face him.

"No problem," he said, surprised to find her eyes brimming with tears. He stepped closer to her. "What's wrong?" he asked in a low voice.

"I don't know," she said, slowly shaking her head. "I'm usually not like this. It's…it's you, I guess."

"I'm sorry, Katelyn," he said, looking away. "Whatever I did, I'm sorry."

"I don't understand you," she said. "Since the day I started at the firm, you've despised me. Why?"

"I don't despise you," Andrew said, turning to her. "That couldn't be further from the truth. You should go," he added, reaching for the door. But Katelyn ignored him.

"Really?" Katelyn asked. "Then what is it? It's not my work, is it?"

"Of course not," he said, impatiently. "You need to go. *Now.*" All he could think of was how much he wanted to kiss her.

"Not until you answer my question," she said, refusing to leave.

"Stop, Katie. Really. I'm mean, *Katelyn*," he corrected himself.

"Fine," she said, brushing by him. "You're a coward *and* a bully," she muttered under her breath.

"Wait," he said, gently placing his hand on her arm.

"Why?" she asked.

Andrew said nothing. Before he could talk himself out if it, he lowered his lips to hers. The kiss was soft and gentle at first, but it wasn't long before Katelyn was kissing him back. When he felt her arms slowly wind around his neck, he pulled her closer to his body. Her response surprised him, and he couldn't help thinking how good she felt in his arms. It took every bit of his willpower to slowly push her away.

"You should go," he whispered, his mouth hovering over hers.

"I don't want to," she said, breathlessly. He knew he should put her in the car and walk away.

"Are you sure?" he asked, searching her eyes.

Katelyn nodded, reaching for his hand. "Tell the driver to leave, please."

Chapter Thirty-Three

The sound of purring was loud enough to wake Katelyn. She felt the warmth of Smokey's body pressed against her and absently reached to stroke him. Her eyes fluttered open, confused, when she didn't feel him there. When she remembered where she was, she decided she'd been dreaming.

Andrew was sleeping on his stomach, his face only inches away from hers. She watched him for a moment, as her eyes grew accustomed to the dark. He was beautiful, she thought. He seemed younger, too. She wanted to touch him again but resisted the urge. Turning slowly, she slid off the bed and gathered her clothing from the floor before tiptoeing into his bathroom.

She paused, eyeing her reflection in the mirror. Her hair was a mess, and her mascara was smudged, but she couldn't stop grinning at herself. She could still feel Andrew on her skin. Could smell him on her body. She brushed her fingertips over her swollen lips and told herself not to think about the consequences of last night. Not yet anyway. There was a hairbrush resting alongside the sink, and she picked it up; quickly running it through her hair. A dark bar of soap rested on a dish, and she absently reached for it, holding it to her nose. It smelled like Andrew.

She reentered the bedroom, relieved that Andrew hadn't moved. Part of her wished she could slip back under the covers with him, but she knew she needed to get home. The idea of going to work today in the same clothes she'd worn yesterday was out of the question. Her eyes lingered on him a few moments longer, as if needing to convince herself that last night really did happen. As quietly as she could, she picked up her shoes and slipped out the door, making her way downstairs.

Her purse was on the table in the hallway. She dug out her phone, forgetting for a moment that it had shattered. Stepping into her shoes, she decided she'd walk over to one of the hotels near the park, where there was always a steady stream of cabs. First, she needed to leave Andrew a note. She searched her purse for something to write on but came up empty. A door off the hallway was ajar and she peeked inside, happy to discover it was a cozy looking study. There was a desk in the room, and she made her way towards it, spotting a pad of paper on top.

Her eyes were drawn to the overstuffed shelves of books. She knew she should scribble the note quickly and leave, but they were far too tempting not to take a quick look at. Most of them were biographies and the classics, and many appeared old and rare. There were no legal books of any kind, which she found interesting. When she spotted an old copy of *Treasure Island*, she carefully pulled it out and opened the cover. The name "Andrew Madden" was written neatly inside in cursive. She grinned, imagining him reading the book when he was a child.

"So you *were* a little boy once," she whispered. She loved the fact he'd held onto his childhood books. She tucked *Treasure Island* back on the shelf, alongside *King Arthur and his Knights* and retrieved the pad of paper before stepping back into the hall.

Andrew,
I didn't want to wake you. I needed to get home. See you at the office.
Katelyn.

She left the note on the table and turned towards the front door, just as a sound drew her attention back to the study. She eyed the front door, knowing she should be on her way, but something told her to go back and check the room first. When she spotted the copy of *Treasure Island* on the floor, she froze.

"How did that happen?" she mumbled, rushing over to pick it up. She inspected the spine, relieved she saw no damage. Still, she couldn't understand how it had fallen from the shelf. The room was dimly lit, so perhaps she hadn't placed it back properly?

"Or maybe it was the spooky ghost of old Billy Bones," she giggled, slipping it carefully back onto the shelf. "I could hardly blame a creepy old ghost for wanting to live in this room," she added, turning away.

Her body pitched forward, and she stumbled to the floor landing hard on her hands and knees, just inches from the fireplace. She remained motionless on all fours, startled by the fall. Had she caught her heel on the carpet fringe, she wondered, turning slowly to inspect the area?

"Strange," she said, unable to figure out how she'd been so clumsy. Still, she was grateful that she hadn't hit her head on the marble hearth. She stood up, coming directly face to face with the solitary photograph resting on the mantle.

Who are you? she thought, inching closer to her to the woman sitting on the bench. The room was so still, she half-expected to hear a response. When she heard footsteps coming down the stairs, she quickly darted out of the room.

"Where are you going?" Andrew asked as he reached the bottom step. Katelyn noticed him cast a curious glance at the study door. "Were you just in there?"

"I was looking for something to write on," she said, motioning to the note on the table. "I'm sorry. I didn't have anything in my purse."

"You don't have to apologize. I just thought I heard something. And I'm glad I did, or I might have missed you sneaking out," he added, reaching for the note. After reading her message, he placed it back on the table. "Come back to bed," he said, rubbing his face.

"I need to get home," Katelyn explained. "I have to be at work in two hours and I live in Newton."

"Please come back to bed," he repeated.

"I can't go to work in the same clothes I wore yesterday," she explained, inwardly thrilled he didn't want her to leave.

"Oh," he said, finally seeming to understand. "You're right. But it's still too early," he said, holding out his hand. "We'll deal with that later."

"How?" she asked, clasping it.

"You know that Newbury Street is loaded with boutiques, and that it's only a few blocks up from here, right?" Andrew asked.

"Yes, but—"

"I'm going to let you in on a little secret," he said as he led her back upstairs.

"Which is?"

"You don't always have to be the first one at work every morning."

Chapter Thirty-Four

Katherine pulled on the floral gardening gloves that Mariah had given her last Mother's Day, recalling what a wonderful time they'd had that day. They'd started their morning touring private gardens in Beacon Hill that were rarely open to the public. Afterwards, they enjoyed a late brunch at one of Mariah's favorite places on Charles Street. The intimate French bistro was nestled between antiques shops and upscale boutiques, and Katherine foolishly recalled feeling underdressed.

"You look fine, Mom," Mariah had said, urging her mother to relax. "Let's have a glass of champagne."

"I knew we'd be doing a lot of walking, and I wanted to be comfortable," Katherine explained, looking down at her frumpy sneakers and frowning.

The waiter had been amiable and pleasant when he returned with two flutes of champagne, placing them down on the table. "And what have you two lovely ladies been up to today?" he asked with a twinkle in his eye. He'd been charming, Katherine recalled.

How have two Mother's Days without you already passed, Mariah? Katherine thought.

She knelt in front of her daughter's grave, on the small foam pad she placed under her knees when she gardened. The purple and yellow mums she'd planted earlier in the month needed deadheading, and it was time to replace the small pumpkins, too. She knew how much Mariah loved them.

"Those squirrels," Katherine said, reaching for the half-eaten gourds and throwing them into the plastic bin she'd brought with her. "I guess you wouldn't have minded though. Remember the squirrel that nearly frightened me to death? The one you snuck into the house?"

Katherine reached for the bulbs and set herself to work, envisioning how beautiful the yellow daffodils and red tulips were going to be in the spring.

Every few minutes, she leaned back on her heels, inspecting her progress. Occasionally she glanced behind her, hoping that Joseph would appear.

"He's not ready, Mariah," she said, tapping down the loosened soil with her spade. "I'm sorry." Katherine's heart was heavy with disappointment by her husband's absence, but she still carried on, trying not to think of the mistakes all of them had made.

"This worked at our garden at home," she explained, reaching for the half-filled jar of cayenne pepper in her purse. She sprinkled it generously over the dirt. "Hopefully the squirrels and chipmunks here won't like the taste, either. There," she said, looking up when she was finished. She pulled off one glove and tenderly traced the etched words on Mariah's headstone.

Mariah Talbot.
b. 3/24/1990 d. 10/22/2017
Beloved Daughter Taken from Us Much Too Soon,
But Will Forever Remain in Our Hearts.

The sound of crunching leaves behind her caught her attention. She turned, certain that this time, it would be Joseph. When another figure came into view, a stranger dressed in maintenance clothing, she didn't hide her disappointment.

"Can I help you with that?" the young man asked.

"It's not heavy," Katherine said, slowly standing up. "But thank you, anyway."

"It's a beautiful day," the man said, looking up at the sky. "Cool but clear."

"It certainly is," Katherine nodded, pulling off her other glove. She shoved them into her pockets and collected the rest of her supplies. "Are you new here? I haven't seen you before."

"I am. My name is Gideon," he said, removing his soil-stained gloves before extending his hand to hers.

"Nice to meet you, Gideon," she said when their hands touched. His were smooth and soft, she thought, not calloused as she would have expected from a groundskeeper.

"I'm new at this," he explained.

"Well, you certainly have a knack for it," Katherine said, looking around. "I don't think I have ever seen the grounds look this nice."

"I appreciate that," he smiled. "You sure I can't help you with that bin?" he offered again.

"If it's no bother," she said, suddenly changing her mind. Perhaps it was his easy demeanor, or the fact that they both tended to the earth. Or perhaps it was just loneliness. Whatever the reason was, she found herself oddly happy to spend a few moments more in his presence.

"I was just about to walk it over to the wood line to dump them out," she explained, watching him lift the container. "It's just old half-eaten pumpkins and dead flowers."

"Well, the squirrels will have a field day with this," Gideon said. "Family member or friend?" he asked as they headed up the hill to the tree line.

"She was both. My daughter," Katherine said, softly. Gideon paused, turning to look at her before responding.

"I'm so sorry," he said. "No parent should ever have to bury their child."

"No," Katherine said. "Thank you."

They continued to walk in silence, and Katherine tilted her head back, enjoying the chilly New England air. She imagined the cemetery blanketed in snow in a month or so, and her thoughts turned to Christmas.

Another year without a tree, she thought sadly.

Mariah always loved decorating the house with her each year and to bake their traditional holiday cookies together. Even when she was in college in Vermont, she managed to make it home for a weekend before the Christmas break just to bake. Jake always got the first plateful. Even before Joseph.

"What type of bulbs did you plant?" Gideon asked, interrupting her thoughts.

"Daffodils and red tulips," she replied.

"I can spread a little mulch over them this week," he said when they reached the woods. "It can't hurt."

"Thank you so much," Katherine said, watching him tip the contents of the bin onto the ground. The pumpkins rolled off a few feet, nestling themselves among the fallen leaves.

"Those won't last long with all these squirrels," he said. "They'll be feasting tonight. Do you usually tend to your daughter's grave alone?"

"I do," Katherine replied, turning to him. She thought it was an odd question but didn't feel offended. "My husband always comes with me," she quickly added, "but he waits in the car."

"I see," Gideon said.

"It's just too hard for him," Katherine explained.

"Is he in poor health?"

"No, I meant emotionally. That's why he doesn't come to the grave when I visit Mariah. That was her name."

"It's a beautiful name," Gideon said.

"Thank you. Mariah was a beautiful person. Their relationship was strained, my husband and Mariah's. My gosh," she said, widening her eyes and covering her mouth with her hand. "I can't believe I just told you that."

"Sometimes it's easier to talk to strangers. Where are you parked?" Gideon asked.

"I guess you're right," Katherine said, shrugging her shoulders. "I'm not too far down the hill."

"What do you like to do?" Gideon asked, walking beside her. "For fun, I mean."

"I...I don't know what you mean," she said.

"I mean, when you're troubled or sad. Do you have a hobby that helps?" he asked.

"Gardening," Katherine said. "Mariah and I had that in common, actually."

"What about your husband? Does he like to garden as well?" Gideon asked.

"Not really," she admitted. "He is more of a behind-the-scenes gardener, if you know what I mean. Helps with the heavy lifting, but not much else, I'm afraid."

"That's too bad, since it can be so therapeutic. You should convince him to give it a try," he suggested.

"I have, believe me. He's a stubborn man and I don't like to push him too much."

"Sounds like he needs it," Gideon said, facing her. "See?" he asked her. "I do it too."

"Do what?" Katherine asked, completely confused.

"Open up to strangers," he said, grinning.

Katherine laughed out loud, deciding that she very much liked this young man. "My daughter would have liked you very much," she said.

"You think?" Gideon said, smiling.

"Absolutely," she nodded.

"What about your husband?" he asked.

"He's a tough man to win over," Katherine said, thinking of all the times she'd tended to Mariah's grave alone. Hadn't Joseph realized how much she needed him? She retrieved the empty bin from Gideon's hands.

"I can take it from here," she said. "It was nice meeting you, Gideon."

"Nice meeting you as well. I apologize for overstepping," he added.

"You didn't," she assured him, holding his gaze a moment longer. But he had, she thought, as she watched him walk away. As she made her way to their car, she found herself smiling.

"Pop the trunk," she said to Joseph, who was leaning out the window, watching her approach.

"How did it go?" he asked. "Gorgeous day," he added, tilting his face to the sky.

"It is. And it went fine," Katherine said, rounding the back of the car. After placing the plastic container in the trunk, she slammed it down and climbed into the passenger seat.

"Everything okay?" Joseph asked, eyeing her curiously.

Katherine turned to look at her husband. The lines around his eyes had grown deeper, and his complexion was pale. He rarely spent any time outdoors anymore and it showed. She slipped her hand in his and looked at his long fingers. They were older now, but they were still strong. And so was he. He'd just forgotten how.

"I was thinking, next time, you need to help me," she said, her eyes still focused on their entwined hands.

"You know it's hard for me just being here," Joseph started.

"And it isn't hard for me?" she asked.

"Please Katherine," he said, pulling his hand from hers.

"I'm still here, Joseph. And I need you. Are you hearing me?"

"Where is this coming from?" he asked, looking away.

"I'm lonely, Joseph. I miss doing things with you. We used to love taking long walks, and now I can barely get you outside. You haven't helped me with my gardens since she died. Do you realize that?" she asked.

"I don't want to talk about this," he said, reaching for the keys. Katherine snatched them from his hands.

"All the pruning and mulching and digging, you haven't lifted a finger helping me. Should I hire someone? Should we sell the house and move in a condo?" she suggested.

"Of course, not," he snapped, turning to face her. His eyes were brimming with tears. "We're never leaving that house. I just need more time."

Part of her wanted to wrap her arms around his shoulders like she always did and tell him that she understood. That he could take all the time he needed. But this time, she held back.

"We're not getting any younger," she said. "And I'm tired of doing things alone. I feel like I've lost you, too, Joseph."

"I am here, aren't I?"

"Not really," Katherine said, shaking her head. She placed the car keys in his hands and buckled her seatbelt. "You haven't been here in a long time, actually."

"Nonsense," he grumbled, starting the car. "Can we finish talking about this when we get home, please? And no more talk about selling the house."

"Fine. Then we're not going home," she decided. "We're going back to the garden center."

"What for? We were just there," he said, confused.

"I've decided to plant a few forsythia bushes on the side of the house. They were one of Mariah's favorite flowers to paint, and you're going to help me. The exercise and fresh air will be good for you."

Chapter Thirty-Five

Katelyn felt a gentle kiss on her bare shoulder and smelled the aroma of freshly brewed coffee. She slowly turned onto her back, opening her eyes.

"Morning," she said, squinting at Andrew. The sheets were soft against her bare skin, and she stretched her arms overhead, savoring the decadent sensation. "I can't remember the last time I had coffee in bed," she said when he handed her the mug. "Thank you, Andrew."

"You're welcome, Katie," he said, sitting down beside her.

Katelyn smiled at him before taking her first sip. "Mmm...this is delicious."

"I'm glad you like it. How are you?" he asked, stroking her bare arm.

"Wonderful." *If someone had told me yesterday that Andrew Madden would be bringing me coffee in his bed this morning, I would have told them they were certifiably insane.*

"What time is it?" she asked, noticing the light streaming through the window.

"Do you really want to know? You're not going to like it," he warned.

"Oh no," she said, eyeing his suit. "You're dressed for work. I didn't hear you get up. How late is it?"

"Don't freak out. Promise?" he asked, hesitating before answering her.

"I promise," she said, drawing the sheet over her breasts and propping herself up on her elbows.

"It's almost nine-thirty," he said.

"What? Why did you let me sleep that long?" she said, shoving the coffee mug back in his hands. She bounded off the bed and headed to the bathroom, dragging the sheet with her.

"I couldn't help it," he confessed, watching her with an amused expression on his face. "You look so peaceful when you sleep. It's nice."

"Not funny," she said, brushing past him.

"It's no big deal. I took care of it," he assured her.

"I need to shower. I need clothes…" she said, ignoring him.

"I'm headed out to pick your new phone. Do you trust me to pick out something for you to wear?" he asked.

"Wait, what did you just say?" she asked, turning to face him. "What do you mean you took care of it?"

"I called in and said you'd be late today," he explained.

"You did *what?*" Katelyn said. "What exactly did you say?"

"I'm sorry," he said, confused. "We all know how you like to be on time. I thought I was helping."

"Will you please tell me exactly what you said?" she repeated, clutching the sheet tighter. She sat down on the bed, waiting for him to answer.

"I said you were exhausted from a wild night of sex and debauchery at my house, and that you'd be in when you damn well felt like it," Andrew said, matter-of-factly.

Katelyn folded her arms across her chest. "This really isn't funny, Andrew."

"I said that you were having car trouble," he said, smiling. "That you reached out to me to let me know because we were supposed to be on the same conference call this morning. That's all."

"Oh, that's good," she said, relieved.

"You're not mad at me?" he asked, sitting beside her. "I did okay?"

This is certainly a switch, she thought.

"No, I'm not," she assured him, reaching for his hand. "I'm sorry if I flipped out there for a second. It's just, well, this is awkward."

"Good. Now that that's settled…what about those clothes?" he asked. "Can I pick something out for you?"

"Seriously?" she said. "*Andrew Madden* is going shopping for me?"

"It would appear that I am," he said.

"Fine. But nothing crazy. I just need a blouse. Something simple."

"I'm on it," he said, nodding confidently. "Anything else going on in that head of yours?"

"We work together," Katelyn began.

"We do," Andrew nodded.

"This isn't exactly an ideal situation," she said, *for me,* she almost added. They both knew exactly what she was getting at.

"Do you like me, Katelyn?" Andrew asked.

"Apparently, I do," she admitted, reaching for his hand.

"I've never been with someone in the office before. Have you?"

"Never," she said, shaking her head.

"Then I guess we're both in unchartered territory," he said softly.

"I don't think it's as simple as that," she said. "You're a partner."

"I understand," he said. "And I'm not insensitive to that, Katelyn. Believe me. I guess what I am trying to say is we'll figure this out together. That is, if you want to."

Katelyn regarded him carefully. There were a million reasons to say no. How many times had she told herself that she would never, ever date anyone she worked with? It was career suicide. And yet, all she could think of, when she looked into his eyes, was that she had never felt this way in her life before.

"I do," she said.

"Then as long as we're always honest with each other, I'd like to see you again. Outside the office, I mean," he said.

"Me too," she said, slowly wrapping her arms around him. The sheet dropped to her waist and the feel of his suit pressed against her bare breasts was surprisingly erotic. "Kiss me," she demanded.

"Finally," he sighed. "There's been far too much talking this morning," he said, pressing his mouth to hers.

Katelyn moaned, drawing him closer. She straddled his lap, running her palms up his back. When Andrew paused to remove his jacket, she stopped him.

"No," she said, catching her breath. "You'd better go. You have back-to-back meetings after lunch. And I need clothes."

"Ugh," he said, hanging his head, dejectedly. "I could call in and say I have car trouble, too?"

"You walk to work, silly," she smiled.

"Oh, right," he said.

Katelyn held his gaze. "Just promise me we'll be careful, okay? Don't start being nice to me at work."

"I'll try my best," he said, planting one, long last kiss on her lips before standing up. "Man are you disciplined," he muttered.

"I have very demanding bosses," she replied.

"They sound like a bunch of idiots. Grab a tee-shirt or something from my drawer if you like and go downstairs and find something to eat. This might take a while," he said, before leaving the room.

"I will," she said.

When she heard the front door slam shut, she peeked out the window and watched Andrew until he was out of sight.

"I'm about to put one of Andrew Madden's shirts on me," she said, laughing, as she turned towards his bureau. She laughed even harder when she opened the top drawer, noting the perfectly folded crisp white undershirts, lined in neat rows.

"Neat freak," she said, still smiling, removing a shirt towards the back. A small red leather box caught her eye. A box that looked like that was special, she thought. Katelyn stared at it, wondering what was inside. Placing the shirt back on top of it, she chose one from the front instead.

She made her way downstairs, forcing the image of the box from her mind. She'd find something quick to eat and take a shower before Andrew returned, she decided. The door to the study was ajar, however, and she only hesitated a moment before stepping inside. The picture of the woman was gone. An unsettling feeling washed over her as she looked around the rest of the room. The copy of *Treasure Island* was exactly where she remembered it was and so was the pad of paper on the desk. But there was no sign of the photograph.

Instead of heading for the kitchen, she bolted back upstairs. Before she changed her mind, she entered the bedroom and pulled the top drawer open and reached for the box. She knew what she was doing was wrong, even as she opened the lid. The exquisite, simple diamond ring took her breath away. She didn't dare remove it but stared at it a moment longer before placing it back in the drawer, exactly where she'd found it. Suddenly, she wasn't hungry anymore. She spied the mug of coffee on the bedside table and took a sip, but it had turned cold.

"My own fault," she mumbled, heading towards the bathroom.

She stepped inside and turned the shower on, watching the steam rise to the ceiling, forming a misty haze overhead. She gazed at it, realizing that something more than the ring was bothering her. It was the image of Andrew entering his study while she slept in his bed, quietly removing the photograph.

Chapter Thirty-Six

"Scotty's latest paintings are marvelous," Katherine said to Joseph, carefully spreading them out across their kitchen table. "Look at these."

"Let me see," Joseph said, putting on his glasses. "He's still painting Mariah, I see."

"He is," Katherine said. "Terry warned me before mailing them to us. He has really made progress, hasn't he?"

"They are amazing," Joseph agreed.

At first, Scotty had worked in simple colored pencils. After a while, he'd switched to watercolors, then to pastels, and now to acrylics. Art materials were expensive, Katherine knew, which is why she made a point of sending him care packages each month loaded with palette paper, brushes and large tubes of paints.

Katherine picked up a woodland scene of a woman, strongly resembling Mariah, holding Scotty's hand. She was wearing a long skirt, as Mariah so often did, and her feet were bare.

"Isn't that interesting," Katherine said, pointing to the lady's bare feet.

"Just like Mariah," Joseph said.

"But how could Scotty have known that?" Katherine asked.

"It's just a coincidence, Katherine. You know what the shrink said."

"They're called therapists, darling, not shrinks," Katherine corrected him. "And yes, I know. The theory is he paints Mariah because she saved his life."

Katherine remained unconvinced of the therapist's explanation. It had been more than two years since Mariah had pinned Scotty to the floor, saving his life. How could he still remember exactly what she looked like? He'd even made her eyes hazel. And now the bare feet?

"Let's take some of the older ones down and put these up," Joseph suggested. "Did you see this one? There's even a pumpkin here. She loved the fall."

"She did. And Christmas, too. Like Jake," she added, tentatively.

They both knew that Jake wasn't going to be with them much longer. He'd been to the vet numerous times the past few months and other than keeping him comfortable, there was nothing more that could be done for him. He seemed to be holding on only for them.

"I was thinking it might be time to put a tree up this year," Katherine said. "For Jake. I could bake his favorite cookies…"

"I'm not sure I'm ready for that and besides, it's barely November," Joseph said.

"What if he doesn't make it to Christmas? Wouldn't it be nice to give him one, final holiday? Mariah would have liked that."

"Can we talk about this another time, please?" Joseph asked.

"Sure," Katherine said, reaching for Terry's note. "Just start getting used to the idea."

She'd been pushing Joseph harder lately, and it seemed to be working. He was more engaged, even happy to take a stroll around the neighborhood with her from time to time.

Dear Katherine and Joseph,

Scotty and I hope this letter finds you well. As you can see, the art lessons you have so graciously gifted to Scotty are truly making a difference. And we can't thank you enough for the supplies! You are far too kind and generous. Any chance you'd like to take a ride up north? The foliage looks spectacular, and we'd love to have you visit. Jake might like it, too!

Fondly,
Terry.

"That sounds lovely, doesn't it? A ride up north. We could find a little B&B and make a weekend out of it," Katherine suggested, eyeing him hopefully.

"I'm not so sure," Joseph replied. "Like you said. Jake isn't well. Probably best if he stays put."

"We could bring him," Katherine added.

"I'll think about it," Joseph said.

"Don't we have Mariah's old easel in the attic?" Katherine asked, still staring at the artwork.

"Yes. Why?" he asked, turning to her curiously.

"I think she'd love knowing Scotty was making use of it. Don't you?"

"But...but it's Mariah's," Joseph said, blinking hard. "I want to keep it."

"Do you honestly think Mariah would have wanted her easel collecting dust in an attic for all eternity?" Katherine asked.

She knew how much Joseph treasured Mariah's easel. Knew that he'd memorized each bit of old dried paint that still clung to it. She wrapped her arms around her husband and rested her cheek against his. "I know this is hard," she whispered. "But it's the right thing to do."

"I'll think about it," he said. "I'll go up to the attic and take another look at it. Maybe dust it off."

"Want me to come with you?" Katherine asked.

"If you like," Joseph said, eyeing her suspiciously.

"Good," she said, as she helped gather up the drawings. "I want to see what we have up there in the way of Christmas decorations."

Chapter Thirty-Seven

Mariah sat on one of the old steam trunks in the attic, watching her parents dig through boxes of Christmas decorations. They were reliving old memories, but thankfully there was more joy than sadness in their stories. At one point, her father even laughed. It was one of the most beautiful sounds Mariah had heard in a very long while.

"Remember this old thing?" her father said, unwrapping her snow globe. "Mariah loved this."

"I remember," Katherine said, carefully taking it from his hands. She shook the globe and watched the snow swirling around the tiny little cabin nestled in the woods.

"We should bring this downstairs, don't you think?" Joseph said. "It's not right to keep it up here in an old box."

"I agree" Katherine nodded. "And I know just where it should go. Come on," she said.

Mariah loved the way her father carefully helped her mother down the narrow set of folding stairs, closing the attic door behind them. *You were always a gentleman,* she thought.

Her easel stared at her from the corner. It was wonderful to be alone with her old friend again. She ran her palm along the base of the narrow tray that had supported so many of her canvases. She'd watched her father do the very same thing, too.

"How long has it been?" she murmured, confused, knowing she was starting to lose track of the days. Yet, she could still remember which paintings coordinated with the dusty dabs of long dried-out paint. One color, oxide of chromium, particularly stuck out in her memory. She'd used it in a landscape she'd painted during the Thanksgiving break of her senior year of college. It was a memorable holiday that year, but not in a good way.

She'd been in her room that morning, so absorbed with her canvas that she'd hardly heard her father knock on her door.

"Can I come in?" he'd asked, peeking inside her room.

"Of course," she'd said. "Come, take a look. I'm just putting the finishing touches on this little study. What do you think?"

"Well, let's have a closer look," he said, reaching into his pocket for his reading glasses. There were a few leaves taped to the Masonite board behind the canvas. "What are those for?" he asked.

"Inspiration," she replied.

"Ah," he nodded, glancing down at her palette. Shades of fiery reds and burnt oranges were dotted on her palette, as well as a shade of green he had found fascinating.

"What's that called?" he asked her, pointing to the rich green hue.

"Oxide of chromium. One of my new favorites."

"Well, it certainly captures the trees. I don't think I have ever seen that color before. I love the sky, too."

It had been an early twilight scene, Mariah recalled. Somehow, she'd managed to capture the receding sunlight, and the results had been wonderful. It was as if the dimming light had set off an explosion of colors in the foreground. The fallen autumn leaves had almost appeared backlit.

"This is beautifully executed," he said. Mariah remembered how proudly he'd beamed at her work.

"It's just a study, Dad. I'm not that good."

"No," he disagreed, shaking his head. "You are, Mariah. What you have, can't be taught. It's raw talent. A real gift."

"Stop," she said, embarrassed. Then he said the four words she'd been dreading all weekend.

"We need to talk. This is what you need to be doing with your life, and you know it. Your mother mentioned something about you and Mark opening a business of some kind? Some kind of decorating store, is that true?"

"We're just talking about what to do after graduation. Nothing is definite," she said defensively.

"Good. Never forget that you are an artist. I know Mark cares deeply for you, but he doesn't know you the way we do."

"I don't want to talk about this," Mariah said, placing the brush down. "I should probably go help Mom with the turkey."

"You do that every time I bring this up, you know that?"

"Do what?" she snapped.

"Avoid the subject. I don't want there to be tension between us, Mariah. And I don't want to ruin Thanksgiving. But you graduate in less than six months and to think you'll be selling draperies or furniture or whatever decorators sell is mind-boggling. You are an artist!"

"Not today, Dad," she begged. "I don't want to hear it."

"When you were in high school, all you did was talk about how much you wanted to be a real artist," he said, ignoring her. "And when you started college that was still your dream. What changed? You could open an art studio right here in Wayland. We could help you financially. You could teach and have studio time for yourself. You love kids, too," he added excitedly. "You're so good with them, so patient. I remember when you gave art lessons at camp back when you were in high school, they loved you."

"I wasn't thinking about needing to earn a living then," she said. "Maybe someday, after I've made my own money, I'd like to teach but not now. Why can't you understand that?"

"I hate to see you put your talent on hold. Is this Mark's influence?" he finally asked.

"For the last time," she said, firmly, "Mark and I are a team. We make decisions together. Do we have to do this every time I come home? Can we please not ruin Thanksgiving?"

He stormed from her bedroom, and she sulked the rest of the holiday, barely engaging either of her parents.

Looking back now, she wished she hadn't behaved so childishly. Especially, since he'd been right. Mariah took a last long look at her easel, happy knowing it would soon find its way to Scotty.

"I'm sorry we argued so much," she whispered to her father. "And for what it's worth, you were right, Dad."

Chapter Thirty-Eight

"What's up with your car?" Grace asked Katelyn over lunch.

"Huh?" Katelyn replied.

"Your car?" Grace repeated. "Someone said that's why you weren't in on time."

"Oh! I got a flat on my way in this morning," Katelyn said. "That, and I also broke my phone last night. Had to get a new one this morning."

"Well, that doubly sucks," Grace said. "Nice top by the way. I don't think I've ever seen you wear red. It's a good color for you."

"You think so?" Katelyn asked, looking down at the silky blouse Andrew had bought her that morning. "Thanks."

No man had ever bought her clothing before. It was a color she never would have picked out for herself, but she loved it.

"How boring," Grace said.

Katelyn frowned. "What?"

"Your reason for being late. The broken phone, remember? I mean, I was hoping to hear you were hungover or tired from all the wild sex you had last night."

Katelyn felt a rush of heat to her face. "Excuse me?" she said.

"I know your secret," Grace whispered, grinning mischievously.

Katelyn didn't know how to respond.

"Stephen showed up at the bar last night and swept you off your feet. Any of this ringing a bell, hon? Kenny told me all about it. It's the only reason I'm not pissed at you for ditching us last night," she said, laughing.

"Oh!" Katelyn said, relieved. "He did actually."

"So, I didn't know you were *seeing him* seeing him," Grace said, leaning in closer. "You never told me. You never tell me anything juicy, actually."

"That's because there isn't much to tell. It's just casual. You know that already," she said, shoving a large forkful of food into her mouth so she wouldn't have to answer anymore of Grace's questions.

"Uh-huh," Grace said. "Whatever you say."

"What about you?" Katelyn asked, switching the subject. "You have a good night? Anything happen?"

"Actually," Grace replied, lowering her voice and smiling seductively. "Kenny *happened*."

"What?"

"After you left," Grace continued, "he wouldn't leave me alone."

"Is that so?" Katelyn said.

"What is your problem with him?" Grace asked. "Could you sound any less thrilled for me?"

"I didn't mean to sound that way, really. I'm sorry. He's just, well, he's sort of intense, don't you think?" It was the nicest way she could think of to say the guy was a creep.

"He's a good guy, Katelyn. Just a little rough around the edges," Grace said.

"I'm sorry," Katelyn said. "I'm happy for you, really."

"Apology accepted," Grace said, standing up and carrying her empty plate to the trash.

"It's just," Katelyn whispered, following her, "what if things don't work out between the two of you? You'll have to see him every day. Doesn't that worry you?"

"Not at all. We're all grown-ups, for crying out loud," she said, rolling her eyes. "I'd bet you half the people in the office are screwing each other. It's really no big deal."

"Really?"

"*Really*," Grace repeated. "Hold on a sec," she said, pulling out her phone. "It's Kenny," she said, with a giant grin on her face. "He wants to know what I'm doing tonight. Catch up later?"

"Sure," Katelyn said, watching her leave. As soon as Grace was out of sight, she pulled out her own new phone.

KATELYN: Thanks for the new phone.

ANDREW: NP. I like the blouse on you.

KATELYN: Me too.

ANDREW: Dinner tonight?

KATELYN: Need to go home. Was abducted last night and abandoned my cat.

ANDREW: You have a cat?

KATELYN: I do.

ANDREW: Hope he likes me.

KATELYN: Why wouldn't he?

ANDREW: How about I drive you home after work and find out?

KATELYN: Sure!

Katelyn tucked her phone back into her purse. She looked down at the delicate, red silk blouse she was wearing, imagining Andrew picking it out for her in some boutique just hours ago. It made her feel sexy. As she walked back to her desk, she forced the image of a perfect diamond ring from her mind.

Chapter Thirty-Nine

"You have to be kidding," Carlos said, staring wide-eyed at Sue. "Candace Trainor wants us to do another room for her?"

"Isn't that great?" Sue said, ignoring the sour expression on his face. "Apparently, she is in the process of hiring a nanny and needs to convert the second-floor office we did two years ago for her into an *au pair* suite."

"Might I remind you, the woman threatened to call immigration on me?" Carlos barked.

"And might I remind you, the commission we made doing her entire house? Not to mention the referrals we got from that job?" Sue shot back.

"Mariah would not have cared," Carlos snapped, shaking his head. "Money never mattered to her. The way people treated us, treated me, mattered."

"That's not fair," Sue replied. "This is strictly business, Carlos. If you don't want to see her, you won't have to, but you will need to work with me on this. In fact," she said, excitedly, "we should still have the old work orders for the pieces she wants re-covered. How much easier could this be?"

"As long as I don't step foot in that house," he warned, "it's a deal. But I mean it, Sue. Don't try to push me on this one."

"I won't and agreed," she said. "They've got to be here somewhere," she continued, opening the middle drawer of the overstuffed filing cabinet. Carlos watched as she pulled a stack of old work orders out of one of the binders and sat on the floor, spreading them out to get a better look.

"Is it there?" he asked.

"Hmm. I don't see it," she said, shaking her head. "That's funny because I know I didn't throw anything out."

"Could it be in another spot?" Carlos asked.

Sue yanked on the heavy lower drawer, pulling it out completely. Instead of the hinges catching as it should have, the drawer crashed right onto her foot.

"Damn that hurt!" she hissed.

Carlos flipped the drawer over, emptying its entire contents onto the floor. "You're going to have some bruise there," he said, eyeing the damage. "Should I find some ice?"

"I'm fine," she said. "Just hoping it didn't scratch my shoes. You know how much these cost me?" she said, examining the fine Italian leather pump.

"No, and I don't want to know," Carlos said as he began sifting through old paperwork.

"Wow," she said, standing up. "I've opened this drawer a million times. That's never happened before."

"Maybe it's a sign we shouldn't do the job," he mumbled, spotting a thick file with a swatch of blue fabric sticking out of the side. "That looks familiar," he said, pointing to the folder.

"Ah-ha," Sue said, reaching for it triumphantly. "That wasn't too hard."

"I remember this," Carlos said, frowning at the pale blue and cream cloth stapled to a work order. "That was on the couch she went crazy over."

"You mean the one you screwed up?" Sue reminded him, sweetly.

"Yes, Sue. The one I 'screwed up'. She ended up not paying a dime for it, as I recall."

"The past is the past, Carlos," Sue murmured, flipping through the pages. "Let it go."

"I miss her," he whispered, looking at Mariah's handwriting.

"Me, too. She must have meant to file all these when she got back," Sue said, lifting the stack of loose papers. When she stood up, a white envelope slipped from the pile onto the floor. The name "Andrew" was written across the top.

Sue bent down to pick up the letter. "What the heck is this?"

"You cannot open that, Sue. It isn't addressed to you," Carlos warned.

"Why not? You think that asshole gave a damn? He didn't even go to her funeral."

"Remember what he said to you?" Carlos said. "At the wake? He couldn't do it. It's addressed to him, so he should be the only one to open it."

"Are you kidding me?" Sue nearly screamed. "Are you actually defending him?"

"No. But we shouldn't judge him either," Carlos said, snatching it from her hands. "I will get this to him."

"And how are you going to do that? He didn't answer any of my calls two years ago, wanted nothing to do with us or Scotty. The guy's a loser," she said, grabbing it back.

"Stop!" Carlos yelled. "I'll throw it into the trash before you open it!"

The sound of breaking glass coming from the showroom stunned them both into silence.

"Did you hear anyone come in?" Sue asked, rushing to the front of the store.

"No," Carlos said, looking around. "No one is here," he confirmed.

"I don't get it. That sound came from inside the store for sure," she said. She walked to the front door, opening it to check that the bells hanging from the knob worked. "Is anything broken?"

Carlos scanned the room. "Look," he said, pointing to the blank space on the wall. "Mariah's painting. It's gone."

"Oh my goodness," Sue said, covering her mouth. "That was her favorite. Do you know how many people have asked to buy that?"

"Hold on," Carlos said, pulling the loveseat from the wall. "I think I know what happened. It's here," he said, spotting it wedged between the wall and the back of the sofa. "It must have fallen off the hook."

"But how?" Sue asked, staring at the blank wall.

"Who knows," he said, looking back up at the wall. "The hook fell out as well. It's an old building," Carlos reminded her, gently pulling the couch away from the wall.

"I just don't get how this could happen," Sue said, shaking her head.

"The glass shattered," Carlos said, cautiously lifting it off the floor. "But the frame is still okay."

"Oh, thank goodness. Did the actual pastel get damaged?" Sue asked.

"I don't think so," Carlos said, inspecting it carefully.

"We'll have to get it repaired right away. I can bring it to the framers down the street on my way home today," Sue offered.

"Okay," Carlos said, carefully propping it against the wall.

"Do you think we should give the painting to the Talbots?" Sue asked.

"Maybe someday," Carlos said. "But for now, I'd like to keep it in the store. I feel like a part of her is still here whenever I look at it."

"Me, too," Sue admitted. "I don't want to argue with you, Carlos. Mariah wouldn't have liked it."

"No, she wouldn't have," Carlos agreed.

Sue sighed, looking down at the picture. There wasn't a single day that she didn't think of Mariah. "She really captured the light in the trees, didn't she?"

"She did. I hope wherever she is, she's painting," Carlos said.

Sue reached for Carlos' hand and gave it a quick squeeze. "Me, too," she said. "What about the letter?"

"I won't open it, and neither should you," Carlos said.

"Fine," Sue sighed. "Andrew should be the one who opens it."

"Agreed," Carlos nodded.

"I just have one condition partner," Sue added. "*I* want to be the one who puts it in his hand."

***

Mariah wasn't pleased. While she was relieved that Sue and Carlos had finally found the letter, she wasn't thrilled that Sue had bullied Carlos into taking on Candace Trainor as a repeat client. That didn't mean Mariah had purposefully intended the drawer to smash down on Sue's foot, however, or for her painting to come crashing down off the wall.

She needed to do a better job at keeping her emotions in check. *Most of the time, anyway,* she thought, smiling as she recalled Katelyn's face plant in Andrew's study.

Candace Trainor, she thought, stroking Pinky's back.

She could see the miserable woman now, perched on her couch like a queen holding court. And she was sitting on the very sofa she ended up keeping for free. Even in death, it still irked her.

She watched as Candace motioned to her housekeeper that it was time for tea. The maid carefully lowered an ornate silver tray on the small butler table in front of the sofa. There was a young woman sitting beside her.

"Thank you, Josie," Candace said to the housekeeper, dismissively.

"Thank you, too," the lady beside Candace repeated, smiling, as Josie quickly exited the living room.

"May I pour for us, Sheila?" Candace asked, smiling sweetly at the young lady.

"That would be lovely. Thank you," Sheila replied in a thick Irish brogue. "What a lovely pot," she added to Candace's delight.

"Thank you," Candace said, beaming proudly. "It's quite old. Been in my family for several generations. Cream or sugar?"

"Neither, thank you," Sheila replied, reaching for the dainty little cup that matched the pot. "These look quite old as well."

"They are. You have an excellent eye, Sheila," Candace said, patting Sheila's arm as if they were old friends. "I must say, I find your brogue quite charming. We have relatives in Ireland, you know."

"How nice," Sheila said. "What part?"

"I'm not exactly sure," Candace said. "So, as I was saying, you would have every Sunday off and, most likely, every other Saturday as well, depending on Maddie's schedule. Does that work for you?"

Ah, Mariah thought. *The nanny.*

"It should be fine," Sheila nodded, taking a sip. "The tea is wonderful."

"Thank you, it's French. The dried rose petals in it are from Versailles. There's a delightful little tea shop in Salem that sends it to me every month."

"How nice," Sheila nodded. "And what does little Maddie do on the weekends?"

"She has gymnastics, ballet, piano lessons and scheduled museum visits each weekend," Candace explained.

"That's quite a schedule," Sheila remarked.

"Not really," Candace said, shaking her head. "Studies have shown that children as young as four years of age that are exposed to art on a regular basis develop quicker, intellectually. And to be clear, the aquarium is *not* a museum."

That poor kid, Mariah thought.

"Really?" Sheila said, raising an eyebrow as she reached for a tissue just before she sneezed. "Excuse me," she said, blowing her nose as quietly as possible.

"Bless you," Candace said before continuing. "And we like for Maddie to listen to French music as often as possible. We have our music stations preset for her. The best way to learn a foreign language is to hear it starting from a young age."

Sheila dabbed her eyes and sniffed, nodding in agreement. "I have heard that theory as well. I am actually fluent in French, by the way."

"You are?" Candace nearly yelled. "Wonderful!"

There's your French tutor, Candace, Mariah wanted to shout.

Sheila's eyes had begun to water and her nose was turning red.

"Is there a problem?" Candace asked warily. The artificial smile that had been plastered on Candace's face suddenly dimmed. "Oh my," Candace said, inching away from Sheila. "You aren't sick, are you? Do you have a cold?"

"I don't," Sheila assured her. "I don't know what is happening, to be honest. Feels like an allergic reaction of some kind. Do you own a cat, by any chance?" Sheila asked, looking around the room.

"We do not. Nor do we allow any pets in our home. The last thing we need is for a dog or cat to scratch up our furniture and rugs."

"I can see that. The house is beautiful. I don't think I've ever sat on a couch as fine as this one, either," Sheila said.

"Well, it's Scalamandre," Candace explained, nodding in agreement.

"I'm sorry," Sheila said, shifting uncomfortably. "I don't know what that is."

"It's a very good brand of fabric. Perhaps the best."

"Oh, I see," Sheila said. "May I use the powder room?" she asked, but not before sneezing again.

"Of course. It's just down the hall. I can have Josie show you if you like."

"That's not necessary. I'm just going to put a little water on my eyes," she explained, rising from the sofa. "Perhaps I'm allergic to something in the room."

"Let's hope that's all," Candace mumbled, clearly disappointed in how the interviewing was progressing and convinced she'd be sick with a cold in two days. "As if I'd ever let a cat claw these carpets," she mumbled under her breath.

Candace reached across the tray for the teapot, refilling her cup when Pinky brushed against her arm. Mariah had to cover her mouth for fear of bursting out laughing when Candace sprang from the couch, dropping the teapot onto her fine Italian silk fabric.

"Josie!" Candace yelled, her eyes darting around the room in bewilderment. Her momentary confusion was replaced with outrage, however, when she spied the damage to the couch. "No!" she cried, frantically searching for something to absorb the growing stain.

Josie came rushing to the entrance of the living room and gasped, covering her mouth with her hands.

"Don't just stand there," Candace cried. "Do something!"

172

"I'll get a towel," she said, rushing away.

Candace grabbed the linen napkins that were folded on the tray and quickly began to blot the couch. "What a brilliant idea," she called after her. "Are you sure you didn't want to just stand there and gawk some more? It's not absorbing the stain, Josie!" she screamed louder.

Josie rushed back into the room with a towel and offered it to her employer. "Are you kidding me?" Candace snapped, grabbing it from her hands. "One? Does this look like a one towel job to you?"

"I'm so sorry," Josie said, who looked as if she were about to cry.

"Just go find the girl, will you? For all we know, she's shoving whatever she can find into her pockets," Candace hissed.

Josie turned, coming face-to-face with Sheila, who had witnessed the entire scene. She scowled at Candace, who was on her knees dabbing the carpet now.

"Lord knows why you work for her," Sheila said to Josie.

"Excuse me?" Candace asked, looking up. "What did you say, Sheila?"

"You heard me," Sheila replied forcefully, turning to leave. "I wouldn't work for you if you paid me a million dollars."

"And *you* won't work in this town again for speaking like that to me, young lady," Candace warned her.

"Are you threatening me? Because I've got three other women begging me to work for them. You can take your fancy teapot and your lousy Scalamandre and shove them up your arse!"

Mariah's hand was still covering her mouth, certain if she'd laughed out loud, everything in the house would fall off the walls. And as much as she despised Candace, she didn't want to be responsible for her mental breakdown. She wished she could high-five Sheila, who stormed from the room without so much as a backwards glance.

Fabulous, Mariah thought. The only thing that would have made the moment perfect is if Carlos had been here to see it.

Chapter Forty

Andrew's first impression of Katelyn's apartment was that it suited her. It was clean and organized, but there were books scattered everywhere.

"And this is Smokey," Katelyn said, picking up the large gray cat. "He's probably going to pout the whole night."

"Well, you did abandon him for an entire day," Andrew said.

"Yes, and as you can see, he nearly starved," she laughed.

"You have a nice place," Andrew said, looking around. There were photographs everywhere, he noticed "Was this you and your dad?" he asked, pointing to one of Katelyn standing next to man in front of a Christmas tree.

"It was," Katelyn said, smiling at the memory. "Just before he died."

Andrew stared at it a moment longer. Katelyn had spoken of her father's passing but seeing how young she'd been at the time was something he hadn't fully grasped "You were just a kid," he murmured.

"I was fourteen," she said.

It made sense, he thought to himself. Her strong work ethic and determination. She'd been a puzzle to him that he was finally starting to piece together. "That's still pretty young," he said softly, carefully placing the photograph down.

"Wine?" Katelyn asked.

"Sounds good," he said, still looking around the room. "You could use a bookcase, or two," he added.

"It's on the list," Katelyn said.

"I think your cat likes me," he said, when Smokey started to rub against his leg. Andrew leaned over and scratched him on his head.

"He's just trying to get a can of wet food out of you," Katelyn said. "Sorry to burst your bubble."

"Not nice," Andrew sighed, walking towards her and shaking his head. "Not nice at all."

"Just teasing," she said, handing him a glass of wine. "He does like you, actually," she added, watching Smokey follow Andrew into the kitchen.

"That's because I'm likeable," Andrew said jokingly.

"Apparently, you are," Katelyn said. "Who'd have thought?"

"Come here, and I'll show you," he said, placing his glass down. He slowly untucked her blouse, running his palms up her bare back. Her skin was smooth and soft, and he felt her breath quicken as he reached to unfasten her bra.

"I wanted you to do this all day," Katelyn whispered, kissing him hard.

Just as she'd started unbuttoning his shirt, someone banged on her door.

"Who the hell is that?" Andrew groaned, as she pulled away from him, tucking in her blouse.

"That could only be Stephen," Katelyn explained. "Shit, I forgot to call him last night."

"Stephen who?" Andrew said, as she opened the door.

"Where the hell were you last night?" Stephen said, marching inside. "I was worried sick about you! I called and called, and you never answered. I was beginning to think that rent-a-cop kidnapped you!"

"What the hell is *he* doing here?" Andrew snapped. "What 'rent-a-cop'?"

"Never mind," Katelyn said, casting Stephen a murderous glare. "Andrew, this is my friend, Stephen. Stephen, this is Andrew."

"Hold on a sec. You're the guy Katie made out with in the street last night, aren't you?" Andrew said.

"I am," Stephen admitted. He watched Stephen turn to Katelyn and wink. It was as if they'd shared some secret that he wasn't in on. Andrew didn't like the feeling one bit.

"Well, I'm the guy she went home with," Andrew announced proudly, taking a step closer to him.

"Is that a fact," Stephen said, grinning. "Should we have a pissing contest now or something?"

Katelyn's face turned a bright shade of pink, but she said nothing. Instead, she gulped her wine.

Stephen smiled appreciatively at Andrew, then turned back to Katelyn.

"Okay, exactly what the hell is going on here, Katie?" Andrew demanded.

"You little hussy," Stephen finally said, bursting into laughter. "You're right," he said to Katelyn before reaching into the cabinet for another glass. "He's absolutely gorgeous."

Chapter Forty-One

Mariah sat opposite Terry in Dr. Mitchell's waiting room. Apparently, Scotty's teachers were growing concerned with his drawings. After the shooting, Scotty had been in counseling several days a week. The treatment he'd received had been wonderful and as a result, he hadn't needed to be seen for nearly a year. Until now.

Dr. Mitchell was a doctor that Scotty had never met before. Neither had Mariah. She couldn't help feeling guilty that she was the reason they were all here today. She had no idea how Scotty was able to see her when others could not, but it had been that way with him from the very beginning.

"Sorry, fellas," Terry said to the tropical fish, slowly circling the glass aquarium. "Never thought it was right to pluck you from some nice ocean and stick you poor guys in a tank."

Neither did I, Mariah agreed.

Pinky's whiskers twitched and her pupils enlarged with excitement. Her tail flicked wildly at the tempting morsels swimming just feet from them. *Not for you,* Mariah warned.

When the door finally opened, Dr. Mitchell greeted Terry politely. He appeared to be in his early fifties and wore a crisp white medical coat over his clothes. None of Scotty's former doctors had done that.

This immediately bothered Mariah.

"Thank you for coming, Mrs. Bartlett," the doctor said.

"No problem," Terry replied, standing up. Mariah knew Terry was trying her best to appear relaxed, but there was no hiding the concern in her eyes. "Where is Scotty?"

"He's just down the hall," the doctor explained. "I left him in the capable hands of our intern for a few minutes so we could talk in private."

Mariah was certain she disliked the man.

"Fine," Terry said, following him inside.

"I've just had an interesting conversation with Scotty," Dr. Mitchell began. He sat behind his desk and motioned for Terry to take a seat as well, as he absently straightened a stack of papers on his desk. He then sharpened a pencil for no apparent reason.

"Oh?" Terry asked.

"Before we get to that, however, I'd like to say he certainly doesn't seem as traumatized by the shooting any longer," he began.

"Well, that's a relief," Terry said, smiling.

Wonderful! Mariah thought.

"But he's not completely out of the woods yet," doctor said, holding up his index finger. "He still suffers from A.C.E, or, Adverse Childhood Experiences," the doctor explained. "From witnessing a violent act. Unfortunately, that trauma will always be with Scotty."

Mariah felt her heart sink. She wished there was something, anything, she could do to erase the experience from Scotty's memory.

"Are you sure of that, doc?" Terry asked. "Because he seems pretty happy to me. He never talks about what happened that day anymore. He hasn't in nearly a year. You know that Scotty was always shy and quiet, even before the incident. I've noticed he's been a little more outgoing, lately. I take that as a positive sign," Terry said, optimistically.

Dr. Mitchell did not like being questioned. He was shaking his head before Terry even finished speaking. "That might be the case, but my diagnosis stands. As you know, Scotty's teachers are growing concerned with the extent to which he talks about his 'lady' friend. I take it you were made aware of this?"

"I was," Terry said, shifting uncomfortably in her seat.

"Apparently, he continues to depict her in his art. Scotty's teachers sent along a few of his most recent works," the doctor said, opening his desk drawer. He proceeded to remove a few of Scotty's drawings, spreading them across his desk for Terry to see.

"Beautiful," Terry said, proudly.

"Be that as it may, his teachers are concerned that the woman here strongly resembles Mariah Talbot. Would you agree?"

"Yes," Terry said, eyeing the sketches. "I've seen these before. But I have no idea why. He seems so happy these days, I don't understand..."

Mariah leaned over the doctor, admiring them. She'd encouraged Scotty to draw, knowing how therapeutic it could be. But she hadn't told him to sketch her. If the therapist was going to dissuade Scotty from that now, she was not going to be pleased.

"I think I can put everyone's mind at ease," Dr. Mitchell explained, his tone professional and calm. "I'd like to ask you some questions about Scotty's mother."

It was not what Mariah had expected to hear.

"Do you have any contact with your daughter?" the doctor asked after a slight pause.

"I do not," Terry admitted. "It saddens me deeply."

"Do you know if she has ever reached out to Scotty through another relative, perhaps?" he continued.

"The only other relative I have is my sister in Maine. If my daughter had contacted her, she would have told me," Terry explained.

"I understand your daughter was an addict," Dr. Mitchell said, stacking Scotty's sketches back into a neat pile.

"Yes," Terry said, looking away. "She was. I did everything I could…"

"I'm sure you did," he said.

"She abandoned Scotty to me when he was barely three years old," Terry added.

Dr. Mitchell leaned back in his chair and cupped his chin in his hand, nodding. "This must be painful for you," he said.

Brilliant observation! Mariah nearly screamed.

"It is," Terry said.

"It's my belief that the lady Scotty draws, despite bearing an uncanny resemblance to Mariah Talbot, is actually his mother. Of course, he's imagining that his mother looked like Mariah, because she protected him."

"I'm sorry, I'm not following you," Terry said, confused. "My daughter looked nothing like Mariah Talbot."

"That's what I'm attempting to explain. These drawings…they are manifestations of a coping mechanism Scotty has put in place to insulate himself from undoubtedly feeling a maternal void in his life. You're clearly much older than most of the other mothers Scotty sees at school. Despite being his sole caretaker, it's clear Scotty doesn't view you as a mother figure."

Mariah gasped at the insult, quickly covering her mouth.

Terry stared at the doctor and said nothing.

"Mrs. Bartlett?" the doctor asked.

"That's an interesting theory," Terry said, nodding politely.

Mariah felt a wave of relief, knowing Terry wasn't buying the ridiculous theory. Nonetheless, she wished more than anything that she could speak up on Terry's behalf. To remind the good doctor that Terry, who was clearly taking the high road, was the one who raised Scotty. She was the one who held him in her arms when he was sick, made sure there were clothes on his back, food on his plate, and worked her fingers to the bone providing the best possible life that she could for him. If that type of unconditional love wasn't the epitome of a motherly figure, what was?

Moron, she thought, wanting to slap him across the back of his head.

"My advice to you and to his teachers is to not make such a fuss when he mentions his imaginary friend. I'm confident he'll outgrow it," the doctor continued, standing up.

"Well, I can't tell you what a relief this is," Terry said, rising from her chair. "Thank you, doctor. You've made such an *impression* on me."

As they walked out of the office together, Mariah carefully proceeded to tilt each diploma on the wall with the tip of her finger until they all hung crookedly.

Chapter Forty-Two

"I'm going to walk down to the stream, Grandma," Scotty said after dropping a handful of leaves into a giant bag in the middle of his backyard.

"Are you asking me or telling me?" Terry asked, pausing to rest a hand on her aching hip.

"Sorry," Scotty said. "Grandma, may I *please* go to the stream?"

"Now, that's better," Terry smiled, pulling Scotty's woolen hat down over his ears. "You may. But no further. You are getting more handsome every day. You know that kiddo?" she said, planting a kiss on the top of his head.

"Grandma," Scotty said, looking around him, embarrassed.

"Aw, come on, no one saw," Terry chuckled. "And I don't care how grown up you get, young man. I'm always going to kiss you so you'd better get used to it."

"Fine," Scotty said, rolling his eyes before darting off.

Mariah followed Terry's gaze as she watched her grandson walk into the woods. She knew that Terry was wondering if Scotty was off to meet her.

"Remember what I told you about moss?" Mariah asked, when she caught up to him. "It mostly only grows on the north side of trees. This way, if you ever get lost without a compass, you can figure out what direction you're headed in. See?" Mariah said, pointing to a soft mound of green on the base of the tree. "If you join the Boy Scouts, like I told you, they'll teach you all about it. They'll even give you a compass. I'm pretty sure there's a club in your school. You could meet kids that love the outdoors, like you."

Scotty ran his hand over the squishy patch. "I think I'd like to do that," he said after a slight pause. "Join that group I mean. I love the way this feels."

Mariah crouched down beside him. "If you like that, you'd love another one of my favorite plants. It's called lamb's ears, and it feels a lot like velvet. We had it in my mother's garden, growing up. Whenever I was sad or nervous,

180

I'd stroke the leaves. It always made me feel better. You should tell your grandmother about it. I'm sure she'd love to plant one with you."

"Why can't *we* plant it?" Scotty asked.

Mariah placed a soft kiss on the top of his head. "I can't do that, Scotty. You know I'm not...not..."

"Real? That's what everyone says. But they're wrong," he said, kicking a rock.

"Come on," Mariah said, slipping her hand into his. "Let's see if those baby trout got any bigger."

"Don't leave me," Scotty whispered, turning to face her. "Please?" he added.

The truth was, she didn't want to. But she couldn't tell him that. "I'll stay as long as I can," she promised. "How are things in school?" she asked, changing the subject.

"Fine," he said.

"Are you trying to make friends?" she asked.

"Not really," Scotty said. "No one talks to me."

"Well, why don't you try talking to someone first?" Mariah suggested.

"I can't," he said, shaking his head. "It's hard for me."

"You talk to me just fine," Mariah said. "What's the difference?"

"That's because you're nice. Most of the kids at school aren't," he explained.

"Hmmm," she said as they made their way down the small embankment to the stream. "There has to be at least one kid you like. Can't you think of anyone?"

"Well, there is one," Scotty said, reluctantly.

"Will you do me a favor?" Mariah asked, pausing. "Will you try talking to him? For me?"

"I'll try," Scotty said.

"Good," Mariah smiled.

"Any trout?" Scotty asked, looking at the stream.

"I see some," Mariah said.

"There!" Scotty said, pointing excitedly. "And there, too! There are so many of them," he said.

"I'll bet," Mariah nodded. She sat down by the edge of the stream, watching Scotty closely. He'd collected some twigs and was launching them down the brook, watching them disappear just as Mariah had taught him. "You can make sails for those with dried leaves, too."

"Good idea. Man, those trout are getting bigger," he said, collecting more twigs.

"You're getting bigger, too," she murmured, wondering how she was ever going to find the strength to leave him.

Chapter Forty-Three

"This is pretty," Andrew said, running his fingers along the edge of Katelyn's ivory silk camisole. She lowered the crossword in her hands and smiled at him.

"I'm glad you like it," she said. "Thank you for the coffee and Sunday paper in bed."

"You're very welcome. What should we do today?" he asked, stretching his arm across her body.

"It's such a blustery, gray day," Katelyn replied, looking out the window. She ran her fingers through his hair and snuggled closer to him. "How about we start with a huge breakfast? I'm starving."

"Not exactly what I was hoping to hear, but fine," he said, turning onto his back dramatically. "Food over me?"

"Absolutely," Katelyn laughed. "I'll make us some eggs."

"Why don't we go out to eat," he suggested. "Maybe brunch somewhere?"

The idea of running into someone they knew still worried her. They were careful in the office and Katelyn was certain no one knew about their relationship. She wanted to keep it that way.

"It's so gross out," she said, getting up. "Today is the perfect day to stay inside."

"Then let's do an early dinner somewhere," he said, pushing himself up on his elbow, watching her. "Some little restaurant tucked away where no one will see us."

"I'm seeing my other boyfriend tonight, remember? We made dinner plans," she reminded him.

"Stephen," Andrew said, sighing, getting out of bed. "You still haven't told me why you made out with him, by the way. Don't think I've forgotten," he said.

"I've already told you," Katelyn said, rolling her eyes. "It's a long story. We were playing a joke on someone we thought was watching. That's all."

"Some joke," Andrew muttered, walking across the room to retrieve his gym bag from the closet.

Katelyn had no intention telling Andrew about Kenny. The last thing she needed was for him to intercede on her behalf. And besides, the kiss with Stephen had seemed to work. Kenny rarely bothered saying hello to her anymore.

"So, you really have a dinner date with him tonight?" Andrew asked.

"I do," Katelyn nodded. "Since you and I have been together, I've hardly seen him. He's one of my few good friends."

"That's not the reason we are not going out to eat, though," Andrew said under his breath.

"No. It's not," she admitted. "Hitting the gym?"

"Since I can't burn calories with you, yes," he said. "Do you mind? I'm trying to make it a habit. Getting healthy and all."

"Not at all," Katelyn said. "I think it's great."

"Good. I'll be back in an hour or so," he said, getting dressed. "Want me to bring something in?"

"No, thanks," she said. "I'll take a shower and whip us up something later."

"That sounds great," he said, giving her a quick kiss on the lips before leaving the room. "Don't miss me too much," he called to her, as he bounded down the stairs.

"I'll try not to," she laughed.

Her eyes lingered briefly on the top drawer of his bureau before she made her way into the bathroom to shower. She regretted opening the ring box and tried not to think of it, even though she still found it unsettling when she did.

After making her way to the kitchen, she grabbed a banana and wandered into the study. There was still no trace of the mysterious photograph. The mess in the fireplace had still not been cleaned which surprised her, knowing how neat Andrew was.

"So unlike him," she murmured. The firewood in the copper bin appeared old and dried out, and a plan suddenly formed in her head. She looked around the room and smiled before hurrying to kitchen and setting herself to work.

After rummaging through Andrew's cupboards and pulling a mishmash of ingredients from the refrigerator, Katelyn quickly assembled a vegetable frittata. While it was baking, she carried the trash can into the study and cleaned out the fireplace. The cheesy aroma of the baking frittata wafted into the room, and she checked the time, calculating that Andrew would just be getting back when it was ready.

Perfect, she thought, excited to see the look on his face when he came home.

The logs caught easily and in no time at all, she created a roaring fire. The room filled with warmth, and she quickly turned on some music before stretching herself out on the sofa. When she heard the front door open, she called out to him.

"I'm in the study, Andrew dearest," she said, in a playful, flirty tone.

"What smells so good?" he asked.

"Come into the library and find out," she replied, suggestively.

The moment he stepped inside his smile faded. "What did you do?" he asked.

"Don't you like it?" Katelyn said, following his gaze to the hearth. "I thought I'd surprise you," she explained, standing up. "I have a frittata baking in the oven, and I thought we could have a picnic in front of the fire."

"I don't use the fireplace anymore," he said, clenching his jaw. "You had no right to touch it."

"I cleaned it out first," she said, panicking. The expression on Andrew's face was startling. "What did I do wrong?"

"Forget it," he said, turning away.

"Talk to me!" she pleaded, following him out of the room. "Please, Andrew?"

"I need to shower," he said, keeping his back to her.

"No!" she yelled, feeling like she was about to burst into tears. "I saw your face when you stepped in that room, and you looked like you'd seen a ghost or something," she cried. "What is this all about, Andrew?"

"Drop it, Katelyn, please."

"Is it about the woman in the photograph that you hid after our first night together? Or the diamond engagement ring tucked in the back of your top drawer?" she blurted out before she could stop herself.

"Excuse me?" Andrew said, slowly turning to face her.

"I didn't mean to snoop. I was looking for a T-shirt," she quickly explained. But she knew the damage had already been done. The icy expression in Andrew's eyes said it all.

"The ring was for her," Andrew said, glaring at her.

"I'm sorry," Katelyn cried. "Stop looking at me like that. I barely recognize you!" she screamed. The smell of burning eggs filled the foyer, and she remembered the frittata baking in the oven.

"I'm going to take a shower, *Katelyn,*" Andrew said, turning away.

She watched him disappear up the stairs without speaking another word. After she heard his bedroom door slam shut, she rushed into the kitchen and opened the oven. Smoke poured out, filling the room. She grabbed a towel, waving it frantically, hoping the fire alarm would not go off. Choking back tears, Katelyn scraped the ruined meal into the trash before slamming the baking dish down into the sink. She pressed the towel to her face as a sob escaped her throat.

"What the hell just happened?" she cried.

All she could think of was that she wanted to leave. Wanted to get back to her apartment and crawl under the covers as soon as she could.

Keep it together, she told herself. *Keep it together.*

She walked back into the study to retrieve her phone. The flames had died down, but the fire was burning steadily. Her gaze rose to the center of the empty mantle.

"You win," she said.

She walked out of Andrew's home without looking back.

Chapter Forty-Four

Andrew marched through the lobby of the building early Monday morning, determined to find Katelyn. He'd called her half a dozen times since yesterday, but she'd refused to answer her phone. He had a meeting scheduled across town in just a few hours, but he wanted to see Katelyn first. He needed to apologize.

When he'd discovered that she had left while he was showering, he could hardly blame her. His behavior had been inexcusable. Seeing the fire burning in the study had taken him by surprise, but learning she'd snooped through his bureau and found the ring had sent him over the edge.

He needed to tell her about Mariah.

"Andrew Madden?" came a sharp, clear, female voice from behind him.

He turned and found himself face-to-face with Susan Davis. Even after two years, he hadn't forgotten what she'd looked like. She was the last person he expected to see on today of all mornings.

"Hello, Sue," Andrew said, coolly. He wanted to ask her what the hell she was doing there but suppressed the urge. After the funeral, she'd left several messages on his phone, all of which he'd ignored.

"You remember me?" she said, bitterly. "I'm flattered."

"What can I do for you?" he asked, ignoring her sarcastic tone.

"Is there somewhere we can sit? Care for a cup of coffee?" she asked, motioning to the *café* in the lobby.

He wanted to say no and to tell her that her timing could not be worse, but he was also curious as to why she was there. Besides that, the determination in her eyes told him it would be futile to deny her. "Sure," he replied, leading the way.

"Wonderful," she snickered.

"What could you possibly want after all this time?" he asked after taking a seat.

"Just as charming as ever, I see," she said.

"Cut the nonsense, will you? Why are you here, Sue?" he demanded. "You couldn't have picked a worse day for a surprise visit. I'm already pressed for time today," he said, looking down at his watch.

"Carlos and I own Back Bay Décor now," she explained, leaning back in her chair.

"Congratulations. So?" he said, folding his arms across his chest.

"So, we came across a letter addressed to you from Mariah," she finally spat out, reaching into her purse, and slapping the envelope onto the table.

Andrew stared at the letter bearing his name in Mariah's handwriting but didn't reach for it. If Sue had meant to shock him it had worked.

"You know, I will never understand what she saw in you. Did you ever think about contacting her parents by the way? Ever wonder how Scotty or his grandmother are doing?" Sue asked.

"Why?" Andrew asked, slowly reaching for the envelope.

"Unbelievable," she muttered, scowling. "Did you love Mariah, Andrew? Because I know for a fact, she loved you."

"I did," he whispered, staring at the letter in his hands.

"Then I don't understand why you ran out of her wake. Her parents were told at the hospital that you had been there, did you know that? And that you told the nurse you two were engaged. Was that true?" Sue pressed.

Andrew felt his throat tighten but remained silent.

"I'm leaving," Sue sighed, standing up. "I delivered this for Mariah's sake, not yours," she added, turning away.

"Wait," Andrew heard himself say. "I never should have let Mariah drive to New Hampshire alone. I couldn't face them afterwards."

Sue paused, considering him carefully before slowly sitting back down. "She was at the wrong place at the wrong time, Andrew."

"No," he said, forcefully. "It was my fault. If she had been in my car with me, or if I had been with her in that diner…"

"Then you might have both been shot, for all you know," Sue said. "Bad things happen in the world. Someone could walk in this *café* right now and shoot us all. It's the world we live in."

"That fucking meeting in Hartford," he said, squeezing his eyes shut. "I never should have gone."

"No one could have predicted what happened," Sue said. "It wasn't your fault."

"There was so much I didn't know about her. The photographs at the wake… I didn't know she had been married before. I was angry she didn't tell me she was divorced," he admitted. "I felt like a fool. They were just a couple of kids. I wouldn't have cared."

"What the hell are you talking about?" Sue asked, puzzled.

"The wedding photo of her," Andrew repeated.

"Oh my god, Andrew," Sue said, covering her mouth. "Don't you know? Mariah was never divorced."

"What? Was she still married when we were together?"

"No, you don't understand. Mariah's husband was killed in a car accident by a drunk driver a few months after they were married."

Andrew felt his mouth go dry. "My god," he said.

"They were college sweethearts," Sue explained. "It was awful."

In all the scenarios Andrew had invented in his head, Mariah having been widowed was never one of them.

"Why didn't she tell me?" he asked. "I don't understand."

"It was hard for her," Sue explained. "You didn't know her back then. It was so painful for her to talk about Mark, to talk about her feelings. Even to me. You have no idea what that poor girl went through. She wanted to tell you about him, but she didn't know how. Can you try to understand that?"

"I actually can," he said, softly.

"I only wish we'd spoken sooner," Sue said.

"Me too. Thanks for bringing me this," Andrew said, tucking the envelope into his breast pocket.

"You're welcome," Sue said, smiling. "So. How have you been, Andrew?" she asked.

"I'm getting better. You?" he asked.

"I still miss her every day," she said.

"She was an amazing woman," Andrew said, smiling weakly.

"The best," Sue said, as her eyes filled with tears. "The world is a little less bright now, isn't it?"

"It is," Andrew agreed, leaning back in his chair. His mind was still reeling from everything Sue had told him. There was always some part of Mariah he couldn't reach, he thought. It all made sense now. "It must have been hard for you to come here today."

"That's an understatement," Sue laughed, reaching across the table and patting his hand. "I need a tissue," she lied, standing up.

"Let me," Andrew said, pushing his chair back.

"I want to stretch my legs anyway," Sue insisted, standing up.

Andrew watched Sue grab a napkin from the counter, dabbing her eyes before turning back towards their table.

"She's exactly how you described her, Mariah. Proud," he whispered.

***

After walking Sue back to her car, Andrew made his way to his office, locking the door behind him. He sat at his desk and removed the letter. After taking a deep breath, he carefully opened the envelope and unfolded Mariah's note.

Dear Andrew,

I can't believe it's only been eight weeks since we met. It feels like I've known you forever. People say that when they fall in love fast, but in my case, I truly mean it.

I was in love with a wonderful guy named Mark who died five years ago. He loved the outdoors, was smart, funny and had big dreams about our future together. We both did. You remind me so much of him even though you're very different. I know that doesn't make sense.

Mark and I got married the day before we graduated college together. We hadn't told our parents we were doing it, and when my father found out, he was furious. He caused a terrible scene in front of all our friends and didn't even watch me graduate. It was awful. We didn't speak that entire summer. Mark knew how unhappy I was and drove to my father's house one day to try and make amends. He never got there.

I didn't tell you about Mark at first, because it was simply something I never shared with anyone. I never saw myself falling in love again. Later, I didn't want you to feel sorry for me.

I blamed my father for the car accident, even though it wasn't his fault. I was angry and spiteful and wanted him to hurt as much as I did. I'm ashamed of myself for that.

I received a letter from my father in this morning's mail. It's not the first letter he has written me, but it's the first letter from him I have read without anger in my heart. I've changed. And it's all because of you.

I love you, Andrew. I'm so sorry I didn't tell you everything sooner. I'm going to see you in just a few hours and writing this letter feels silly, but I had to get my thoughts on paper. (I'll probably rip this up come Monday morning!)

Love,
Mariah.

Andrew read the letter two more times. The only thing he could think in that moment was what a gift it was. He thought of Mariah's father. The anguish in his eyes the day of his daughter's wake had haunted him for months. It suddenly became clear what he needed to do.

First, he needed to tell Katelyn everything and reached for his phone to text her.

ANDREW: Please pick up. I need to talk to you. Heading out for a long meeting soon.

He watched for a reply, but none came.

Andrew walked to her desk, knowing in his heart that she wouldn't be there. He thought about leaving a note for her, but hesitated. She might not like that, he decided.

On his way out of the building he stopped at the security desk.

"Hello, Mike," Andrew said. "Hi, Kenny."

"Hi, Mr. Madden," Mike replied. Kenny mumbled hello.

"I'm looking for Katelyn McGraw," Andrew said. "It's urgent. Did she come in today? I stopped by her desk, but she wasn't there."

"I don't believe she's come in today. I can call H.R. if you like, see if she called in sick?" Mike offered.

"No thanks, Mike," Andrew said, quickly. The last thing he wanted to do was to get Human Resources involved. "This is a personal matter," he said, lowering his voice. "It can wait."

Kenny raised his head. "Is there a problem with Katelyn?"

"Excuse me?" Andrew asked, regarding him curiously.

"Katelyn," Kenny repeated. "I can text Grace and ask her if she knows where Katelyn is, if you like."

Damn, Andrew thought. He didn't like the way Kenny perked up at the mentioning of Katie's name.

"That's not necessary," Andrew said dismissively. Something didn't feel right. Andrew recalled an off-handed remark that Stephen had made when they'd first met. Some joke about a security guard.

"It's actually a work-related matter," Andrew said, eyeing Kenny directly. "Nothing more. I'll try her number again."

"Sure," Kenny said, smirking. "I'm going to text Grace anyway."

Andrew wanted to wipe the knowing look off his face.

Chapter Forty-Five

Katelyn couldn't bring herself to look at her phone. She wasn't ready to speak to Andrew. After calling into work earlier this morning, explaining that she needed to take a personal day, she'd turned it off completely.

"It's just you and me today, Smokey," she said, stroking the cat's back. He hissed at her and jumped down. Katelyn pushed herself up on her elbows, watching him disappear under the bed. She couldn't understand why he'd been acting so strangely the past twenty-four hours. He hadn't touched his food bowl and hid under the sofa most of the day yesterday, too.

Mice, she wondered?

"I can't deal with that now," she groaned, dragging herself out of bed. She needed coffee. Eyeing the empty bottle of wine on the kitchen counter, she wished she'd taken an aspirin last night before crawling into bed. She tried not to think of her horrible fight with Andrew as she made her coffee. What was he not telling her?

"It doesn't matter anymore," she muttered.

She couldn't imagine their relationship ever recovering. Oddly enough, the last thing she was worried about was how awkward she might feel seeing Andrew around the office. Instead, she felt only loss. The revelation surprised her.

"Can someone really fall in love that fast?" she whispered to herself.

Absolutely, said a voice in her head.

"Wonderful," Katelyn said, rubbing her temples. "Now I'm talking to myself."

When she heard a knock at the door, her first thought was that it was Andrew. That he'd managed to get into her building and was standing outside her door now, waiting to apologize. She paused and stared at the door. Was she ready to face him?

"Are you in there?" she heard Stephen asked.

"Coming," Katelyn said, feeling a pang of disappointment.

"You look like crap," Stephen said, stepping inside. He was dressed for work and carrying his laptop case. "What the hell happened to your eyes?"

"Thanks," Katelyn said, flicking him on the arm. "I'm hungover. Why aren't you at work?" she asked.

"You didn't show up last night," Stephen said. "I wasn't too worried, I figured you'd spent the night at Andrew's again. But then I just saw your car outside. You should be at work by now. You playing hooky?"

"Yup. Coffee?" she asked.

"No thanks," he said, confused. "I never thought I'd see the day when Katelyn McGraw blew off work."

"Me neither," she said. She felt her eyes welling up and bit her lip trying not to cry.

"Come on," he said, dropping his bag to the floor and giving her a hug. "Tell me what happened."

"Don't you need to get to work?" she asked, pulling away and wiping her tears.

"Work is overrated," he said. "Sit."

"Fine," she said, reaching for a box of tissues.

"Where's my friend Smokey?" Stephen asked, looking around the room. "This is the first time I've been here that he didn't rush out to say hello."

"He's completely freaked out by something," Katelyn explained, shrugging her shoulders. "I seriously have no clue."

"Maybe it's your ugly red nose," Stephen said, patting the seat beside him for her to sit down.

Katelyn proceeded to tell Stephen about everything. Including the diamond ring hidden in Andrew's drawer.

"I'm not proud of what I did," she admitted. "But clearly, the engagement didn't happen. I guess he never got over her," she said, blowing her nose.

"You don't know that," Stephen said, disagreeing.

"Whatever. It really doesn't matter anymore," Katelyn said. "You should have seen his face...he was furious with me. All I did was light a damn fire."

"Back up a second," Stephen said. "We don't know anything about the woman in the photo. I can't imagine being rejected by someone but keeping their photo on display. It doesn't make sense. Not unless he's some serial stalker, anyway. And we're pretty sure he's not, right?"

"He's a lot of things," she said, burying her face in a pillow. "But not that."

"Great. Then don't you think you should at least let him explain himself? I mean, you really like him. You could be blowing a really good thing here."

"I guess," Katelyn said. "I'll just never forget the expression in his eyes. It was a completely different Andrew."

"I care about you, Katelyn," Stephen interrupted. "What I'm about to say might sting a little."

"Uh oh," Katelyn moaned.

"In all the time I've known you, you've never seemed really happy. And you've certainly never cared about anyone like this guy."

"That's not true," Katelyn said. "I'm extremely happy."

"You may think you are," he said, "but you're not."

"Bullshit," she said, defensively. "I love my life, I love my job, or I did, anyway."

"You're driven. That's not the same as being happy. Your sole purpose in life is to make your mother proud of you. Everything else is secondary. And now, a guy comes along that you're crazy about, and you're ready to throw in the towel after one fight."

"Whose side are you on?" Katelyn asked. "I'm not exaggerating. You should have seen the way he looked at me."

"And *you* shouldn't have gone snooping," Stephen shot back.

"Agreed. But I did and I apologized. And what's so terrible about being driven? I'm all my mother has. Is it so wrong for me to want to help her? She worked three jobs after my father died, did I ever tell you that? Worked her ass off and never complained. We never traveled anywhere or did anything crazy...I want to give her all that now."

"Has she asked you for those things?"

"Of course not," Katelyn said. "My mother is the most selfless woman I know."

"Exactly," he smiled. "You know what I think your mother would *really* love? Seeing her only daughter enjoying her life. Not taking her to Disney Land."

Katelyn slumped her shoulders, not wanting to hear anymore. She'd barely slept, and her head was spinning. "I'm having serious brain fog. Please just let's drop this for now?" she asked.

195

"Sure," Stephen said, gently. "Go get some sleep. I'll hang out here and do some work on my laptop. When you wake up, we'll grab a bite to eat, and I promise I won't say another word."

"A nap sounds good," she said, yawning. "Thanks."

"Go," he said, pointing to her bedroom.

Katelyn patted Stephen's shoulder as she walked past him towards her bedroom. "I'm glad you're here," she said.

She could barely keep her eyes open when she closed the door behind her. A flash of something red on her pillow caught her attention. She wondered if her mind was playing tricks on her.

"That's not possible," she said, as the item came into focus. It was the blouse Andrew had purchased for her. Her eyes wandered to the closet door. Had she taken it out last night after drinking the bottle of wine? *I must have,* she thought, searching her memory. There was no other logical explanation.

Remember the morning he gave it to you?

Katelyn smiled fondly, recalling the memory. He'd been so excited to show her the blouse he'd selected, and a little nervous, too. It was a side of Andrew she'd never seen.

"I don't ever wear red," she'd said, when she opened the bag. She hadn't meant for it to sound like a complaint.

"Oh," Andrew had replied. "I can take it back then. It's not a problem."

"No," Katelyn said, touching his arm. "It's beautiful. I want it. It looks like the right size, too. Thank you, Andrew."

Andrew looked at her relieved. "I did good, then?" he asked.

"You did," she nodded. "I'll just go run up and change."

"Wait," he said, handing her a small bag. "I also bought you a new cell phone. I added my personal number to your contacts."

"Are we ready for that?" she teased. "I mean, that's a big step, don't you think?"

Andrew had replied by kissing her firmly on the lips. "You're going to be late for work, Ms. McGraw. Go get dressed."

That was the Andrew she'd fallen in love with, she thought. The *real* Andrew.

Chapter Forty-Six

Gideon found Mariah sitting in Katelyn's apartment, long after Katelyn had left for work Tuesday morning. "What are you doing here?" he asked.

Mariah ignored the question. She was sitting on Katelyn's couch, her bare feet on the coffee table, holding Pinky tightly on her lap. "She doesn't like other cats," she explained, eyeing Smokey staring at the three of them from across the room.

"You're terrifying that poor cat, you know. This is ridiculous. Andrew has the letter. It's time for you to leave," Gideon said.

"Nice to see you, too," Mariah murmured, "She looks good in red, doesn't she?" she added, rising from the sofa, still holding onto Pinky.

"Who?" Gideon asked, perplexed. It was clear to him that Mariah was agitated.

"Katelyn," Mariah said. "This is a nice apartment, too. Lots of books. I like that."

"Mariah," Gideon started. "Listen to me, please?"

"But what a neat-freak!" Mariah laughed. At that, the hair on Smokey's back stood straight up and he shot back into Katelyn's bedroom. "Poor kitty," Mariah said. "He's had a fright."

"You're not getting it," Gideon sighed, frustrated.

"I hear you, Gideon, alright?" Mariah said, turning to face him. How could she explain to him that she wasn't ready to leave? That there were still too many things she needed to do?

"They found the letter," Gideon repeated. "You're done here, Mariah. Unless you prefer to continue frightening former clients and performing silly parlor tricks," he added.

"What 'parlor' tricks?" she asked defensively.

"Do you really want me to list them? Because I will."

"Stop spying on me," she snapped, pacing around the room.

"Katelyn didn't need your intervention. She was always going to give Andrew another chance. They love each other, can't you see?"

"I do," she said. "But they still needed my help." Mariah insisted, still pacing.

"Do you know how long you've been dead?" he asked, bluntly.

The question brought Mariah to a stop. She didn't know the answer. "A few months?" she guessed.

"It's been over two years, Mariah. And in all that time, what have you accomplished? Not much," he said, before she could answer.

"Two years?" she repeated, slowly. "No way," she said.

"Why would I lie?" Gideon asked.

Mariah sat back down on the couch. "I didn't know I would feel like this," she said. "I love him," she finally whispered. "I don't want to leave him. It's not fair."

They both knew who she was talking about, and it wasn't Andrew.

"Tell me, Gideon, where is Scotty's mother?" Mariah asked, turning to him. "I know you know the answer to that question. Is she alive? Is she dead like me? Because I sure as hell haven't bumped into her on this side."

"Stop," Gideon said, putting his hand up. "Don't go down this road, Mariah."

"If I had been blessed with a child like Scotty," she continued, "I never would have abandoned him."

"No one has the right to judge, Mariah," he reminded her.

"I know," Mariah said. "I'm sorry."

Gideon remained silent, staring at her before sitting down beside her. "Like old times, huh?" he said.

"Has it really been that long?" she repeated. "Two whole years? It doesn't feel like it at all."

"Longer even," he said, slipping his hand into hers. "You would have been a wonderful mother, Mariah. I'm sorry you never got the chance."

"Scotty still needs me," she insisted softly. "Terry isn't going to be here forever. Who else does he have?"

"You can't stay, Mariah," he sighed, exasperated. "There's only so much I can do to help you."

"Do you think Katelyn will be a good mother?" she asked.

"You're confused," he continued. "This is exactly what I warned you about. Remember? Please focus on what I am saying."

But Mariah ceased to listen. Instead, she looked around the apartment, eyeing the stacks of books everywhere and all the photographs hanging on the walls. "We never got this," she murmured. "Mark and me, I mean. Not for long, anyway."

"You can have this, now. Don't you want to see him again? He's still waiting for you."

"I want them both," she said. "I want to be with Mark *and* with Scotty. It's not fair. Look at all of Katelyn's wonderful photos," she said, pointing to the photos around the room. "All these accomplishments. She's achieved so much in her short life, hasn't she?"

"You're really starting to worry me, Mariah," Gideon admitted, looking away.

Mariah failed to respond.

"Mariah?" Gideon repeated, looking around the apartment.

Mariah was gone. Pinky was sitting on the kitchen counter, alone. His worst fears about Mariah were coming true. "Sorry, girl," he said, walking towards Pinky. "You're coming home with me now."

Chapter Forty-Seven

Katelyn walked into her building Tuesday morning wearing the red blouse. She hadn't expected to find Andrew waiting for her in the lobby but was disappointed, nonetheless. She'd texted him last night, apologizing for ignoring him, explaining they should talk at the end of the day today. Andrew had apologized for his behavior again and agreed they should meet.

Kenny was watching her as she approached the security desk.

"Morning, Katelyn," he said.

"Morning, Kenny. Morning, Mike," she said.

"Where were you yesterday?" Kenny asked.

Mike turned to Kenny and scowled disapprovingly.

"Out," she said coolly, scanning her I.D.

"Because your *boyfriend* was looking for you," Kenny said, sarcastically, bringing her to a halt.

Katelyn slowly turned to face him. "Excuse me?" she asked, her eyes narrowing on his as she stepped towards him.

"Andrew Madden," Kenny said, smugly.

Katelyn wasn't frightened. She was pissed. "Stay out of my *fucking* business, Kenny," Katelyn warned.

"So, it *is* true," Kenny said, rounding the desk. "It was only a hunch but thanks for confirming."

"What the hell are you doing, Kenny?" Mike interrupted. "Get back here, now."

"I'm not surprised you'd set your sights on a partner," Kenny said, his voice loud enough for everyone in the lobby to hear.

"You think that's why I turned you down?" Katelyn shouted back. "Really? It had zero to do with your profession, Kenny, and everything to do with the fact that you're a creep. You're also a bully and you have no manners. Don't talk to me ever again."

Kenny stared at her, speechless.

"Mike, I'm going to be lodging a formal complaint against Kenny with the security company," Katelyn continued. "I just wanted to give you both a heads up."

"I'm already on it," Mike said, reaching for the phone.

***

By the time Katelyn reached her desk, she'd texted Andrew twice. Their conversation could no longer wait until the end of the workday, and she needed to warn him about Kenny.

"Morning, *Katie*," Grace said, appearing at her desk.

"Hi, Grace," Katelyn replied, curtly.

"Where were you yesterday?"

"I took a sick day," Katelyn said, knowing full well that if Kenny had found about her and Andrew, then Grace most likely knew as well.

"You look fine to me," Grace said.

"Is there something you'd like to say, Grace?" Katelyn asked, folding her hands across her chest. She was tired of playing nice.

"You know what I find interesting? That you have the nerve to caution me about dating Kenny because he works in the building, yet you're screwing Andrew Madden," Grace said. "Kenny's just texted me, by the way. Apparently, he has quit, thanks to you."

"Don't be vulgar, Grace. It doesn't suit you. And if Kenny quit, it was because he was most likely going to be fired. It was his own doing. He crossed the line. The guy's no good, Grace, how can you not see that?"

"Come on," Grace said, bitterly. "You never liked him. Clearly, we know why now."

"You have it all wrong," Katelyn said, shaking her head.

"I thought we were friends, Katelyn," Grace said.

"I did, too," Katelyn replied.

"Then why didn't you tell me?"

"Because it's no one's business, that's why," Katelyn stated. "Period."

"Fine," Grace said. "Whatever. You know he was really messed up after his girlfriend got killed a few years ago, right? That decorator from Back Bay? Rumor has it they were very much in love."

201

"I need to work," Katelyn said, looking down at her laptop. What the hell was Grace talking about? The diamond ring flashed in her head, and she hoped she didn't look as shocked as she felt. "We're done here, Grace."

"We are," Grace said, walking away.

As soon as Grace was out of sight, Katelyn reached for her keyboard and googled 'Back Bay Decorator Killed.' Within seconds, dozens of articles appeared on the screen. "Oh my god," Katelyn whispered, clicking on one of the links. Mariah Talbot's smiling face filled the screen.

"It's you," she said, recognizing her from the photograph in Andrew's study. She scrolled down the article, reading the horrific details of Mariah's death as her eyes blurred with tears. All she could think of was that Andrew had been through hell.

"Katelyn?"

She turned to find him staring at her screen.

"Andrew, I—" she felt her face burn with embarrassment. His posture stiffened and his eyes remained on Mariah's image. "I don't even know where to begin," Katelyn said, rising from her seat. "Can we go somewhere private and talk? Your office?"

"I came because of your texts," Andrew said. "They sounded important."

"It doesn't matter anymore," she said. "Let's leave. Come on." She reached for his hand, not caring that they were being watched.

"Where no one can hear us or see us?" Andrew asked.

"I didn't mean it like that," she said quickly. "I don't care about them. Grace said some things to me this morning, and I looked up what happened online...to that...that poor woman..."

"Mariah Talbot," he said, softly. "That was her name. I loved her."

"I'm so sorry, Andrew."

"Aren't you worried?" Andrew asked, looking down at their joined hands.

"That you still love her?" Katelyn asked, confused. "Because I'm not."

"No, not that. About what they think," he said, motioning to the people sitting at their desks. "Because they don't matter, Katie. When will you ever figure that out? Life is short," Andrew said, pulling his hand from hers.

"Please," Katelyn begged, as her eyes filled with tears. "Let's go somewhere."

"I'm sorry about what happened on Sunday. My behavior was inexcusable," he said, turning away.

"Wait," she said, reaching for his arm. "Don't go."

"I have to. There's somewhere I need to be, and I need to do this alone."

Chapter Forty-Eight

Mariah sat perched on the old stone wall in Scotty's backyard patiently watching for the school bus. Most of the trees had lost their leaves and the afternoon sky had turned a gloomy shade of gray. The sounds of birds chirping overhead caught her attention, and she tipped her head back, looking for them amongst the bare branches. But she only saw the darkening sky. An overwhelming sensation of loneliness gripped her, and she began to weep. The more she cried, the louder the birds squawked.

Even before she saw him, she sensed Gideon by her side. He was holding Pinky in his arms.

"What is all the clacker about?" he asked, looking upwards. "Are you scaring all the birds away?"

"I didn't mean to," Mariah replied, averting her eyes. She wiped the tears from her face before reaching for Pinky. "I wondered where you'd gone," she said, forcing a smile.

"She missed you," Gideon said. "We all do. We are worried about you, you know."

"I'm fine," Mariah assured him, sniffling hard. Pinky jumped from Mariah's arms and dashed into the woods. "Even she's pissy with me," she mumbled.

"Not so," Gideon said. "She's been stuck in the cabin, waiting for you. Just needs to stretch her legs a bit."

Mariah ignored the reference to the cabin and bent over and to pick up a leaf. Holding it by the stem, she twirled it between her two fingers, trying to count all the color variations. "I think I miss painting," she stated.

"Then leave this place once and for all. I'll go with you."

"I can't," Mariah said, shaking her head. "Scotty still needs me. I know that's why you're here, Gideon. Why can't you understand that? I...I..."

"You love him," Gideon said, finishing her sentence.

"I do," Mariah admitted. "More than you realize. I can't help it."

Gideon placed his hand on her arm. "He's doing really well, Mariah. Don't you see that? He's even made friends."

"But a lot of the kids at school still tease him. I know it," she said.

"All kids get teased, Mariah," Gideon replied. "Scotty's made amazing progress. You're just not seeing it."

"He's not ready for me to go. He begs me to stay," she stated firmly.

"Can you recall the last time he asked you not to leave him, Mariah? Do you honestly think this is helping him make more friends?" he said, motioning to the woods around them. "You, lingering around here, day after day, playing with leaves and waiting for his bus?"

"He doesn't want me to leave," she yelled, flinging the leaf to the ground. She slid off the wall and stormed into the woods. "I've asked him," she said over her shoulder when he followed her. "He gets upset."

"Are you sure about that?" Gideon asked. "When is the last time you really asked him? You're confused."

"I'm not," she screamed, whipping around to face him. A pair of squirrels screeched in fear and dashed up a tree beside them. "Go, Gideon. Please."

"And now you're scaring the squirrels," Gideon said, cracking a smile, watching as they disappeared into their nest. "And you call yourself an animal lover?"

Mariah laughed. "I didn't mean to do that," she said, feeling the fight drain out of her. She wasn't a fool. She knew Gideon was there to help her, and that she had been feeling lost lately, but that didn't mean she was ready to go. Nor did it mean Scotty wanted her to leave. When she heard an approaching school bus, she brushed past him quickly.

"Go, Gideon. He might see you," she warned him.

"He won't," Gideon said, slowly following her.

"Well, *I* don't want to see you anymore," she snapped, wishing he'd just disappear.

"Fine. I'll leave. But this time, Mariah, I won't be back."

"Good," she said, ignoring the pang of anxiety at the thought of never seeing him again. *He's bluffing,* she thought.

"I'm not," he called to her.

"I hate when you do that," Mariah yelled over her shoulder.

"He's growing up, Mariah. He doesn't need you anymore. He hasn't needed you for some time, in fact."

"How can you say that? He still loves to explore these woods with me. Just yesterday, we made boats out of twigs and floated them down the stream together."

"No," he said, shaking his head. "That was months ago, Mariah."

But Mariah was no longer listening to him. Her attention was fixed on the school bus coming to a stop in front of Scotty's house. She wanted to hear how his day was and to walk down to the stream with him. When a boy she didn't recognize stepped off first, she was momentarily confused. Had the boy gotten off at the wrong stop, she wondered? He was a little shorter than Scotty and had curly red hair. Scotty bounded down the steps behind him.

"Do you want me to show you the trout I found in the stream in the woods?" she heard Scotty ask the boy.

"Sure," the boy replied, excitedly. "But can we have a snack first?"

"We have brownies," Scotty said, leading him to the front door. "Homemade. My grandmother loves to bake. She's really good at it."

"I love brownies," the boy shouted. "They're my favorite."

Mariah stood motionless as she watched them walk inside the house together. Scotty hadn't so much as glanced in her direction. "He didn't see me," she murmured, completely bewildered. "I don't understand. He didn't even look over."

Gideon placed his hand on Mariah's shoulder. "He hasn't in a long time," he said, gently. "Now, do you understand? You need to leave this place."

"No," she said. "It can't just end like this. It can't..."

"It has to," he stated.

"Wait," she said, turning on him. "Did you cause this? I know you can do anything, Gideon...did you make him not see me?" she cried.

"You know I would never do that," he said. "I'm only here today to show you what you cannot see."

Mariah didn't want to believe him. She was angry and confused and trying to recall her last conversation with Scotty. Had she said goodbye to him? She remembered explaining that she needed to go to the cabin, but hadn't she said she would be right back? She couldn't remember anymore.

"You don't believe me," Gideon said, defeatedly. "After all this time you still don't trust me?"

"I don't," Mariah screamed, squeezing her eyes closed. "Leave me alone, please. I just want to go home!"

"Then goodbye, Mariah. And good luck," Gideon said, his voice filled with sadness. He watched Mariah run into the woods, knowing she would never see him again.

Chapter Forty-Nine

Andrew sat in his car on the street outside the Talbot's home, holding Mariah's letter in his hands.

"I should have called them," he murmured, staring at the white clapboard house. He'd walked out of his building this morning after seeing Mariah's face on Katelyn's computer and drove directly here. For all he knew, the Talbots might not even be at home.

"Only one way to find out," he said, taking a deep breath as he opened the door. Just as he approached the brick walkway, a car pulled into their driveway. He watched intently as Mariah's mother emerged from the passenger side. Their eyes locked on each other, and he could tell she was trying to place him. It took a few seconds, but the flash of recognition in her eyes followed by her quick smile put him at ease.

"Can you lend us a hand?" she called out to him.

"Of course," Andrew said, walking towards them.

"We need to carry Jake into the house," she explained, as Joseph exited the driver's side. "We were just at the veterinarian's office."

"This is Andrew Madden," Katherine explained to her husband. "*Mariah's* Andrew."

"Oh," Joseph said, slowly extending his hand to Andrew's. His expression was both surprised and guarded.

"Our dog isn't well," Katherine said. "Can you carry him into the house?"

"Sure," Andrew said. As he rounded the back of the car, he caught Joseph frowning at his wife. It was clear the man didn't want him here, and Andrew didn't blame him. Andrew lifted the rear hatch and spied the resting dog who barely lifted his head. "Hey there, buddy," he murmured, leaning over him. "Nice to finally meet you."

"He's fourteen years old," Katherine explained. "He can't jump down."

"I understand," Andrew said, bending over the dog. "Mariah told me all about you," he whispered. "She said you had the sweetest face. She was right."

"I can carry him," Joseph insisted. "We don't need *him* to do this," he snapped.

"It was hard enough the first time," Katherine said. "Let Andrew help."

"Fine," he grumbled.

Andrew scooped Jake up, surprised by how light he felt. He adjusted him carefully in his arms before following Katherine and Joseph into the house. When they entered, Katherine instructed him to place Jake on the couch in the den. "We want him to be as comfortable as possible. This is his last night with us," she whispered.

Andrew placed Jake down slowly, stroking the old dog's head. "I'm so sorry."

"He's had a wonderful long life," Katherine said. "Our vet is coming over tomorrow. We just, well, we just needed one more night with him."

"I understand," Andrew nodded. He looked around the room, noticing it was already decorated for the holidays. There was even a Christmas tree in the living room.

"I know it's barely November," Katherine explained. "We were in the mood to decorate early this year."

"Nothing wrong with that," Andrew said, smiling. He eyed the five stockings hanging from the mantle. There was one for Jake, with a large bone sticking out of it. Andrew's eyes softened, reading Mariah's name on another.

"Why are you here?" Joseph asked bluntly.

"Joseph," Katherine said, glaring at her husband. "Don't be rude."

"It's a reasonable question," Andrew said. Joseph's posture was stiff, and he stared at Andrew with a mixture of hurt and mistrust. "I don't blame you for hating me, Mr. Talbot."

"He doesn't hate you, Andrew," Katherine interjected.

"They told us you were engaged," Joseph blurted out. "But you didn't even come to the funeral."

"I didn't," Andrew said, looking down at the floor. "And I deeply regret that. I was in a bad place."

"We understand," Katherine said. "But you're here now. That's all that matters. Let's go into the kitchen. Can I make you coffee, Andrew? I made Christmas cookies for Jake this morning. They were always his favorite."

"Thank you," Andrew said, following her.

He saw so much of Mariah in Katherine in that moment, her kindness and strength, her determination and compassion. The similarities were comforting. A large bay window behind the sink was loaded with various sized terra cotta pots filled with vibrant looking plants. They reminded him of the first time Mariah had sat in his kitchen.

"Were you really engaged to our daughter?" Joseph asked.

"I was planning to ask your daughter to marry me the night she was killed," Andrew answered truthfully. "I guess the answer to that question depends on what Mariah's reply would have been."

"She would have said yes," Katherine smiled, as her eyes glistened with tears. "She loved you."

"Tell us why you're here," Joseph asked, blinking hard. "After all this time?"

"Sit down, Joseph," Katherine said. "Now," she added sternly when he failed to move. "I apologize, Andrew," she said, placing her hand on his shoulder. "This has been an emotional day for us."

Andrew reached into his jacket pocket, withdrawing the envelope. "Mariah wrote this letter to me the day she died," he explained. "You need to read it."

"I don't understand," Joseph said, staring at it. "It's addressed to you."

"Just read it, please," Andrew said, holding it out to him. Joseph stared at it a moment longer before reaching for it. Andrew noticed his hands were shaking and looked away.

"Should I read this now?" Joseph asked, turning to his wife.

"I'm not so sure," Katherine said, eyeing the letter worriedly.

"It's good news," Andrew said, looking back and forth between them. "I promise."

"Then why don't you get your glasses and read it somewhere private," Katherine suggested, "unless you want me to come with you?"

"No," Joseph said. "I'll be fine." She watched him walk away, with a concerned look in her eyes.

"It will make him happy, Katherine. I swear to you," Andrew said reassuringly.

"Thank you, Andrew," she said. Her eyes remained on the hallway where Joseph just disappeared from. "How do you take your coffee, Andrew?"

Katherine asked. "Andrew?" Katherine repeated, turning, when he failed to answer.

Andrew was staring at the artwork taped all over the kitchen. A woman who looked exactly like Mariah was in all of them. In one, she stood by a well in front of a cabin, surrounded by pine trees. She was even holding a pumpkin in her arms. In another, she was walking in the woods holding the hand of a little boy with an orange cat following them.

"I don't understand…" Andrew began.

"Oh, dear," Katherine said. "You're white as a ghost. I should have warned you."

"Who…who painted these?" Andrew asked.

"Here," Katherine said, quickly handing him a glass of water. "Drink this."

Andrew raised the glass to his lips, but his eyes never left the detailed sketches. "You need to tell me," he said. "Please."

"Scotty," Katherine stated. "They are all from Scotty."

"How is this possible?" Andrew asked.

"He just likes to imagine her," Katherine said, just as Joseph reentered the room. His eyes were damp with tears, but he was smiling.

"Is he okay?" Joseph asked Katherine, motioning to Andrew.

"The artwork," Katherine explained.

"I'm fine," Andrew said, carefully placing his glass down onto the table. His brain was reeling. How could this boy have created such incredibly accurate renderings of Mariah in real places? It wasn't possible.

"You remember Theresa Bartlett?" Katherine asked. "The waitress at the diner?"

"Yes," Andrew nodded.

"We've kept in touch with her," Katherine explained.

"The boy has no other family," Joseph said. "Mariah loved to paint. Did you know that?"

"I did," Andrew said.

"So does Scotty. We like to encourage him, so he sends us paintings from time to time," Katherine said. "He has amazing talent as you can see."

"I still don't understand," he repeated.

"Clearly the boy has a wonderful imagination," Joseph said. "We believe it's how he wants to remember her."

"The psychologists assure Terry it's all perfectly normal," Katherine added.

It's not normal! Andrew wanted to scream. *That cabin is real! That well, that pumpkin…even Mariah's scarf…Scotty couldn't imagine those things. It's not possible!*

"Are you okay?" he heard Katherine ask.

"I need to sit down," Andrew admitted, pulling out a chair.

"I believe my wife was talking to me," Joseph said. Andrew turned to find Katherine embracing her husband.

"You need to read the letter," Joseph said to his wife. "It's the greatest Christmas gift we could ever wish for. And to think it came today of all days. Mariah made this happen, I know it. You need to read it."

"I will," she said. "Just as soon as I'm sure Andrew doesn't pass out and hit his head."

"I'll try not to let that happen," Andrew said, trying to regain his composure. "Can I have Theresa's phone number?" he asked.

Katherine opened a drawer and removed an address book. After copying Theresa's number on a piece of paper, she handed it to Andrew.

"Thank you," he said, folding it carefully.

"And thank you for this," Joseph said, holding the letter up.

Andrew looked into Joseph's green eyes and saw so much of Mariah. "Could I, maybe, come back another time?" he asked. "I'd like to hear about Mariah. What she was like when she was younger."

"We would love that. You're not planning to drive up to New Hampshire today, are you?" Katherine asked Andrew, eying him suspiciously.

"I most certainly am," he nodded, smiling. "If Theresa doesn't mind, that is."

"I had a feeling you might," she said. "And she won't. Would you mind bringing something to Scotty from us?"

"Not at all," Andrew said. "I'd be happy to."

"It's in the attic. Do you mind?" Joseph asked.

"Of course not," Andrew said. "Can I say goodbye to Jake before I go?"

"Certainly," Joseph said. "Take your time."

Andrew walked back into the den where Jake was sleeping peacefully on the sofa. He bent down, kissing the dog on the top of his boxy head. "You're going to be with Mariah soon," he said, petting him tenderly. "She loved you so much. In fact, it's because of you we met. Thank you," he said. When he turned to face Joseph, there were tears in his eyes. He quickly wiped them away.

"It's alright, son," Joseph said, patting him on the arm.

The word 'son' made Andrew smile. He was nearly part of this family, he realized. He would have liked that. Although there was no changing the past, who and what he became in the future was up to him. He thought of Katie and the future he might have with her. Life was precious, and he didn't want to waste a single minute more of it.

"Mariah was the most wonderful woman I'd ever met," Andrew said, his voice raw with emotion. "I loved her with all of my heart."

"I'm grateful she knew you, Andrew," Joseph said, embracing him.

"Okay, you two," Katherine said, dabbing her eyes. "We have a pre-Christmas party to get started, Joseph. And Andrew has a long ride ahead of him."

"One question," Joseph said, as he led Andrew to the attic stairs. "How big is the trunk in that fancy little race car of yours, anyway?"

It was the last thing Andrew expected to hear. "Like father, like daughter," he said, laughing.

Chapter Fifty

Mariah loved seeing Andrew helping her father carry her old easel down from the attic. The scene had caused her such unimaginable joy; she felt as if she were glowing. The sensation had brought with it a lightness and clarity she hadn't felt in a very long time. She looked around the house, delighted by the holiday decorations and more importantly, the happiness she saw in her parent's eyes. The magic she'd felt in this house as a child was back.

"Look at Jake," Joseph said, after Katherine placed a plate of cookies beside him on the couch. It was the first time all day he'd lifted his head. "He still can't resist your Swedish jam treats."

"He never could," Katherine said, grinning. Jake licked his lips and looked at them both, even managing to wag his tail.

"That's the most he's eaten in days," Joseph said.

"It is," Katherine agreed. "I know it was silly...decorating the house for him. But I really think he likes it. Don't you?"

"Absolutely," Joseph said, taking his wife's hand. "Let's let him be," he said, leading her to the Christmas tree in the living room.

Mariah watched her father thumb through his holiday albums before selecting one to place on their vintage record player. Another Talbot Christmas tradition, she thought. Bing Crosby began to sing 'White Christmas,' as Mariah snuggled up against Jake.

"Wait until you see the cabin," she whispered, stroking his back. "You're going to feel like a puppy again. I promise," she continued softly, kissing his head. Jake sighed with pleasure and looked up at Mariah. His tail thumped against the couch.

"You finally got to meet Andrew and you got your favorite cookies, too. I'm sorry you didn't have them the past few years," she said, laying her head against his. "Let go, Jake," she said, gently. "Mom and Dad are going to be fine. I promise. You can come live with me now."

His breathing started to slow down within minutes. Mariah continued to murmur in his ear, stroking him until he closed his eyes for the very last time. She kissed him on the head before standing up.

Now for the hard part, she thought, bracing herself.

She needed to leave this house forever. It was time. She peeked into the living room, where her father was showing Katherine the letter again. Mariah longed to enter the room and sit beside them but didn't dare. Instead, she lingered in the doorway.

"I feel her here," Katherine said. "Do you?"

"I do," Joseph nodded. "But I more than feel her," he whispered, glancing to where Mariah was standing.

Can you see me, Dad? Mariah thought.

"There's such an odd glow in here, isn't there? I thought it was the lights from the Christmas tree, but I'm not so sure anymore," Katherine admitted, following her husband's gaze.

"I don't think it's the tree," Joseph said, as Mariah stepped into the room. "Look at the mantle," Joseph added.

Are you talking to me, Dad?

"She loved that thing," Katherine said, smiling. "I still remember the day you gave it to her."

Mariah turned to see what they were talking about. *It's my globe.*

"So do I," Joseph said. "She thought it had magical powers."

The cabin, Mariah thought, eyeing the tiny house inside. She pressed her palm against the smooth glass. *I want to be at the cabin.*

She turned one last time and looked at her parents. The image of them sitting together, their arms entwined, filled her spirit with the courage to finally let them go.

"I think we should keep it on the mantle always," Joseph said. "Do you agree?"

"I do," Katherine said.

It was the last thing Mariah heard before the room went dark.

"I do," Mariah said, feeling the sun on her face.

"I do, too," Mark said, holding her hand. "Forever and ever."

There was soft grass under her bare feet. The air was sweet and clean, and Mariah inhaled deeply, savoring the woodsy scent. She squeezed Mark's hand tighter.

"I've missed you, Mark."

"I've missed you, too, Mariah. Let's go home."

Chapter Fifty-One

Terry agreed to meet Andrew at the diner. Her demeanor on the phone had been warm and friendly, and he was relieved that she seemed eager to speak with him.

It was for that reason alone that he hadn't suggested another location. The idea of walking into the place where Mariah had drawn her last breath was unnerving. After her death, he'd read that the diner had closed for renovation, but to him, no amount of new flooring or a fresh paint could erase the horror that had occurred there.

He braced himself as he reached for the door, stepping inside. To his surprise, the diner was bright and cheerful, and he was amazed to feel almost instantly at ease. It was crowded and noisy with people enjoying meals with their families, as servers hustled busily back and forth from the kitchen. It didn't take long for Andrew to spot Terry. She looked exactly as he remembered. She'd been waiting for him, he realized, leaning up against the register and laughing with an older man wearing an apron. He watched her carefully as she approached.

"How have you been, Andrew?" Terry asked, cheerfully.

"Well, thank you," he said. "And you?"

"We're doing just fine, thanks. Cup of coffee?"

"No thanks. But I'm happy to sit if you have time," he said, motioning to one of the retro-looking booths. "Nice place," he added.

"Thanks. It's a little busy now as you can see…"

"I do," he agreed. "I can come back later?" he started to say.

"Actually," Terry said, after a slight hesitation, "why don't you follow me back to my house? My shift is nearly done, and I've already checked with the boss," she said, nodding to the man behind the register who winked back at her.

"Great," Andrew said. He took one last long look at the diner but avoided gazing down at the black and white floor.

"Everything is new," Terry said, casually, as she reached for her coat and purse from behind the counter. "The floors, the booths…all new. Better zip up," she added. "Feels like snow tonight."

It did feel like snow, Andrew thought, following her outside.

"That's me over there," Terry said, pointing to an old pick-up truck. Andrew couldn't help thinking that it had seen better days.

"Great," he said. "I'll follow you."

The ride to Terry's house took less than ten minutes. The first thing Andrew noticed about the tiny ranch home was that it was in desperate need of repainting. There was also rot along the base of the narrow deck. There was no garage, either. He imagined Terry having to clear the snow from her truck in the biting cold all season.

"Come on in," she said, leading him to the house. "I keep the heat down during the day," she explained, stepping inside. "No sense wasting all that money when no one is home."

"Makes sense to me," Andrew said, as Terry reached for the thermostat. The house was neat and tidy, he noticed, but sparsely furnished and freezing cold.

"Coffee?" Terry asked.

"No thanks," he said. A cup of coffee sounded great right about now, but the last thing he wanted her to do after a full day's work was to wait on him.

"Let's sit then," she said, leading him towards one of the two chairs across from a small television set in the den. "What would you like to talk about?"

"As you know, I was at the Talbot's house," Andrew began.

"Ah," Terry said, nodding. "You saw the artwork?"

"I did." When Terry made no explanation for Scotty's paintings, Andrew continued.

"They said that Scotty imagines her. But those places Scotty draws…the are real places." The words sounded strange, even to his own ears.

"Are they now?" Terry said, matter-of-factly.

Andrew looked around the room, not knowing what to say next. The tiny kitchen opposite them was bare. There was no artwork taped to the refrigerators and cupboards, no bowls laden with fruit or knickknacks on the countertops. Just a simple toaster and a coffee pot.

"I don't see any art here," Andrew remarked.

"Well, we put most of them away," Terry said, following his gaze. "It hasn't been easy for him. Making friends, I mean. He's just starting to come out of his shell. The pictures, well, they were hard to explain, I guess. He's exceptionally bright and gifted," Terry added. "And artistic beyond belief."

"I know," Andrew agreed. "It's remarkable, in fact."

"He's just quiet. Always been quiet. His mother was, too."

"Do you mind if I ask what happened to her?"

"My daughter, Scotty's mother...she was a drug addict. She couldn't handle the responsibility and just disappeared one day. I don't tell too many people that," she admitted.

"I'm so sorry," Andrew said. "Do you ever hear from her?"

"Not in years. But I still hope every day that I will. I have a sister in Maine," she said, changing the subject. "I don't see her as much as I'd like, but we talk a lot," she said, smiling.

"I'm glad to hear that. It's good to have people to talk to," he said. He couldn't begin to imagine the grief in not knowing if your child was dead or alive.

"It is," Terry nodded.

"I have something for Scotty. It's actually a gift from the Talbots," he said.

"They've already done so much," Terry said, shaking her head.

"Will he be home soon?" Andrew asked, hesitantly.

Terry glanced at her watch. "The bus should be here in a few minutes," she said, standing up. It suddenly occurred to Andrew that Terry might not want him to meet Scotty again.

"I want to help you," he blurted, before being asked to leave. "You and Scotty."

"We appreciate that Andrew, but we have everything we need," Terry said, proudly.

"I know," he said, looking around the room. "You have a lovely home and, I know Scotty must want for nothing. But, nonetheless, I want to help. Particularly with his education."

"Excuse me?" Terry said, raising an eyebrow.

"Clearly, he has incredible talent," Andrew explained. "He should be in a school that helps foster that."

"Scotty likes his current school. The teachers there are great."

"I'm sure they are," Andrew agreed. "But what about when he's older? Don't you think a small high school with a strong art program might benefit him? Mariah would have wanted this."

"I don't know," Terry said, shaking her head, unsure.

The sound of an approaching school bus ended the conversation.

"I can leave through the back door," Andrew said, "if you don't want him to see me again. I totally respect your decision. My behavior at the wake was unforgivable, I know."

He started to walk past her, as she placed her hand on his arm. "Why do you think I asked you back here? Yea, I wanted to set eyes on you, first, make sure you were in a good place and all," she confessed. "The wake was a horrible day for all of us, Andrew."

Andrew opened his mouth to reply, just as the front door flew open. An exuberant, taller boy than he remembered, entered the house, tossing his backpack to the floor. Scotty's coat was lightly dusted in snow, and he stomped his feet onto the doormat. "Whose car is that, Grandma?" he asked just as he spotted Andrew. Andrew watched the excited expression on Scotty's face immediately vanish.

"This is a new friend of ours," Terry explained, rushing towards him. "Let's get that coat off and get some hot cocoa into you. What do you say?" she asked, bending down to help him.

"I can do it by myself, Grandma," he said, his eyes still fixed on Andrew.

"I remember when everyone used to fuss over me, too, after school," Andrew said, hoping Scotty would crack a smile. "It's nice, isn't it?"

"I guess," Scotty said.

"Scotty, this is Mr. Madden," Terry said.

"Call me Andrew," Andrew said, extending his hand.

"I remember you," Scotty said, flatly.

"You do?" Andrew replied. "I think maybe I didn't behave so well the last time we met. I apologize for that."

"Why are you here?" Scotty asked.

"Excuse me, young man," Terry said, sharply. "Manners, please?"

"Sorry," Scotty said, looking down at his feet.

"I was recently visiting the Talbots," Andrew explained. "They gave me a gift to bring to you. It's in the back of my car. I might need a little help getting it out," he said. "It's kind of big."

"Grandma? Can we go get it?" Scotty asked.

"As long as you put that coat back on," she said, "you can skip the hat and gloves, but don't think I didn't notice you weren't wearing them when you got off the bus."

"I'm never cold," he mumbled, casting a sideways glance at Andrew. "She doesn't understand that."

"I wasn't either when I was your age," Andrew said, waiting for Scotty to pull his coat back on. "Let's go," he said, opening the door, surprised to see the snow was now sticking to the driveway.

Scotty ran to the back of the Audi, staring at the car with a boyish enthusiasm that made Andrew grin. "This is a nice car," he said. "Looks like it goes fast."

"It does," Andrew replied. "Which is why I drive extra cautiously," he added, knowing Mariah would have wanted him to add that, even if it wasn't completely true. When he popped open the trunk, Scotty's eyes widened in disbelief.

"Is that an easel?" he said, barely able to contain his excitement.

"It is," Andrew said, reaching inside. "Here," he said. "You grab one end and I'll grab the other."

They carried it into the house, down the narrow hallway into Scotty's room.

"It was hers, wasn't it?" Scotty said, when they carefully sat it down. "Mariah's. I know how much she loved to paint."

"It was. How do you know that?" Andrew asked, curiously.

"I just do," was all Scotty said.

Andrew didn't blame the boy for not trusting him. He looked around the room, struck by the sparseness. A twin bed with no headboard and a tiny desk were the only pieces of furniture. There were no toys, no books, and no art on the walls.

"I used to have stuff on the walls," Scotty said, following Andrew's gaze. "But we put it all away."

"Oh?" Andrew said, just as Terry entered the room.

"That's amazing!" she said, looking at the easel. "You're one lucky young man. We'll need to call Katherine and Joseph right away."

"I will. But first, can I show him, Grandma?" Scotty asked. Terry looked at Scotty but didn't answer him. Andrew could tell by her expression that she wasn't entirely comfortable with whatever he was asking.

"Show me what?" Andrew asked, looking back and forth between them.

"Sure," Terry said, turning to Andrew. "After all, Andrew is our new friend, right?"

"I hope so," Andrew said, still confused about exactly what Scotty wanted to show him. He also understood that Terry was asking him if they could trust him.

"Hold on," Scotty said, opening the closet door. There was a large plastic container that he dragged to the center of the room. When he removed the lid, he came face to face with a beautifully detailed sketch of Mariah holding a large orange cat.

"Scotty, this is…this is beautiful," he whispered, reaching for the drawing.

"Did you know she had a cat?" Scotty asked.

"Yes," Andrew managed to say.

"Pinky is her name. She's always getting into trouble. Mariah has to watch her constantly," he said. "Especially in the woods."

Andrew stared at Scotty, unable to speak. *You speak to her?*

"There's more," Scotty said, pulling other paintings from the container.

All were of Mariah. Mariah in the woods, Mariah sitting on a stone wall, Mariah bending over a stream…Andrew was so overwhelmed, he sat down on the floor.

"I like this one," Andrew said, after a while, pointing to a sketch of a tiny boat made from twigs and leaves.

"Mariah taught me how to make those," Scotty said. "She's an expert at making things."

Terry stared at Andrew, but also remained silent.

"You have a gift, Scotty," Andrew said, trying his best to remain composed. "It's something you should be very proud of."

"She used to tell me the same thing," Scotty replied, pulling out another sketch. It was of Mariah standing outside a cabin. *Their* cabin. Andrew's hands were shaking when he reached for it.

"Can I ask," Andrew slowly began, eyeing Terry cautiously. "I'm just wondering, have you ever seen this cabin?"

"No," he said. "But she told me about it so many times. That's where she was going that night."

Andrew felt as if the wind had been knocked out of him.

Scotty looked at Andrew and laughed. "Is this scaring you," he asked. "Don't worry, I don't see her anymore."

"You don't?" Andrew repeated.

"Nope. Mariah finally went back to the cabin."

Chapter Fifty-Two

Andrew promised Scotty and Terry that he would be back before Christmas. He was going to go on one hell of a shopping spree and that was just the beginning, he vowed. There were details to work out, but with Terry's permission, he planned to look after Scotty for the rest of his life.

By the time he got into his car, the snow was falling more steadily. He knew he should head to Boston, but when he saw the sign for 93N, towards Franconia, he changed his mind. He needed to see the cabin.

He also needed to talk to Katie and reached out for his phone.

"Katie?" Andrew said, relieved that she picked up on the first ring.

"Andrew, where are you?" she asked.

"I'm sorry I never told you about Mariah. And I'm sorry about what happened that morning, the way I treated you."

"It doesn't matter," Katelyn said. "Can you come over? Or I can come to you?"

"I'm in New Hampshire," Andrew explained. "I needed to see someone."

"Who?"

"The boy Mariah Talbot gave her life to save. His name is Scotty. I'm going to help him," he explained. "I've been so blind."

"I think that's a wonderful idea," Katelyn said. "I...I read about him. And what happened. I'm so sorry, Andrew. And I'm sorry I didn't take your calls on Sunday. I needed time to think."

"I know you did," Andrew said.

"I've been worried about things that don't matter, and I feel like such an idiot. I don't care who knows about us anymore."

"You don't have to worry," he interrupted her. "I'm leaving the firm."

"What? Don't say that."

"I haven't been happy there in a long time. I don't even know if I want to practice law anymore."

Snow was sticking to the windshield, and he turned on the wipers. "Can we talk about all this tonight? I can come over if it's okay...wait up for me?" Andrew asked.

"I will," she said. "I'm falling in love with you, Andrew. You should know that."

"Good. Because I think I've loved you from the beginning," he said.

"Really?" she said. "You had a funny way of showing it."

"That's because I wasn't ready for you," he said, laughing.

His hands gripped the wheel tighter when he took a turn a little too sharply, feeling the antilock brakes kick in.

"Promise you'll come straight here tonight?" she asked.

"I promise," Andrew said. "Just wait for me."

***

Andrew had no idea where he was. There were no lights on the road, and he thought he might have taken the wrong exit for the cabin. His GPS was useless which struck him as odd, since it had worked perfectly in the same area two years ago.

When the small service station came into view, he breathed a sigh of relief. He pulled just as a young man stepped from the garage. Andrew watched him withdraw a knit hat from his pocket, pulling it over his head as he approached.

"Hello, there," Andrew said, lowering the window. "I think I'm lost."

"How can I help?" the man asked with a friendly smile.

"It's this unexpected snow and the lack of lights on these highways," Andrew said, frustrated. He hated asking for directions. "Were they even calling for snow?"

"The weather up here can change on a dime," the man said. "Are you looking for the cabin?"

"How did you know that?" Andrew asked, surprised.

"It's a popular destination," he explained. "Popular with the tourists, I mean. I noticed the Massachusetts plates."

"Huh," Andrew said, regarding him more closely.

"My name is Gideon," he said. "You have a reservation there or something? Because I happen to know the owner, and I don't recall him saying the place was rented for the night."

"Andrew Madden," he replied. "And no, I don't," he said. "Just wanted to take a quick look at it."

"May I ask why?" Gideon asked.

"I'm thinking about booking a weekend there," he lied.

"Looks like this car drives pretty fast. How does it do in the snow?" Gideon asked, ignoring Andrew's explanation.

"Not great, I'm afraid," he replied impatiently. "Look, I just want to walk around the place. I'm not intending to break in or anything."

"It's just an ordinary cabin, Andrew. There's nothing much to see. You sure you don't want to head back to Massachusetts?"

"I'm sure," Andrew said. The familiarity with which Gideon spoke to him felt odd, but Andrew reminded himself that he wasn't in Boston anymore.

"Hold on then," Gideon sighed, turning away. "You'll never find it on your own. Not in this weather. You can follow me there."

"You really don't have to," Andrew called to him. "Just give me the directions."

"It's no problem," Gideon called out to him. "These roads are tricky. Wouldn't want you to end up in a ditch."

"Fine," Andrew said, wishing Gideon had simply given him directions. He wanted to see the cabin alone.

Within minutes, he was following Gideon's truck slowly down the darkened roads. After a few turns, they finally reached the driveway of the cabin. Andrew felt his mouth go dry as he lowered his window. It was so quiet, so still. Everything was exactly as it was two years ago. The old well was just where he remembered it, too. Gideon stepped out of his truck, making his way towards him.

"Everything okay?" Gideon asked, when Andrew remained in his car. "This is what you wanted, right Andrew? Well, here you are."

Something didn't feel right, and it wasn't just the way Gideon spoke to him as if they were old friends, it was the overwhelming sense that he wasn't supposed to be here.

"What the hell am I doing here?" Andrew muttered. He thought of Katelyn waiting for him back in her apartment.

"I can give you a quick tour of the inside, seeing how you came all this way. Ready?" Gideon asked.

"Sure," Andrew replied, following him.

"We don't bother locking our homes around here," Gideon explained, as they approached the front door. "It's a pretty safe community."

"That's great," Andrew said. His heart was racing as he followed Gideon inside. The room was dark and he could barely make out the furniture.

"Looks like I need to flip the circuit breaker," Gideon said, placing his hand on Andrew's shoulder. "Don't move, okay? We don't need you taking a tumble or anything. Lord knows how you lawyers are always itching to sue people."

The last thing Andrew thought before hitting the floor was that he'd never mentioned he was a lawyer.

***

Andrew woke to the sound of a crackling fire and the delicate notes of piano music. Sunlight streamed through the windows, filling the cabin with a rich, warm glow. Mariah was sitting on the couch, a wine glass dangling from her fingers. She was just as beautiful as he remembered. Her hair was long and loose, and her smile was radiant. Jake was at her feet, stretched out as she rubbed the side of his body with her foot.

"Such a good boy," she said, laughing, when he flipped onto his back so she could focus on his belly.

"Someone is getting awfully jealous," Mark said, motioning to the top of the stairs. An orange cat was peering down at the scene below. "More wine?" he asked, turning towards Mariah.

"Not yet," Mariah replied.

There was no mistaking the love in their eyes, Andrew thought. It filled the entire room.

"We're going to need more wood soon," he heard Mark say, as he stoked the fire.

"Don't throw another log on just yet," Mariah said, standing up. "Let's take a quick walk in the woods while there's still daylight."

Andrew watched as Mariah finished the last of her wine, placing the glass down on the table. She walked directly past him towards the closet, as Jake jumped up from the floor, following her.

"Does he ever get tired of walks?" Mark asked, laughing.

"Nope," Mariah replied brightly. "Here," she said, tossing Mark his coat. Andrew watched as they each pulled on their boots.

"Come on, boy. Let's go," Mark said, opening the door.

"You protect the house, Pinky," Mariah said looking up, before stepping outside. "We'll be back soon."

Andrew followed Mariah's gaze to where Pinky remained, flicking her tail, staring down at him. When the door slammed shut, he moved towards the window, watching Mark and Mariah hold hands as they tromped through the snow. Jake was wagging his tail and following them. He could still hear their laughter when they disappeared into the trees.

***

"Andrew?" he heard a voice say, "You okay?"

Andrew parted his lips to speak but was unable to form a single word. His lack of a response had little to do with the pain in the back of his head, which he realized was still resting on the floor. *Mariah,* he remembered, struggling to open his eyes. *She's here!* He pushed himself up on his elbows and blinked hard, as Gideon's face came into focus.

"Ah," Gideon said, hovering over him. "Welcome back," he smiled.

Andrew regarded him briefly before scanning the room. There was no sign of Mariah or Mark, no fire burning in the hearth and no piano music playing. "What happened?" he whispered.

"I told you not to move before I got the lights on," Gideon explained. "Guess you didn't listen. Looks like you tripped or something. Is your head okay? It wasn't too bad of a fall, but you're going have a whopper of a headache."

"I just saw...just watched..." Andrew said, trying to finish his sentence. "They were here. *Both* of them. Even Jake," he stammered.

"Slow down a minute," Gideon said. "You look pale. Want some ice for that bump?"

"My head is fine," Andrew shouted, trying to comprehend what he'd just witnessed. "Something just happened...I just saw...I saw..."

"Saw what?"

Them! Andrew wanted to scream.

228

"I need to get back to the garage and close up for the evening," Gideon explained, squinting at the watch on his wrist. "Unless you think you need to see a doctor…"

"I *saw* them," Andrew yelled, standing up and pointing to the couch. "I felt the heat from the fire," he added, looking at the empty hearth. "I don't need a doctor! I didn't trip on anything. What I saw, well, it just isn't possible."

"Why not?" Gideon said.

"Excuse me?" Andrew asked. He faced Gideon and held his gaze. "What did you just say?"

"I said, why not?" Gideon repeated.

Andrew stared into Gideon's eyes.

Gideon stared back, folding his arms over his chest. "Why isn't, whatever you think you just saw, *not* possible?"

"Because things like that don't happen," Andrew said. "They just don't. You know me, don't you? You know I'm a lawyer. How?"

"It's time to go home, Andrew," Gideon said. "You're not supposed to be here."

"You know what happened here," Andrew pressed. "I know you do."

"I know you bumped your head. And that you're tired from driving all day. You've been on this journey long enough, don't you think? Come on," he said. "I'll walk you to your car."

There were so many questions Andrew wanted answered. Whatever had happened here had been real, he knew. He felt it in his heart and soul. Scotty was right, Mariah *did* return to the cabin.

"Fine," he said, following Gideon outside. The snow had stopped, and he turned back to look at the cabin one last time.

"I'll never understand…"

"What was your real reason for coming here, Andrew?" Gideon asked. "What did you think you'd see?"

He thought of Scotty's painting. "I don't know," he said. "I lost someone I loved. You know who I'm talking about, don't you?"

"If I *did,* my only advice would be to consider whatever just happened back there a gift. Someone must truly love you."

"She looked so happy," he murmured. "They both did."

"Are you happy, Andrew?" Gideon asked.

Andrew thought of Katie waiting for him at her apartment. "I wasn't, for a very long time," he said. "But I think I could be."

"Everyone deserves to be happy," Gideon continued. "If we're lucky enough to find someone to love, who loves us back, we need to hold onto that person for as long as we can. Don't you agree?"

"I do," Andrew nodded.

"It was a pleasure meeting you, Andrew," Gideon said, extending his hand. "I don't intend to run into you for a very, very long time."

"Good to know," Andrew said, reaching for his hand.

Andrew glanced at the cabin one last time.

If you can hear me, Mariah, I'm happy for you. You'll always have a special place in my heart.

"You know how to make your way back to the highway?" Gideon asked, walking back to his truck.

"I do," Andrew said.

"Good. Drive safely now. Oh, and one last thing."

"Yes?" Andrew asked, pausing before opening his car door.

"She feels the exact same way."

The End